Scalpel

Scalpel

A Novel by

Joel Berman

Visual Managing Publishing
Mission Viejo, California www.VisualManaging.com
For information, email: VisualManaging@gmail.com

© 2006 by Joel Berman

ISBN : 978-0-578-61662-9

Library of Congress Control Number: 2006934187

Printed and bound in the United States of America

Second printing: December 2019

ACKNOWLEDGMENTS

I am thankful to Faith and Adrian Van De Ree for reading, reviewing and commenting on the manuscript. The late Dr. Louis Smith, a fine obstetrician and gynecologist, and mystery aficionado was immensely helpful in his editorial comments.

The pendulum of justice swings both ways.
                    Count Dvorak Pendenture (1712-1746)

The scalpel sees no evil deeds,
It only does what the surgeon needs.
Although its guilt is insurmountable,
It never is held at all accountable.
                    Raphael Dubrovnik, M.D. (1831-1931)

I jiz wanna put all them attorneys in a blender.
                    author unknown

The Law is the true embodiment,
Of everything that's excellent. It
has no kind of fault or flaw, And I,
my Lords, embody the Law.
                    from *Iolanthe,* Sir William S. Gilbert (1836-1911)

– 1 –

New York City

Septimus McClymonds, Mac to his friends and just about everyone else, was not generally impressed by anything anymore. At fifty-eight he had seen the morbid and the dead for half his lifetime. But this was different. The body was nude, only partially hidden by the underbrush in the park, and lying face up on top of a white sheet. The arms were out to the sides, and there was no blood. It looked like a patient on a surgical table, perhaps a bit paler than usual. The eyes were closed and, above them, in the middle of the forehead, was a small, round bullet hole. The chest was hairy, as were the legs and arms, but the abdomen had been shaved clean. In the midline of the belly was a vertical incision, closed with surgical skin staples.

"Clean and neat!" Mac muttered to himself.

Dr. Norman Birdwell, the county medical examiner, was standing to one side with two police officers who were securing the site with yellow police tape. They were talking with a young man in running shorts and tee shirt, who apparently had found the body and called the authorities.

"What have you got, Norm?" Mac said, stepping up to the body, careful not to disrupt anything.

"Nothing yet. Clean-shaven, middle-aged guy, probably about fifty-five, shot in the head with a 22 caliber pistol at close range.

1

No blood. Probably about four or five hours ago. Already some rigor mortis and lividity."

"And the sheet? What's with the sheet?" asked Mac.

"That's the way he was found." Birdwell pointed to the young man in running shorts. "This guy was doing a morning run and spotted him from the road over there. Didn't touch anything. Called us on his cell phone. He hasn't seen anyone or anything else. The patrolmen were here within three minutes and called me immediately." He held out a card with a string attached. "This was tied around his right big toe."

The card had a computer printed message. It read:

The Defense Rests!
Lacks Intestinal Fortitude---Lacks Intestine!

"What's that mean?"

"Don't know."

"And what about the belly? New or old cut?" Mac walked around the body, bending over to examine the neatly shaved abdomen and the stapled skin.

"That's the peculiar part. At first I thought it was a recent surgery, but if you look closely there's no blood at all in the incision. It looks too new. Almost as if it were made after the guy was dead."

They looked at each other. Mac said, "Well, there's always a first time for everything."

The photographer finished his pictures after going over the entire area. Birdwell motioned for them to get the body into the wagon and take it downtown.

He watched as two uniformed officers started to lift the sheet. "We'll look into that belly once we get him to the morgue."

The words were hardly out of his mouth when a plastic bag slipped from under the body and moved along the sheet to the end held by one of the policemen. It moved so fast that it hit the

2

officer's hand and broke open, splattering blood and tissue into the officer's face and onto the floor. He dropped the sheet and the body fell off onto the ground.

"Damn," he cried, trying to wipe the mess from his face. Mac moved in quickly and appraised the situation with Birdwell, who looked down at the blood and tissue on the ground near the opened baggie.

"Geez. It's the guy's intestines or something," said Mac.

Birdwell bent closer, and then stood up. "Almost, Mac. It's his colon. You know, the large intestines. The guy's colon was in the plastic bag."

One of the other men brought over a towel for the bloodied officer, who moved away waving his right hand. "Oh, my God!...someone else can carry this one. I'm going home and clean up." He was shaking. "I hope the son of a bitch doesn't have AIDS or something."

Birdwell signaled to another man and pointed to the body. "Get him outa here and don't drop him." He looked at the retreating officer. "Hey Benson, I'll run an HIV test on him. Don't worry. I'm sure you'll be fine."

Benson looked back at him. "What do I tell the wife? I mean, Jesus, I'm a bloody mess." Birdwell shook his head. "Just keep your pecker in your pants for a day, and I'll call you right away. I'm sure there's nothing to worry about."

Benson walked towards his car, got in, and drove away.

The body was already in the wagon, along with the plastic bag and the tissue. The formerly-pristine site was now a bloody mess, and a crowd was forming. The dew was starting to disappear from the grass, and Mac looked at Birdwell. "*Now* I've seen it all."

"Hey," said Birdwell, "this guy probably didn't know if he was comin' or colon. Get it? Coming or colon." He glanced at Mac who hadn't changed his expression of disgust.

"You're sick, Norm. Let's get some breakfast."

"Chitlins?"

— 2 —

The morgue was always immaculate. It may have smelled a bit funny, but, except when the bodies were out of the cooler, it was spotless: stainless steel tables, everything in its place, recording machines with hanging microphones for the examiner.

"This place always looks clean as an operating room," commented Mac.

"Oh, yeah? Have you been in an operating room, Mac?" said Birdwell.

"No. But I've seen 'em on TV."

The body lay on the dissecting table, and the morgue assistant had all the equipment prepared for Birdwell, who had changed into greens to keep from contaminating evidence and soiling his clothes. He uncovered the body and described the findings from head to toe, then removed the staples in the belly. The entire abdomen fell open.

"This is not a surgical closure, Mac. Someone just stapled the skin and left all the underlying muscles and tissue unclosed. In surgery, these layers are all sewn individually. This guy was apparently opened and closed by the perp."

Mac looked at the body cavity, which was slowly opening wider of its own accord. "Yeah, I know. I read that book, *Understanding Surgery,* you gave me. It talks about wound closures. This guy must have had a lousy surgeon."

5

Birdwell countered. "Actually, not. Aside from the wound closure, which would have taken a good while to accomplish, the rest of the procedure was done quite well."

"What do you mean, quite well?"

"You remember that colon and fluid in the plastic bag? Well, this guy has had most of his colon removed, and I don't mean just ripped out. He's actually had a surgical resection of his large intestine and had the divided ends sewn and stapled back together. You know, they can staple intestines together pretty fast with the new stapling devices. I watched a video of a surgeon friend of mine connecting a colon together in five minutes using those things."

"So this guy is shot by a surgeon, and then has an operation after he's dead and has his colon removed? That just doesn't make sense."

"Unless he's making some type of statement. Remember the note. You know some doctors are off the deep end."

"Yeah," said Mac, "but this is pretty deep. And I thought I had seen it all. This is what keeps me interested. There's no end to the weirdoes out there."

Birdwell continued his examination, dictating as he rapidly went from organ system to organ system. When he got to the head, he cut through the scalp down to the skull, then took an electric saw and began cutting through the bone with a loud grinding noise, eventually removing a skull segment and exposing the brain.

"That's it. I'm outa here," said Mac. "Let me know what else you find, and I'll have 'em start on the bullet as soon as you have it out."

He turned and walked out of the room, the door swinging behind him as Birdwell continued his examination, pausing every few moments to dictate into the hanging microphone. There was no exit wound, so he lifted and cut the brain out of the skull and placed a probe through the bullet track, slicing into the farthest end and retrieving the splayed out bullet. The surrounding brain had extensive hemorrhage and could only be examined after the brain had been pickled properly for a few days.

6

After he finished, his assistant wrapped the remaining body, placed it on a trolley cart and wheeled it back to the cold storage. He slipped it into place and slammed the cooler door. The paper on the door read: JOHN DOE #354 case 2006-578.

— 3 —

It was a fine eating establishment. Not just a place to pop in and find a table, but one where you had to make reservations a few weeks in advance, be a big shot or know somebody important. He considered himself all of the above as he and the attractive, buxom young woman with him were ushered to a table in the far corner.

"A pleasure to have you with us this evening, doctor," said the maître-d', nodding at the woman with the long, brown hair and helping her into a chair.

"Thank you, Charles. This is Felice."

"A distinct pleasure. The good doctor has excellent taste in all areas." He smiled and bowed, retreating from the table.

The doctor felt elated; his entire body tingled, almost the way it did after the first two glasses of wine he took each evening upon arriving home. But this was different. It was like having a continuous orgasm, his throat almost into his chest and his breathing a little quicker than usual. Felice was his latest female find. She was a divorced nurse from the intensive care unit, twenty-eight years his junior; a bright, cheerful woman who hadn't quite gotten used to calling him by his first name after several years of addressing him as "Doctor".

He was the scion of a cultured Australian landowning family and had been raised in Sydney and, later, Paris, Oxford and London. His credentials were impeccable, and his practice had progressed and grown rapidly.

This evening they were having a late dinner after a fine performance of *Die Meistersinger*. The music rang through his brain, augmenting the natural high he felt alongside this beautiful woman. Life was indeed good for the doctor. He was admired by his colleagues and adored by women. He had had two marriages. The second one lasted for fifteen years with no children. His second wife had died quite suddenly six years before during a hiking trip in the mountains of Switzerland. He had withdrawn from the public for three months after the episode before returning to work.

The doctor was six feet two inches tall, with a full head of silver-gray hair and piercing blue eyes that captivated women. Although he had been an athlete as a youth, in recent years he had stopped all outside sports, except for his twice a week workout with a trainer, Patrick, in his home gym, and his morning laps in the pool. He refused any offers for golf or tennis after his wife died.

He was mild-mannered and rarely lost his temper except for the occasional times in the operating room when something went wrong because of the equipment or a careless nurse. When he lost his temper, he was quick to apologize at the end of the case, leading most of the operating room staff to think of him as a paper tiger. When a nurse or fellow physician had a family financial problem, he was always the silent supplier of assistance, although he never spoke of this to anyone and wanted no overt recognition.

The doctor's surgery was quick, efficient and of the highest standards. He rarely lost a patient on the table and was known as the surgeon's surgeon. His hands were long and large with strong fingers and well-cared-for nails, which he had done every other week.

This evening was a first. He thought there would be some regret or fear or reservation, but he felt none. Just the sensuous excitement and restlessness that he found both exhilarating and sexually uplifting.

He looked forward to a fine dinner followed by a late evening of sexual fantasy with this woman. He had been with her intermittently for almost three months, and they were well-suited to one another. She was the caretaker and love giver, and he was the needy lover, willing to go to any lengths to satisfy both their pleasures. While she was strikingly beautiful, she appeared somewhat reserved to her friends and colleagues, and while he seemed formal and asexual in demeanor, they both exploded in passionate exchanges when they were alone in the night. And tonight he would reach heights never before attained. Tonight would be a perfect ending to a perfect day.

— 4 —

Birdwell ran the fingerprints through state and federal files for forty-eight hours with no identification. He was almost ready to leave the office for the day when his associate, Ben Parks, came through the door with a big smile on his face.

"Got a call from Los Angeles twenty minutes ago. It's just about two o'clock there. The same character, Sergeant Bill Braverman, got it."

"Got what?" asked Birdwell, tired and already slipping away from the cases of the day.

"The guy with the colon removed, the John Doe from two days ago. His name is Clark Devereaux and get this...he's an attorney from Placentia, California. That's somewhere near Los Angeles. Anyway, he's divorced. When they called his ex, she sounded almost happy to hear about his demise. Apparently, he was a real asshole."

"What was he doing in New York?"

"Well, he has his own law practice, and Braverman went to speak with his secretary. He says she's quite a number. The way she broke up in tears, he figures there was more than a professional relationship. Devereaux was in New York for the National Medical Malpractice Attorneys' Conference at the Hilton last Thursday through Saturday."

"Oh, great. Did you let McClymonds know about this?"

"Yes. He's been bugging me all day, and he's on his way over here now. I told him you hadn't left yet, so stick around for a few minutes. He's just around the corner and wants to talk to you about this Devereaux character."

Birdwell shook his head. Another dinner reservation shot to hell. He'd have to call Margot and tell her he'd be busy. He'd been late the last three times anyway, and she was just barely tolerating him and his schedule. He went over to the phone to make the call and left a message on the answering machine. Maybe she was in the shower. Better for him not to have to explain priorities to her in person. He spoke to the phone recorder and then went back to his office and pulled the DOA John Doe, now Clark Devereaux, file.

Mac showed up a few moments later with another officer.

"So the guy's a medical malpractice attorney, and the killer's probably some kind of surgeon who finally got pissed off enough to get even. That narrows the field quite a bit."

"Seems that way," said Birdwell. "There's nothing else on the postmortem except the 22 caliber bullet, which is pretty well destroyed after going through the skull…and, of course, there's the surgical procedure."

The two policemen started taking down notes. Mac spoke to his junior assistant. "Get a list of all the medical malpractice cases for the last three years in the New York and Los Angeles areas. See if Devereaux has anything to do with a case here and run down everything else he's done for the last few years. Can't be that many. If we're lucky, maybe we can find a surgical case with a big settlement and a supremely pissed-off doc."

"Don't they all carry malpractice insurance?" asked the assistant.

Mac answered. "Most of them do, but the letters they get from the attorneys are really bad. I saw a case once and reviewed the documents. They start out with a *letter of intent* from the attorney to the physician, stating all the things he alleges the doctor has done. They really lay it on heavy. The case I had was an emotional, single young doctor, just starting out in private practice, who had a relatively minor complication on a surgical case.

"After a hard day in the office, he received the letter stating that he essentially destroyed some patient's life, and a lot of other bullshit. He took it all to heart, went out and had a few drinks, went home and took an overdose of sleeping pills. The attorney actually felt sorry. Said it was just a form letter he had to get in to beat the statute of limitations."

"What's that?" asked the assistant.

"In most medical malpractice cases," said Mac, "the defendant has to be notified within one year of the plaintiff knowing about the alleged event. Of course, they can usually get around that by saying they didn't know there was a problem until much later, which may actually be the case."

Birdwell piped up. "Most of the malpractice attorneys are on the up and up, but some of them are just looking for an easy few thousand bucks and will sue a doctor over next to nothing. It's cheaper for the malpractice company to settle the case for a few thousand dollars than to go through a lot of expensive investigations only to have the case settled later or even thrown out. And most doctors would just as soon have the matter out of their hair."

The assistant shook his head. "Why don't they sue the attorney for malpractice?"

Birdwell commented, "It's expensive, almost never successful, and the doctor often has to pay for it out of his own pocket. The attorneys know this and don't have much fear of counter-suits. The patients often don't understand that medical treatment isn't perfect and deviations from perfection aren't necessarily malpractice. Many of these scumbag attorneys play on the emotions of these patients and encourage them to continue their suits. They take the cases on contingency, so it doesn't cost the patients anything. But it places the attorneys in a position where they're putting out time and money. They at least want to recoup their losses at any cost. I saw a case of a woman who had a hysterectomy and sued the doctor for leaving a sponge in her vagina. It caused a bad infection. The outcome showed that the sponge was not the kind used in the operating room, and she probably had placed it there herself to get money from the doctor. Even after this was determined, rather than go to court and take a chance with the jury, the physician and the malpractice company settled for five thousand dollars. Pure bullshit."

"No wonder doctors hate attorneys," commented the assistant.

"You haven't heard the half of it," said Birdwell. "There are a few valid cases of malpractice, but a lot are relatively minor stuff. By the time they get the poor dumb doc into court and run him through the mill and out the other end, they have him looking like an intentional axe murderer."

Mac chimed in. "I think one of those docs got pushed over the edge. I've got a few acquaintances who are physicians, and they constantly joke about doing in lawyers. But I've never seen a case where they acted out their aggression. I have heard about a couple of suicides, though—usually unstable guys to begin with. You know, these docs, for the most part, do a pretty good job. Joe Public expects perfection. When something goes wrong, they're at the attorney's door in a flash. If you think criminal law prosecutors are vicious, you should get a load of these guys."

The assistant looked at Mac inquiringly. "So we've either got a disgruntled surgeon who's decided to have his day in his own courtroom or some vigilante doc out to even the score."

"Oh, God," said Mac, "I hope it's not the latter. That's all we need is some nut-case doctor knocking off malpractice attorneys."

Birdwell held up his index finger. "Look at it this way. The guy doesn't just run out and blow away this attorney. He sets the whole thing up very carefully. He shoots him, shaves him and performs his own postmortem. Then he takes the very big risk of transporting him to a public place and leaving the body on a white sheet. This is more like a well-planned operation, if you'll excuse my pun. He had to get the guy to a safe place where he could do all this stuff, have a car to transport him and carry the body to the scene without being spotted. This surgeon's got balls galore."

"And," said the other cop, "he'd have to be pretty strong to carry a hundred-seventy-pound body around."

Mac was taking notes. "So we're looking for some crazy surgeon or bodybuilder with an axe to grind. Well, that certainly narrows the field." He looked at the others. "Let's see what we can turn up here and in L.A. Thanks, Birdwell. I'll be in touch."

"Yeah. I'd be interested in meeting the guy when you get him. I'd like to take him out to dinner."

— 5 —

It was a warm Thursday evening. He would be off for the weekend with no patients in the hospital. He'd had all outpatient surgeries that week and no emergency room call. Free for seventy-two hours, and a strong feeling was rising in him again. He'd done his homework. Like planning a surgery: just a little reviewing, preparation, and the routine history and physical examination.

The American Bar Association had a meeting in New York. It was simple enough to find out about the times, schedules and speakers. Pick a name, any name, and make a few phone calls on a secure telephone. It was easy to find out what the man did for a living. Corporate law? Forget it. Environmental law? Nah. Medical malpractice? Bingo!

David Malmberg, Esq., Philadelphia, Pennsylvania. *What a schmuck*, the doctor thought. *Esquire my ass.* He looked up the guy on the Internet. As he expected, he was listed.

Have you suffered at the hands of an incompetent physician? My law office will FIGHT for you. No fee unless recovery. We can get you qualified medical treatment, and you can be reimbursed for your pain and suffering. Twenty years' experience. If you want the best results, seek out the BEST.

DAVID MALMBERG, ESQUIRE.

The doctor called the convention number and spoke to a receptionist. "Hello. This is David Malmberg. I'll be speaking at the meeting this weekend. What were my hotel arrangements?" Pause for a few moments. "The Hilton? Excellent. Can I have a room number for my office, or can't you give me that on the phone? Oh, wonderful. Thank you. Extension 1054."

He smiled as he wrote down the information in his small notebook. Leather-bound. Fine work. Montblanc pen.

He had cased the area during the week and knew the loading dock and the laundry locations. Timing was all-important. *Get all the details correct before the procedure. Just like surgery*! He had the instruments and would use the bed sheet. *Just like surgery*, he repeated to himself. He felt the excitement growing.

The brown wig made him look twenty years younger, and the cutoff mustache completely changed his appearance. He'd done some acting in college and knew a little about makeup and costumes. He put silicone plugs inside his cheeks, and they gave his face a fuller appearance. The padded belly was the final touch and had special pockets that allowed him to store some of the necessary surgical equipment. He would weigh only fifteen pounds more and could easily manage. He was in good physical condition and could bench press two hundred and fifty pounds with ease.

Just hope the guy isn't too big.

His plan was to abort the whole thing if the guy turned out to be huge. *Hey,* he thought, *why not do a female attorney*? He pondered that, then went back to his original plans.

Friday, he got on the train and made the several-hour trip to Manhattan, where he picked up a delicatessen sandwich, found a small fleabag hotel, paid in cash and checked in for two nights.

Marvin Bowfinch

He signed with his left hand with a shaking scrawl, taking the pen with him into the room.

Everything wiped clean. Keep it surgical. Make it sterile.

He talked to himself as he situated everything neatly in the room. The makeup, hair and padding made him hot, so he turned the air conditioner down to 68°. Had to stay comfortable.

He lay back on the bed, turned on the TV and took a sleeping tablet. He was out cold in twenty minutes.

Saturday found him exhilarated. He cleaned up the disguise, shaving where needed, and left the room at 6 A.M. It was a one-hour subway ride into the heart of the city, and he liked to have plenty of time. If possible he wanted to catch a glimpse of the guy, to gauge what he was up against.

No surprises, no strange anatomy, no hemorrhage. Just like surgery. Keep it simple and neat and quick. Just another case.

He felt a stirring deep within him and remembered Marilyn. Everything always came back to Marilyn. She had great breasts and good legs. Somehow, she was involved in this with him.

Come on, sweetheart, we're on our way. All for you.

He was getting warm, and now he liked the feeling. His body was strong, and even the disguise couldn't completely conceal the strength and stature. He knew he had poise and tried to conceal it with a slight forward bend, staring toward the ground. His eyes were his only giveaway, so he wore slightly tinted dark glasses. He glanced at himself in shop windows and was pleased. The suit that fit the disguise was clean and neat and, although it wasn't his usual Armani outfit, he wore it well, albeit with an extra fifty pounds in appearance. Just another big guy walking around the Big Apple.

He got to the hotel early in the afternoon, entered the main lobby and easily made his way to the service entrance. It was easy to walk in because if anyone stopped him, he would just say he was a hotel guest who went in the wrong door. But he never got stopped. No one cared. He took the staff elevator to the tenth floor and watched the rooms casually. A few people came and went, but no one took notice of this ordinary-looking man. At about 9 P.M. a rather thin, wiry gentleman went to 1054, inserted the key card and went in.

Mr. Malmberg, Esquire, the doctor whispered to himself, smiling beneath the disguise. *He can't weigh more than one hundred fifty in his briefs.* He was pleased with his selection. *Coming, counselor. It's me—your judge and jury! The doctor is making a house call.* He put on his white dress gloves.

But he didn't go near the door. He went to the hotel phone near the elevator and called the hotel operator. "Mr. Malmberg, please."

"I'll connect you with his room, sir."

"Thank you."

The phone rang three times, then the squirrelly Malmberg picked it up. "Yeah. What do you want? I told you I didn't want to be disturbed."

What a complete schmuck, thought the doctor. "So sorry to bother you, sir. The management would like to extend our welcome with a bottle of Mumm's champagne, on the house. Of course, if you do not wish to be disturbed, we could call tomorrow."

Malmberg paused on the phone for a second. "Okay. Yeah. That would be great."

The doctor said, "Shall I have it sent up now, sir?"

"Yeah, now. Send it up."

"Right away. And sorry to have disturbed you."

The doctor felt his excitement rising and took his pulse. One hundred thirty-five. He must learn to control himself. That was not the way to start a case. He hung up the phone and looked at his watch. Ten minutes should be enough time before knocking. He reached into his pocket and pulled out a tiny bottle of Mumm's champagne. "Probably not what you're expecting, counselor," he muttered to himself.

"It's time for surgery, Marilyn."

He walked towards the door. There was no one else in the hallway.

Knock. Knock. "Room service." He held the bottle in front of him and directly opposite the eye hole in the door. There was some movement on the other side. The door handle turned, and the door opened.

"From the hotel," said the doctor, holding the bottle towards the man as he opened the door wider.

Malmberg reached for the bottle, and the doctor forced himself into the room, grabbing the slight man by the throat with his strong left hand.

"Gghuh." A sound barely made its way from Malmberg's throat as he was pushed back. The door closed behind them.

"Greetings from the medical community, Esquire," the surgeon said as he brought the Mumm's down on the man's forehead. The bottle was not heavy and did not break, but the effect caused Malmberg to fall backward slightly, the surgeon's hand still firmly grasping his throat. The doctor felt tremendously empowered, practically lifted the small man off his feet and backward into the room. The blow to the head had stunned him, and it wasn't until he reached the bed behind him that Malmberg started to struggle. The doctor released the neck grip, and his victim fell backward onto the bed, his hand going immediately to his injured throat.

His eyes were wild, and he was gasping for air. "What the fuck's goin' on?"

As he started to get up, his eyes came directly into line with a small pistol equipped with a silencer, which the doctor pushed directly between his eyes. "Please keep quiet, counselor."

The small man began to move, but stopped short when he started to grasp the entire situation. "Hey, man, take my money. It's over there on the dresser."

"You already got *my* money, counselor. Don't you remember?"

"Hey. Who the hell are you? I don't know you."

The doctor pressed the silencer of the gun more firmly into the skin, and the smaller man began sweating profusely. "Of course, you know me, Mr. Malmberg. I'm the medical profession." The doctor removed the dark glasses and stared steadily into the fearful eyes. "I'm here to give you your contingency fee."

"Wha—what?"

The doctor smiled with his lips together and pulled the trigger of the small caliber pistol.

THUNK

The small man's body arched backwards onto the bed and a small amount of blood exited from the wound. There was some twitching from the body for a few moments, then nothing.

The doctor looked at his clothing. All was clean. Just a little blood on the victim's forehead. He placed a gloved finger over the opening for a few minutes, glancing around cautiously and listening for any commotion. Nothing. There was silence except for the TV. He glanced at it—a nude porno scene. He removed a clean sheet from the bed to use later.

The doctor took off all his own clothes and placed them neatly on a chair in the corner. He lifted Malmberg's body onto the bed and stripped him naked. He glanced at it. The man had soiled himself at the last moment and had to be cleaned up. No problem. He was used to fecal material. The man's body was almost hairless, except for his groin and legs. The doctor took out two large blood pressure cuffs to use as tourniquets and placed them high around the upper thighs. He wrapped an Ace bandage tightly around the legs, then insufflated the tourniquets to decrease the blood loss. Even with a dead body, there would be a lot of residual blood in the legs, and he wanted to limit the mess. He took out a marking pen and made lines on the thighs, so there would be large posterior flaps for closure. Operating on the dead was easier. No problem with hemorrhage. He chuckled to himself as he readied the scalpel with a large number ten blade.

Here's for us, Marilyn.

He made a deep incision around one thigh with a minimal amount of blood loss. He carved down through the muscle in an orderly fashion until the blade hit the bone of the femur. He took out a scraping instrument and cleaned the attached tissue off the bone circumferentially with a rasping action. The bone was yellow-white. Without the usual bleeding, it looked like uncarved scrimshaw, he thought. He took a small hand saw, easily divided the bone and removed the first leg. He repeated the process on the other side, placed the legs into a plastic bag and tied the top. Then he took out a needle holder and large sutures and approximated the fascial and muscular tissue from front to back to form the end of each stump. The skin flap from the back was brought forward and attached to the front skin with a stapling device. He completed both stumps and stepped back. It was a fine job, he thought. He took out a pre-printed computer note and attached it to the right thumb.

The Defense Rests
It's in the Bag
The Prosecution Hasn't a Leg to Stand On

The doctor smiled at his artistry and his literary style. He spent the next half hour cleaning the body and himself. He pulled the small dresser to the center of the room and threw a clean sheet over it. He wasn't going to take this one to Central Park; that had been too risky and foolish.

He lifted the body onto the sheet and thought how light it had become without the legs. He pulled the arms out to the sides and left the legs in a bag on the floor. He went to the bathroom and took a shower, carefully rinsing the stall of any hair left after he had finished. Then he placed the towel in a sack and the sack into a pocket of the costume. He dressed, replacing his entire outfit, then glanced at himself in the mirror.

Case well done, Marilyn. One less menace for society to worry about.

He looked at his watch. It had taken almost three hours to finish the surgery and get everything back in order to his satisfaction. He listened at the door and opened it cautiously. The hallway was empty. He stepped out and went to the stairway. He felt ecstatic. He had a broad grin on his face as he made his way down the ten flights to the street, whistling an aria from Rigoletto, and disappeared into the night.

— 6 —

"Absolutely not! The press would have a morbid field day with this. Just keep it quiet for a while if possible." Mac was livid. "And that sick sense of humor to boot."

"There's just no way to keep this out of the press. One more, and we've got a major serial killer." He raised his eyes. Captain Michaels had the room filled with policemen. "I'll handle the press."

Mac was at a small podium in front of a blackboard. "The only thing we have in common is that both these guys were medical malpractice attorneys and, from what we have gathered, they represented the bottom side of the profession. Now, that may be just coincidence or else this surgeon, or whatever he is, is picking on any malpractice attorneys. There's no apparent link between the two guys—one came from California and the other, three thousand miles away in Philadelphia. We've been through their cases for the last five years, and there are no cases or physicians in common. Neither one of these guys has any connection with undesirable elements. They've had no death threats or apparent secret problems from what we can gather. Zilch."

One of the onlookers asked, "Anyone see anyone or anything?"

Mac began again. "Nothing definite. There were several strangers in the hotel, according to the staff, but no one specific. Big hotel like that, you have hundreds of people wandering in

27

and out who have nothing to do with the hotel, and who aren't staying there. Some just like to use the restrooms. Nobody saw anything peculiar. The guy probably took a shower after this murder, but all we have is a few brown hairs, which may not even be his. They may not be human. May be from a wig. He washed the place down pretty well. All the blood belongs to the victim.

"One thing, however. The medical examiner says the man's throat is badly bruised, probably by a large hand. So we're assuming it's a male and a fairly big man at that. He has to be pretty strong to deliver that body to the park on the first case."

Another policeman stood up. "We got a list of all the mal-practice cases over the past five years in the New York area. Several thousand. Mostly small stuff. But it's going to be a huge job to sift through, much less to make any sense relative to these cases."

Michaels walked back to his desk and held up a sheet of paper. "This is a directive from the mayor. He knows all about the situation and says we have to make a public statement later today before the press gets wind of this thing."

"They already have." Sergeant Jamieson walked into the room holding a newspaper in his hands.

Crazed Surgeon Kills Counselors

"Oh, shit," said Mac.

"It's all here. Somebody's opened his mouth." He looked around the room to serious faces. "If I find out who, there'll be hell to pay."

"Always happens, Mac. For a couple hundred bucks the department is full of leaks."

McClymonds set up an information center and assigned jobs to the six men in the room. He did it almost without thinking. He'd been doing this a long time, and he'd gone about as high in the department as he would. No political ambition, no chief or administrative desires. He was content with his job and pretty much wrote his own game plan for work. He left the politics to Michaels and kept his mind on police business and solving murders. He was a private sort of guy, who never socialized much and kept to himself off hours. He'd been married once for fifteen years, had two daughters now grown and married and a wife who'd left him for a more stable life.

McClymonds was a cop's cop. No crap. No favoritism. When he finished the day, whether at three in the afternoon or two in the morning, he went to Shaunessey's Bar and sat in the same booth thinking for hours. He rarely had any company and never dated. He had a few hookers he had known for ten years who occasionally visited, and it was the only time he allowed himself to be pampered to any degree. They understood him and his needs, and no longer demanded anything more.

He saw the city as a seething pit of inequity and misery with an occasional surprise comedy relief, and saw himself as the stability of the law, cleaning up his little turf and somehow feeling that this justified his reason for living. It had been a long while since any superior had raised his voice to him and he was *good ol'* Mac who got the job done. This scenario had repeated itself over and over and never failed to keep him alert and interested.

He tried to put himself inside the perpetrator's mind and, whether or not it helped him in the case, he enjoyed becoming the man or woman he was looking for. He wrote notes to himself throughout the day and assembled them at night by himself in his two-bedroom, six-room flat. When the day was over, he collected every sheet of notepaper and stored it in one of several file cabinets in a back storage room. He had a huge collection of misery, maimings, murder and morbidity, each labeled with the appropriate few words.

That day he left the office late in the afternoon with a pile of notes and papers he had assembled or had been given by his subordinates. At his table in the bar he spent time doodling on a sheet of yellow, lined paper. He drank very little, just an occasional sip of beer and, when he was satisfied, he gathered everything together and headed home. He opened the door to the flat, greeted his aging cat, Georgia, and took the notes into the back room, where he placed them into the newest file box. This one was already labeled. He placed several sheets of paper into it and pulled around the attached rubber band. The label read 'Scalpel'.

— 7 —

The doctor sat at his computer. He had always wanted to write about his life, and at first it came slowly. Some of it he made up as he went along.

I don't know exactly where to begin. I can't go back to my childhood because, for some reason, there's a curtain pulled over most of it before the age of twelve. I suppose there's some psychological defense mechanism or block that occurred at that time, and someone might think I had a dysfunctional family and all that crap. However, the memories I do have are pleasant. We lived in a nice, dark red, three-story mansion in Sydney, Australia. Dad's father was wealthy, making money off the land inherited from his father.

I was the only child, and mom died of heart valve disease when I was in my teens. She was a sweet woman, but I remember her as always sick and bedridden. Before she died, they attempted to do a surgery on her mitral heart valve, but that was the time before open heart surgery and extra-corporeal circulation with a heart pump machine. The procedure consisted of making a hole in the beating heart with a scalpel, inserting a finger with a small knife attached to it and, by feel alone, opening up the tightly closed, diseased mitral valve. She was pretty sick going into the procedure and never woke up afterwards.

Died three days later. Dad was broken-hearted, and he deteriorated noticeably after her death. Basically, I was pretty much alone as far as family was concerned. I had the money and the six house servants to console me.

Martin, an old Scotsman, had run the household for many years and was like a second father to me. Within a year I finished my pre-university studies and went off to Paris for a year with Martin and his wife, leaving my father to his business. Father and I had never been very close, and when mother died he was more withdrawn than ever. In those days your dad wasn't your pal like you see in some modern families. Especially in our family. It was fairly formal, and mom had been the only source of warmth and loving. Anyway, I'm getting off track.

In Paris I spent a year at an art conservatory and initially wanted to become a painter. Unfortunately, my ability was much less than my desire, and after a year the professors urged me to rethink my decision. It was difficult, but I finally decided I would go to the University at Oxford.

Money yields a welcome mat just about anywhere, and I was accepted without much problem, even though I barely made the grade academically. I guess I had some of my father's isolationism, because I never formed any close friendships. I did, however, form a bond with the man who taught anatomy, and he introduced me to the world of medicine. Once I got the bug, it was all over as far as any other profession. He brought me to the anatomy laboratory as an undergraduate, and I took to it immediately. I loved the beauty of the human body and the fact that I could systematize everything and remember the parts so well. I had a broad-based education, including theatre arts, but I knew I wanted to be a physician. After graduating, I was accepted for the following year at an east coast American medical school. That gave me an opportunity to live in London for a year after completing my college at Oxford, and I became quite a dandy and man-about-town. I had money at my disposal and access to my father's townhouse near the British Museum.

I saw my father only three times during those five years and, even then, only for a few days each time. We would talk by phone once a month, but his mind was totally into his business. When he died of lung cancer at age fifty-six, I was only remotely saddened and never shed a tear. I inherited everything, but let Martin manage the business affairs until he died twelve years later. I sold it all and cashed out the Australian business, placing the money in several numbered Swiss accounts. I was financially set for life.

I love the sight of blood. I love the color, and I love the motion of the pulsating arteries. I often sit holding my index finger to my radial artery at the wrist or the carotid artery in my neck, marveling at the magnificence of the human machine. The blood vessels are the highways of life...the conduits of life. They carry the oxygen to the tissues and carry the carbon dioxide back to the lungs to be expired. They carry nutrition to the tiny cells, carry the waste products to be excreted, and have the potential for death when they are cut open.

I remember once having seen a cat severely bitten on the leg by a dog that was then whisked away by the owner. The cat bled profusely for almost ten minutes, and I watched the life ebb from its body. I was paralyzed by fascination with the simplicity of death. One moment, the scion of life, the cumulative evolutionary magnificence of a billion years, and the next, a dead object ready to be delivered back to the earth, fodder for some other creature to grow on.

I think of men and women in the same light. We are a continuum of the life force, and the physician holds sway, if even for a small moment in time. When I went to medical school, I knew immediately I would become a surgeon and handle those organs, that life, which so fascinated me, and so it has been for the last forty-two years.

I do love the sight of blood, and sometimes in surgery when a small amount of blood flows I wait just a fraction of a second to see it pool at the bottom of a wound before securing the vessel with a suture or electrocautery. I am wandering. I often do nowadays. It was never so when Marilyn was alive.

— 8 —

Ellen Freemont, attorney at law, was in her seventh year of practice with the firm of Dearborn, Howard and Sedgwick. She had divorced her husband a month ago, had no children, great legs and a new set of breast implants. Her face had been remodeled twice by Dr. Vanderbilt, and she had smooth skin and a pixie nose. She lived by her looks, and she was good at it. She intimidated men when prosecuting cases; she came on slowly and built to a crescendo. She seemed pleasant enough at the beginning, almost friendly. No matter how many times the defense warned their male clients about her, each one thought her innocuous and charming. Charming like the black widow waiting in the web.

She saw no reason to withhold her obvious charms in court, but kept just within the bounds of propriety. Judge Martin was an early conquest; she, the innocent, demure and virginal new lawyer who went into his chambers, ending up with the judge in *her chamber*. She knew which ones to warm up to and which ones to be professional with. Like the Northwest Mounted Police, she always....

Simon Beaujolais, a surgical resident, was in his last year of training. After twenty-four hours on duty, he was called to the emergency room with his junior house staff just fifteen minutes before his shift ended. It was the kind of case every surgical resident hated because it might tie him up for another exhausting three hours.

A mathematics professor's sixteen-year-old son, Herbert, was returning from a party on Saturday night with two older friends when their car was struck by a drunk driver on the wrong side of the road. Fortunately, there was no high speed involved or they all might have been killed outright. As it was, the older boys in the front, wearing seat belts, got out with minor scrapes, while the younger boy, Herbert, was thrown through the window onto the street. All three were rushed to the county hospital, where the older boys were treated for bruises and discharged.

Herbert was alert and doing well with a few cuts and bruises, but, surprisingly, had no pain or tenderness except for his face, which required several neatly placed plastic sutures. His x-rays, physical exam, and blood count were normal, and Beaujolais went over him personally. The boy was frightened that his parents would ground him, even though it wasn't his fault, so he didn't mention the mild aching in his left lower ribs.

After a careful exam and with no abnormal laboratory work, Beaujolais sent him home, heaved a sigh of relief and signed out for the day.

The boy began to feel sick with mild nausea and spent most of the day in bed. His parents, reassured by the senior resident, felt comfortable with the situation until five hours later, when the boy complained of abdominal pain and vomited twice.

"What's wrong, Herbert?" asked his mom. "Do you hurt somewhere?"

"A little," said the increasingly pale boy, "just on my left side, like I told the doctor."

He pointed to the spot on his left lower ribs where a bruise had become more prominent. Of course, he had never mentioned anything to the physician, but he felt sick and wanted to tell his mother that he had been a good and reliable patient in the emergency room.

"Well, let's get you back to the hospital right now," said the father.

The boy sat up and immediately passed out. They called 911, and the paramedics were there in a few minutes. Herbert had become unconscious, and the emergency medical technician immediately started an IV as they raced to the hospital. The blood pressure kept falling and was barely present when they arrived.

"He's bleeding inside," said the ER physician. But in spite of resuscitation attempts, the blood pressure stayed dangerously low. Herbert was taken immediately to surgery where the belly was opened and a massive amount of blood was found coming from a ruptured spleen. The operation was completed, but afterwards the boy was severely brain-damaged. He remained on a respirator for the rest of his life (which turned out to be seven years, before he died of pneumonia).

The parents were irate. Their son should have been diagnosed earlier, but that damn resident just wanted to get home. He was responsible for Herbert's condition and he, the hospital, and the residency program would pay. They hired the law firm of Dearborn, Howard and Sedgwick. Ellen Freemont was assigned to the case.

Interview followed interview followed by depositions. No one but the parents had heard the boy complain of abdominal or left-sided pain, but the thing spoke for itself. When they went to court, the boy was wheeled in, bed and all, and the resident was lambasted by Freemont.

"How can you rely on a child for a history?"

An expert witness was called, one of many paid doctors who would testify to anything about anything.

"You should have assumed nothing and gotten a CAT scan of the abdomen, which would probably have shown the splenic injury," the expert said.

It was a difficult case. Freemont summed up by imploring the jury to find for the boy and send a message to *these ill-prepared doctors who are being turned loose on society*. The case went to a jury of his peers. They found for the complainant and awarded five million dollars. It made national headlines in every junk paper and grocery store tabloid, with the resident's picture on the cover. He was put on temporary leave while the case and situation were reviewed for the umpteenth time by the residency committee.

Three days later, Dr. Beaujolais put a gun to his head and blew his brains out!

In a public announcement, Ms. Freemont expressed sorrow over the incident. That was the end of the case. Or was it?

– 9 –

The doctor continued his writing. It had been several months.

I can't stand the American jury system. I have been called many times for jury duty, but never once assigned to a case. Attorneys shy away from professional people, especially doctors. Unfortunately, the jury ends up with a mixture of non-intelligent and intelligent people, among them the unemployed, retired, and every other type of individual. How could they have been influenced by such histrionics and that lawyer dragging a poor lad into the court room? Easy! They were led down a pathway by a vindictive attorney. Damn system. I read about that Freemont case and my blood boiled. That Dr. Beaujolais had four years of college, four years of medical school and five years of surgical residency under his belt and was a damn good surgeon. And he's put before a jury of his peers. Peers, my ass. I doubt whether anyone on that jury had half his brains and integrity.

Oh, you may ask about that case. Well, it was a bit unusual, but one of those things that can happen in a rare situation. But a jury of his peers looked at the poor suffering kid and, egged on by that bitch Freemont, they destroyed a second life. The first life was probably unavoidably lost. But the second was the result of an attorney doing anything and everything to destroy the life and practice of a good physician. There was no maliciousness about the physician. He was given the information, used his best judgment in a difficult circumstance and came out losing a patient. It was a sad situation that might have happened in a hundred emergency rooms in the country. Yes, some physician might have gotten a CAT scan, which might have prevented the disaster, but most would not have, in view of all the findings.

But that bitch of an attorney knew all that and still decided to take the road to hell with the resident. I'm sure she would say she was doing all she could for her client. Perhaps so, but at what expense? The old "end justifies the means" that is hammered into every attorney's head early on. Who will stand up for the doctor? Who will stand up for the medical profession? Who will rid the world of this pestilence and Godforsaken evil?

I sometimes talk to Marilyn when I am home alone in the study or bedroom. She can hear me. I am sure of it. Sometimes, I can feel a small gust of air against my face, and I know she is in the room. She supports me in my times of sadness and depression. I often feel her presence in the operating room and know that she watches my cases.

Am I crazy? I think not. There is sometimes a faint humming sound in my ears, and I know it is her, and she sometimes comes through the void with a single word of love. I do miss her terribly, but she is not completely gone, and I thank God for that.

When I first became aware of her presence, I doubted my senses. I am not schizophrenic, and I was worried about that for a few times. It's like believing in God. Don't try to prove it to anyone. Just look on any dollar bill. "In God We Trust." Is the whole country schizophrenic?

I'm getting off the track. Freemont must be made an example of. I'm smart enough to know I can't continue to do my extracurricular activities by choosing individuals with notoriety. But just this once. It will give me great pleasure to vindicate Dr. Beaujolais. I am sure that in some way his spirit is sensing what must be done. My justice will be indeed punitive. I can smell it. I can hear it, and I can feel the excitement welling up inside me. My hands will be an extension of Dr. Beaujolais's hands, when he was sitting in the defendant's chair and wanting to reach out and squeeze that charming neck. I can almost feel the softness of her skin, her hair touching the backs of my hands. I can see the eyes starting to bulge and the panic in her face.

I can feel my breathing coming more quickly, and I know that it will be done. And now. Yes, I can feel that soft touch of air on my forehead, and I know that Marilyn is here with me.

"Marilyn, I love you. I shall not forget you. My Marilyn. My sweet Marilyn."

He closed the diary and locked it in the safe.

–10–

Mac was tired. It didn't happen often, but he felt the problems of the day. He thought about the murder.

He sensed a long case and saw a whole string of dead bodies before finding the killer—if they ever found the killer. There were a lot of unsolved cases. John and Mary Public didn't realize how many murders went unsolved.

In crimes of passion, the angry husbands and wives usually got caught. But this kind of apparently random killing was a problem. And if this was indeed a surgeon over the edge, Mac figured he might be dealing with someone who had taken more precautions than the usual run-of-the-mill drunk or doper.

He stood in the back hall with his files and went down the list of serial killers with whom he had been involved. Nine in all, and that was a lot for one individual. Three were out-and-out crazy with predictable, though bizarre, behavior and easily traceable: the guy who strangled prostitutes on Sunday nights in Harlem; the woman who left "Catch Me" notes on the bodies of men, all tall, dark-haired teachers; and the psychopathic gang member who was only shooting the opposite gang members on Saturday night.

The others were more difficult. No particular pattern except some vague connection with a relative such as mom, dad or a spurned lover. It usually took several deaths to find the pattern and sometimes the killer just stopped killing, either moving away or getting the urge out of his system.

There were two professional people. One was a lawyer who killed seven women before killing his own wife, followed by one more just to throw the police off the search. Then there was the veterinarian who looked for mistreated animals, then treated the owners in kind. There were a lot of neutered, murdered people before he was finally caught.

But this doctor, or whoever he was, was different. He was knocking off attorneys...malpractice attorneys with no apparent relationship to one another. There must be tens of thousands of those lawyers around, any one of whom was a potential victim. Hopefully, the guy was based in New York and wouldn't decide to take a trip across country.

The cases of the first two victims were at dead ends. There was not a significant clue, not even one potential subject for investigation. He knew they'd have to wait for the next one or two murders, and maybe the guy would slip up. Even a little bit. Mac shook his head and went to the refrigerator for a beer. He sat down in a chair and wrote all the information he had several times. Sometimes, when he did that, something would pop up, something he missed, some angle. It would often be staring him in the face for days, and then he would see it.

This one had to be a man...large strong hands and fast on his feet...relatively good shape...able to lift a heavy body. Maybe there were two individuals? No. He ruled that out as a strong improbability. He was definitely either a surgeon or a technician who worked extensively with a surgeon or in a hospital. There were nurses who did surgical assisting, but then the whole thing about malpractice attorneys wouldn't make sense. That led directly to a physician, rather than anyone else.

He was a firm adherent of the *when you hear hoof beats, don't think first of zebras* philosophy; *the most commonest things occur the most oftenes*t, one of his mentors had once said. But he also kept the *zebras* in the back of his mind...the weird case, the weird perpetrator. But this case was more straightforward.

Vengeance and retribution. The motives were pretty clear he thought, but finding the guy….

So how to go about it? He had three officers working on the malpractice case angle, checking the last five years. Should he go back further? Maybe. No big-name attorneys. No big-name cases. Nothing to hang his hat on. He spent another half hour mulling over the situation, then turned in for the night.

–11–

Ellen Freemont. Mr. Freemont's little girl. I'll bet he was proud of her when she got into law school and even prouder when she passed the bar. He glanced at the newspaper article, one of the grocery store glitz papers. There she was on the cover with a story about the Beaujolais case and, of course, a picture of Herbert. He was in bed hooked up to all sorts of support machines, and Beaujolais was in his apartment on the floor, surrounded by his own blood and brains. Graphic…and a good newspaper seller! And she was going to be on a talk show Thursday night. That probably meant recording it beforehand, maybe Monday or Tuesday. He'd find out when she would come into the city and arrange his own schedule. He could fly in, but that left too many records. Best to take the bus or train. He didn't want to drive. Always the chance of getting spotted or someone seeing the car. Especially his car—too fancy.

He thought about the situation, then called the television station.

"WNOX. How may I direct your call?"

"Public Relations department." He was holding a towel over the phone and talking in a higher than usual tone. The phone clicked and another voice answered.

"Pamela Jones. May I help you?"

"Yes. I'm William Hartford with the Times. I'm interested in interviewing Ellen Freemont, but wasn't able to reach her. I've got a deadline to meet. Is there some way I can speak to her this afternoon?"

The voice on the line hesitated a moment. "Just a moment Mr. Hartford." He heard the line click into a hold pattern and waited a few moments. Then the voice returned. "She'll be at the Wilchester Hotel this afternoon. You could try her there. Of course, I can't be sure she'll want to give you an interview, but that's the best I can do."

He thought to himself with his lips tight together, a smile trying to break his lips apart. Then he answered, "I'm sure I'll get my interview. I haven't failed yet."

"Well, good luck to you." She chuckled and hung up the phone.

"I suppose that makes you an accessory before the fact or something," he said to himself, as he set the receiver back on the hook.

He had packed everything in a small leather carry-on bag and went off towards the train station. Halfway there, he parked in an alleyway and changed his appearance so that he looked like an old man. He took off his good clothes and put on a different outfit: brown pants, tee shirt, and the usual forty-pound bulky appearance around the waist and chest. He placed the mustache and put on a brown wig. He looked at himself in the car mirror; even his mother wouldn't know him. He felt warm inside, sensuous, self-assured, and powerful. He was right; he was good; he was an avenging angel. He flexed his biceps. The workouts had made him solid, invincible.

He drove to the station and took the next train into the city. He sat alone in the compartment with his small Naugahyde travel bag. He kept it on his lap during the three hours and never left his seat. He felt a floating sensation and thought of Marilyn.

"I love you, darling," he whispered to himself a thousand times before the train pulled into Grand Central Station. He disappeared into the four o'clock crowd and made his way to the Wilchester Hotel, a large place with a busy lobby in the center of town. He walked right in.

Just another ordinary businessman, he thought. He lingered in the lobby unobserved, and shortly after 8 P.M. saw Ellen Freemont enter the elevator. He just made it to the door before it closed, and the two were alone going up to the eighth floor. He smiled and nodded to her as she exited. He got out, following at a distance, noticing her going into 826. He walked past and stood for a moment at the door to the linen room. It had worked once, why not try it again? He went back to the elevator, where he picked up the house phone and dialed 826.

He was amazed at how easy it was to fool a person with complimentary champagne from the management. He waited ten minutes and walked to the door. Holding the bottle in front of the peephole, he knocked. She looked and opened. After all, it was the champagne she expected, and there was nothing to fear in a major hotel.

Once the door was open, his left hand grabbed her by the neck and stifled any sound. He pushed her into the room like a rag doll, closing the door behind him. He let her take a breath, then grabbed her tightly again. "One sound, and I'll snap your neck like a twig."

Her pleading eyes assessed the situation, and she nodded her head up and down.

"I'm going to let go of your throat, but I must warn you. Any resistance, and I can break your neck in a second."

She nodded again, and he slowly let her neck go, grasping her left arm as he set his traveling bag onto the floor.

"What do you want?"

"Does it matter?"

"Don't hurt me. Just don't hurt me."

"That's entirely up to you. If you behave, you'll be perfectly all right. If not—" He made a motion with his hands like twisting a wet towel. She shuddered and began trembling.

"Are you going to hurt me?"

"Of course not. I only want to talk to you. I'm really a very gentle person." He smiled and led her into the bedroom.

"Lie down on the bed and keep silent. Remember what I told you."

She thought of the possibilities. She looked at the window and the doors. There was no escape. The windows were closed, and there was a gentle hum of the air conditioning. If she yelled, he'd kill her. Maybe he just wanted to force himself on her, and then he'd leave. She looked at him imploringly. "I'll do anything you want; just don't hurt me."

"Okay," he smiled. He thought, *daddy's little girl is going to be easier than I thought*. "Get undressed!"

"Everything?" she asked, fearfully.

"Down to your underwear."

She began to cry, and he came towards her with his hands opening and closing. She became silent and slowly removed her clothes until she was sitting on the side of the bed in bra and panties.

Nice body of evidence, he thought and pushed her back onto the bed. He bound her arms and legs and tied her to the corners of the bed with strong ropes he had brought along. Then he placed a cloth in her mouth, and she was spread-eagled before him, powerless.

"Are you frightened?"

She nodded her head up and down.

"Are you very frightened, Miss Freemont?"

The sound of her name suddenly stopped all movement, and a new fear came over her. This man knew her name. "Are you as frightened as Dr. Beaujolais, counselor?"

She began to struggle against the bonds and made several sounds through the cloth in her mouth.

"Please be silent, counselor, or I'll have to sanction you. You see, I am the judge, and this is my courtroom." He put his face very close to hers. "And I am also the jury."

He went to the radio and turned on the classical station. "Mendelssohn Octet, Miss Freemont. Do you like Mendelssohn?" He opened his bag and took out a pair of surgical gloves, pulling them easily over his fingers. Before returning to her, he wiped every surface he had touched.

He would like to have performed surgery upon her while she was awake, but it would be almost impossible with her struggling, and he'd have to take care of bleeding. It would be a terrible mess. And without any paralysis, the procedure would be near impossible.

Oh, well, he thought, *lucky for her. I will do it with my hands. Yes, my hands around her neck, whispering Dr. Beaujolais's name as the last words she will ever hear.* He stood before her and took off all his clothes. She was sure he was going to rape her. Then he went over to his bag, then to the window.

Oh, my God, she thought, *maybe he'll just do it and leave.* She tried to talk through the mouth gag. After all, it was her words that always got her through problems, her words and her body. If she could only say something to him. And then she felt a cool draft as he opened the window slightly and came back to her with a tray filled with knives, scissors and other strange instruments. She started sweating and noticed herself shaking with fear and, for the first time in her life, felt a complete and deadly helplessness.

"Isn't this like taking the bar exam, dear?" he asked. "Don't know the questions and hoping you'll pass, make the grade, maybe?" He began placing his hands on her abdomen and feeling around as she moved under his fingers. "The hands of a surgeon. Do you like the touch?" He probed a little deeper into her abdomen in the right upper quadrant. She was in near panic now as he took a marking pen and drew an oblique line about two inches under her right rib cage margin. The perfect gall bladder incision, he thought. Unfortunately, he wouldn't be able to do the procedure laparoscopically. Not enough equipment. No carbon dioxide insufflator, no special instruments.

Then he got on top of her and gently cut off the remainder of her clothes with a scissors. He leaned towards her pallid face and whispered, "Dr. Beaujolais was a fine surgeon. He would have done this procedure very well."

She struggled and twisted her head back and forth as he reached up and gently caressed her neck with his large hands and strong fingers. As he tightened his hands around her throat, she suddenly became aware of what was happening, and her eyes began to bulge as he whispered, "Dr. Beaujolais, Dr. Beaujolais." Then the air was shut off, her lungs became painful, and she knew as he looked at her that she was looking death in the face.

And the last words she was conscious of as she twisted and tried to pull air into her tortured throat were, "Beaujolais, Beaujolais…" and in the distance a muttering of sounds before she lost consciousness.

He held his hands around her throat for almost three minutes after she stopped moving, then felt for a carotid pulse. None. He took out a stethoscope and listened at the heart. Nothing. He got off her and prepared the surgical field. This was the fun part. Almost like doing a dissection in anatomy class when he was a medical student. Yes, some oozing, but no arterial bleeding to worry about. Just clean surgery.

He made a sweeping incision where he had made his mark under the rib margin and carried it through the fascia and muscles and the peritoneum lining the abdomen. He even had a small retractor to keep the abdominal wall open, and he used cloth towels to pack the intestines out of the way. He grasped the gall bladder lying under the liver edge and, using a scissors, dissected it out of the liver bed in which it was positioned. The artery to the gall bladder was dissected out, doubly clipped with titanium surgical clips, then divided. The gall bladder duct was clipped, and the gall bladder was removed and placed in a small sandwich baggie. He removed the packing and the retractor and felt around the still-warm abdomen, just as he was conditioned to do in living patients. *Nothing much except some cysts on the right ovary.* He took out a large suture and closed the abdominal wall fascia. Then he took a skin stapler and closed the skin. He went to the bathroom, got a towel, and cleaned the body. There was no blood on the sheets; he was pleased with his work and his cleanliness, although, without a beating heart, this didn't present such a tremendous accomplishment. He undid the ties on the wrists and ankles and left her spread-eagled on the white sheet. He took the printed message he had prepared on his computer and tied it to the right big toe.

This attorney had a lot of gall to sue Dr. Beaujolais.
She doesn't have it anymore!

He was proud of himself. "Good job, huh, Marilyn?" he muttered as he replaced the instruments in the bag along with the towel. He went to the bathroom and took a shower, rinsing the stall vigorously after he was finished. Then he dressed and glanced once more at the scene. "Goodbye, counselor."

He went to the door, opened it slowly to peek into the corridor. It was almost midnight, and there was no one around. He grabbed his bag, slipped out, took the stairs to the lobby, and disappeared into the night, humming 'La Donna e Mobile" from Rigoletto.

–12–

A crowd was building behind the television vans in front of the Wilchester Hotel. Radio and TV announcers pressed forward as McClymonds came out of the heavily guarded, taped-off entrance. Mac had already spoken to the mayor and the chief and been prepped on a minimal number of words to release to the eager press. This was the part of his job he detested most—not because of the actual reporting to the media, but because he was never quoted correctly. Everything was exaggerated or sensationalized. He was told not to answer questions, but only give a brief announcement.

"Ladies and gentlemen. Thank you for being so patient. I'm sure you can understand the importance of clearing the crime scene and not reporting anything to you except the facts, as we understand them. I'm sorry, but for security reasons I will be unable to answer any questions. I will read a statement that has been prepared by me, along with the mayor and the department chief." He took out a single sheet of paper with handwriting on it and pulled on his glasses. It made him look more erudite and distinguished, and he didn't like the non-cop look it gave him.

"We have three cases of homicide, apparently by the same individual, and all three victims have been attorneys. There are two men and one woman and, as of yet, we can find no significant clues regarding the identity of the perpetrator. We have tried to conceal any facts that only the killer would know because we are already receiving many calls from individuals confessing guilt. None of them has been able to show knowledge of the crimes or crime scenes. We have been in touch with the local chapters of the American Bar Association and have issued warnings to attorneys we feel may be at risk. There does not appear to be a risk to non-attorney members of the community, and we do not want to panic the general populace. We have engaged teams from the city, state and federal government to help in this investigation and will keep you informed of any significant developments in the cases. Thank you."

He turned to leave and was inundated by many questions, which he politely declined to answer. He went back into the hotel as the medical examiner, Dr. Birdwell, left with his staff, who carried the body in a body bag.

Mac turned to him. "Stay away from the vultures. No comments unless it goes through me or the chief."

"Yeah, yeah," said Birdwell. "But you must admit the guy has a charming side, what with *no more gall*. Damn. It's the sort of thing you dream about as a physician."

"Remember. No comments. No leaks. Nothing. Not even your doctor friends. They'd have a field day with this."

Mac went back up to the room where the forensic team had just finished dusting and were gathering their equipment. He asked everyone to leave as soon as they were done, then closed the door and sat in the center of the room on a chair, staring at the floor, his hands falling between his legs. Then he took out his notebook and started writing himself notes. He made his usual plus and minus sides to the investigation. What were the similarities and what were the differences between the cases? Under the plus, he put down: *attorney-malpractice, surgeon, surgery, notes left on the bodies, murders in New York City— need to check out other city possibilities.*

The negatives were increasing. There was a change this time. Apparently the other two were random victims, but this one was obviously selected because of the newspaper notoriety. The last victim was strangled; the other two were shot. This one was female; the other two were male. No particular body type, hair or eye color. Apparently, the killer had called the television station to find out where she was staying. He flipped over his pad and wrote: *characteristics*. These were items he never shared with his colleagues because they were often speculative, but his long career had made him almost clairvoyant in some cases. He wrote down words as they came into his head: *confident, vigilante, thinking*. He underlined the last twice. This guy, surgeon or not, may be crazy, but he wasn't stupid. *Has to be a surgeon. Three different surgeries: colon, leg amputations, and gall bladder. Who would do all the types?* He made an asterisk next to this. It needed a few phone calls. He turned the page again and wrote: *Where? New York. Lives not too far away. Wouldn't take a plane. Must drive, take a bus or train. Three or four hours at most?* He added several question marks. *Just a gut feeling. Probably single or living alone. Had to be able to come and go at whim.*

Mac looked around the crime scene. Nothing special. Typical hotel room with bed, table, and individual bar. There was no indication of any sexual activity. Nothing with the men, either. Mac wrote again: *Anger at malpractice attorneys, tendency for extreme violence, use of words in notes? He's just gotten started. Expect more…many more!*

He folded the pad, placed it in his left hip pocket and started a meticulous search of the room. He knew that several others had done this already, but it was his routine, and he tried to see the room through the eyes of the perpetrator. See what the killer saw, feel what he felt. Sometimes, it gave him ideas, but today he came up with nothing…nothing except neatness and cleanliness. Very unusual for a crime scene, he thought. The man was obviously compulsive. The gall bladder hadn't been torn from the body, but carefully dissected out. It was almost as if the dead body were a sacred calf to be revered and treated carefully, even in death. *Controlled violence*, he thought. *This guy is doing a job, not an immediate and compulsive act. He does his homework and then carries out his action. As long as he can take his time and make the rules, he will continue to escape detection.*

Mac pondered a moment and wrote: *Try to disrupt the pattern. Make him change. Force a mistake.*

He glanced at his watch. Just after 6 P.M. He went over to the television and turned on the news. Then he sat back in a chair and watched the announcer. Sometimes reporters looked at things from a different angle. Anything was welcome. He wasn't proud. He'd accept help from anyone and anything.

The cameras were focused on the front of the very building he was in, with shots of the coroner's team departing and recapitulations of his announcement. He tried to imagine the thousands who were probably glued to their sets waiting for a vision of the macabre or some gruesome fact to latch onto. Face it; murder had appeal, and a good, juicy murder like this had good, juicy appeal. He concluded to himself for the thousandth time it was a sick society.

The camera homed in on Fred Battle, the anchor for KBLH. "Another murder and another attorney. This one was apparently a young woman from Los Angeles whom we have all seen on the front pages of the tabloids. Ms. Freemont graduated Yale Law School and was affiliated with a large firm that specializes in personal injury and malpractice law. She had recently won a large decision for her client and was supposed to appear on Luella French's interview show tomorrow. Ms. Freeman spent yesterday afternoon being recorded for the program. The station has temporarily canceled the airing until an appropriate later date.

"She was found this morning by a hotel maid, and we are unable to get much more information because of the ongoing investigation."

The reporter in the TV studio turned to his left where a gray-haired gentleman in a three-piece suit sat austerely looking into the camera. Fred Battle introduced the man.

"We're privileged to have with us today, on short notice, Professor David Filliger, a prominent New York attorney and a teacher at NSP Law School here in the city. Thank you for being with us today."

The man nodded his head up and down, and his serious look contrasted sharply with Battle's continuously pleasant expression. "Thank you, Fred. Always a pleasure, but not under these circumstances."

"Are we looking at a disgruntled physician out to kill off all the malpractice attorneys?"

"It's always a strong possibility, since these attorneys are frequently threatening the very lifeline of physicians by impugning their work. I have seen some angry doctors, though I don't practice that kind of law. This may be a man who's lost a big case and just flipped. Attorneys generally see physicians as passive individuals who can be threatened and sued at will. There aren't a lot of checks and balances in our profession. Since attorneys often take on cases before they know all the facts, they start out with very nasty threatening letters, which tell a physician how he has committed some bad deed against his client. It's been the way of the profession for years, and I'm frankly not surprised that some loony doctor has finally lost it. It's a tragedy for these three attorneys and their families, but it's a tragedy that's been waiting to happen."

"Do you think the profession should do something to curb these attorneys?"

"Now, wait, Fred. I'm not coming down on malpractice attorneys. Most are very fine professionals, and they are needed to protect the public. I am only saying that this kind of reaction is not a surprising one in view of the negative consequences from what they do."

"I see. Do you see this as a sentinel event which might stimulate more physicians to take action?"

"Oh, I think not, Fred. This is an isolated instance of a mad-man and not the reflection of the attitudes of most doctors."

Mac brought his right hand up to his forehead as he listened to the dialogue. He said softly to himself, "Just what my mad surgeon wants to hear. This idiot is practically threatening him to do it again and as soon as possible. Self-righteous son of a bitch attorney."

The interview then switched to the individual sitting on the other side of Fred Battle, another distinguished-looking man in his sixties wearing a white coat with *Dr. Marsouppeal, Department of Psychiatry* written on it. Battle continued. "After our break we'll be back with a forensic psychiatrist and a close personal friend of mine, Dr. Phillip Marsouppeal, for a few words on the case."

Battle was replaced by a panty shield advertisement: *You won't be drippy with Skippy!* Mac turned away from the TV, glanced around the room again and walked over to the bed. The wooden four corners of the bed had been pulled inward by the woman's struggles, and he examined a few rope fibers left near the headboard. He knew forensics had seen these and taken samples. She had been tied up, but no sexual activity could yet be determined. She was attractive in life; he had seen her pictures. In death she looked awful. A little makeup, hair styling, clothing, and that little feminine extra could do a lot.

Ten years ago Mac had had a woman friend, Penny, who lived in the apartment upstairs from his. He saw her each morning on his way to work and said, "Hello." She was not just plain, she was downright ugly. Then one afternoon he came home early and found a female model at the front door—not just attractive, but gorgeous. It made him stop a moment until she said "Hi" and had to introduce herself as the selfsame Penny who lived upstairs. *My God,* he thought. *That's what makeup can do?* It made a great impression on him, and he realized that disguise could effectively change one individual into another. Descriptions of suspects involving half-intelligent people were often incorrect, and the suspect could change his or her appearance very easily. Small things like a mustache, hair color, glasses, or eye makeup could completely conceal an identity from all but the most observant onlooker. And Mac knew that the average citizen didn't look very carefully or very closely at anyone, much less a stranger.

The television had switched back to the interview, and Battle was talking with the psychiatrist. The doctor was giving a long lecture on serial killers, frequently reminding the viewing audience that this case was different, since only attorneys were being killed, and the public should not get overly alarmed. Mac couldn't take any more. He reached for the clicker and turned off the set. He needed a beer.

–13–

I swim laps in my pool in the morning. Fifty times up and back; it keeps me fit. I have always liked swimming. I usually start at 6 A.M. It wakes me up and prepares me for the day ahead.

I had two cases scheduled in the operating room today, a hernia repair and a partial thyroid removal. I went into the doctor's lounge to change my clothes and found a vacant locker. The dressing room was empty, and I sat on the bench, removed my shirt, tie and trousers and hung them on the hooks. I had to take off my shoes, since the surgical scrub pants wouldn't fit over them, then I put on the green shirt and pants, then the shoes again. I put paper booties over the shoes, a surgeon's cap to cover my hair, and went into the operating suite hallway. I was scheduled in room three and made my way down the hall, nodding to the many nurses and technicians who knew me as Doctor, and finally I put on my surgical mask and entered the operating room.

I said good morning to my patient, a Mr. Harold Humber, and confirmed with him and the nurses that I would be repairing his hernia on the left side. I was strangely excited about cutting into another human body after my busy weekend.

The news reports are increasing in frequency with each of my activities and it gives me a tingling sensation deep inside. I know that few would understand my motivation, and some would label me a senseless murderer, but I expect that.

After having spoken to Mr. Humber, I went outside the room to the wash sink and took a single usage scrub brush from the rack, soaped my hands and began a thorough scrubbing of my hands and forearms up to the elbows. I thought, "Surgery is so neat and clean, so well-defined."

I love the orderliness and the regularity of the obsessive and compulsive attitude often needed to succeed in my line of work. The attorneys just don't understand the time and effort involved in training to become a physician. But I will teach them in a most definitive manner. Yes. A most definitive manner.

"You're smiling doctor!" a nurse scrubbing her hands next to him jarred him from his thoughts.

"Just thinking about my pleasant weekend, Marie."

He finished washing and held his hands up, allowing water to drip from his elbows, and backed into the operating room, pushing the door handle to undo the locking mechanism. He walked over to the "scrub" nurse and she gave him a cloth towel to dry his hands. Then she held up the gown, and it was tied in back by another nurse; then the latex gloves were held out, and he placed his hands into them.

He glanced at the operating table and looked at the patient. It was the exciting moment when he stared at the immobilized body. He gazed on the man lying asleep painted with the orange-brown iodine prep solution. It brought back memories of his first surgery. He felt a sense of strength well up.

It's not the same as when I was working last weekend. I didn't feel the same sensuous pulling deep inside me. How can I explain it? It was not orgasmic, but it was definitely very exciting.

He adjusted the overhead lights after placing the sterile light handles and focused the beam onto the groin.

"Scalpel!"

It was firmly placed in his hand, and he made a short, deep incision through the skin. He reached for the cautery and started to coagulate the bleeding vessels, being careful not to touch the skin itself. That would cause a bad scar. He cut deeper into the wound, through the fat and fascia until the hernia defect was seen. The epigastric artery had a small bleeding branch, and he watched the red blood flow for just a moment longer than usual, then touched the vessel with the cautery stylet.

He thought to himself, *I love to see the blood. It makes me shiver inside to know that this small blood vessel, left to its own resources, could eventually lead to the demise of the patient. We are so strong in many ways and yet so fragile in others. The human body is a miracle, and the surgeon is a privileged interloper. The hernia is simple and straightforward. I have done a thousand before. I isolate the defect and the sac and tie off the protruding tissue and remove the excess. I reinforce the deep wall with strong silk sutures and then start the closure. It has a beautiful symmetry.*

"Even Ellen Freemont had this symmetry."

"Excuse me, doctor?" The scrub nurse looked at him, unable to understand what he had said.

"Oh," he said, surprised that he had been speaking aloud. "Nothing, really nothing. Just talking to myself." He smiled. "Getting old, you know!"

"Not you, doc. Never," responded the other nurse.

He finished sewing up the tissue layers, then the skin and left the dressings for the nurses. He knew that his extracurricular activities would somehow impact his normal activities, but he found it a bit scary to realize he had actually mentioned Miss

Freemont's name aloud. He walked to the recovery room with the chart in his left hand and thought, *The same hand that squeezed the breath from that young attorney can also prolong life. I know God has given me a great talent. I have strong hands. Always had strong hands. Never had to use those little exercise balls. I could always squeeze things well!*

He wrote the post-operative orders and dictated the operative note, then went to the waiting room and spoke to the patient's wife. It was a nice part of the day, he thought, when someone thanked him for what he had done. Appreciation was appreciated.

He sat for a while waiting for his next case to begin. It would be a thyroid operation, and he was already thinking of his next weekend.

Marilyn. A thyroid. He smiled, because part of the surgery was preserving the nerves to the voice box. *I'll have to make some surgical errors on my next one. A surgical error, but acceptable in that case.* He laughed aloud, then thought about his activities.

Am I becoming psychotic? No. Well, I did talk to Marilyn, but that's different, I think. Everyone occasionally hears some voices. I mean, it's not a regular thing, but it does happen on occasion, and I recognize it.

The next case went well, from the bold slash into the neck to the final closing sutures, and something about that neck gave him pause from time to time. He removed his surgical clothing and dumped it in a hamper. He put on his new suit, a soft gray fabric by Zegna, along with a new shirt and tie. He had rewarded himself for a job well done over the weekend. It was important to reward himself when something went well. There was too little recognition for a job well done.

Life was good!

–14–

He thought, *The first thing I noticed about her was her blouse. No, that's a lie; it was her breasts. She had on a loose bra, and when she bent forward to pick up a paper she had dropped on the floor I was sitting ten feet away, and my eyes wandered where they would. She was statuesque and seemed so pure in her white blouse and black skirt.*

It was the medical library, and I rarely came over except to pick up journals to read at home or in my spare time during the day. It was an older library with long tables and several chairs on each side. She sat down across from me, opened her physiology book and began reading and taking notes. She was a first year student, and I was in my fourth and last year. I glanced at her from time to time, and she only looked up once, smiling demurely, going back to her studies as if to say, "Hello, goodbye, and good luck."

After a few minutes I got up and left and didn't return. A few days later, I arrived at about the same time. She was there at the same table, and I made a point of sitting near her again. Still no impact, yet I know she was aware of me. The third time I went later in the evening, just before library closing time, and sat down opposite her.

"Have a coffee with me after the library closes?" I implored in my softest voice.

She looked up, surprised, and then smiled politely. "Thank you. But I don't date medical students."

"Then I'll have to do away with myself! It will be a terrible blow to my parents."

She had not expected this reply, and she laughed a moment, stared at me, and then said, "All right. But just so your parents won't blame me." She looked back at her books.

"Actually, I lied. My mother passed away years ago. It's just my dad who would be shattered." She looked up with a serious expression, then went back to her book.

The remaining half hour moved ever so slowly, and then the buzzer went off indicating closing time, and we both got up and left the library together. We went for a coffee, and then I took her back to her apartment. I knew from that time on that we were soulmates and, as ridiculous as that may sound, it was the first and last time I felt that way about anyone.

I was surprised when she invited me in. She had been rather reserved for the last hour, and I expected just to drop her off and leave. She grabbed my right hand and drew me into her apartment without a word. She held the sides of my face and looked deeply into my eyes for a prolonged few seconds, then brought her face up to mine and kissed me. She pressed herself fully against me with a passion and an urgency I'll never forget.

"Come with me," she said, and led me into the darkened bedroom, where she stared at me as she slowly undressed until she was standing before me completely unclothed. Her large breasts rose and fell quickly with her rapid inspirations. I was completely taken aback, both by her boldness and by her beauty. I stood motionless for a few seconds, until she looked at me and said, "Do I need to ask permission from that father of yours?"

I undressed and went with her into the bed. She unleashed a passion I had never known, and when morning came she was up by 5 A.M. and standing next to me, fully dressed when I opened my eyes.

SCALPEL

"No one will ever love you the way I do," she said. Then she quickly turned, gathered up her books and purse, and left me alone in her apartment. That's how it began.

Her name was Marilyn.

—15—

It was one of the evenings when Mac needed some comforting. He wanted someone to be with and not to argue with, someone just to be there when he felt that all the ends were loose or coming apart. He'd called two of his usual *friends* but they weren't in. He knew he would end up at the bar, sitting alone in the corner until one or two in the morning. On the face of it he was stolid, in control, the man's man. But at times like this something let go, and he felt like the young policeman he had been, leaving the academy so many years ago. It was an unsure, empty feeling brought on by the work. He had been there before when difficult cases were in progress. He didn't know exactly why he felt this way, but thought it might be due to the lack of control. Someone was out there committing these murders, and now he was out there with him—unknown to each other, yet pitted against each other. It was a battle to the death, in his mind, where one would win and one would lose.

Television dramatized these situations too much. It was never so clear-cut or dramatic. He was facing an uphill struggle, starting with three bodies and practically no good clues, and he knew there would be more killings before he finished. His mind felt overburdened with the senseless information, and he couldn't clear his brain for even a few minutes. That's why he needed Rochelle or Billie; they knew him like a book and took care of his needs. Oh yes, there was the physical and sexual side,

71

but he actually saw that as the lesser of his objectives. These women had been friends for many years, way past their prime as hookers; they were friends, comrades, psychologists and geishas. They also had the ability to be just silent partners. Sometimes, they just sat with him for hours, without a word being spoken and perhaps a cup of coffee or tea, and then the peace of mind would come, and he would feel relaxed, if only for one evening.

The next morning he would feel invigorated and face the problems with a clean slate. But tonight his saviors were not available. They were out, trying to make a living in the oldest profession, and he resented their absence. He sat alone at the back of the bar, and his thoughts went to everything and nothing. His wife, long gone, his grown children, and the many cases he had fumbled with over the years. He had seen his friends on the force face that strange depression and had known two who just couldn't stand it and ended it with their own service revolver.

Why couldn't he be a self-sufficient guy like *Dirty Harry* or an uninvolved, unemotional *Joe Friday*? *Bullshit,* he thought. *Those guys are fiction, and I'm making them real.* Fake police, fake doctors, fake attorneys—the airwaves were replete with them to the degree that the real guys measured their abilities and successes against the fakes. He thought of how his son had wanted to be a doctor like Robert Young's Marcus Welby, M.D., or a lawyer like Perry Mason, or a lawman like Matt Dillon. Society measured reality by these fakes, and Mac resented it. He was on the front line taking the risks, doing the work, putting in the tedious hours and getting the chump salary. The actors were making the images, taking the awards and putting their names on the public's lips.

His mind went back to the case at hand. He wanted to catch the guy, but also couldn't help feeling a bit resentful toward the attorneys. He'd had more than one bad guy set loose on a technicality and had seen his efforts twisted and turned to allow some punk or murderer freed by the system. But Mac knew the ropes and knew it was probably the best of the worst. Still, he had to smile at the thought of this surgical vigilante giving it to the attorneys where it hurt most. If it put some fear in them, so be it. He'd catch the guy eventually—he usually did—but he would also stand back and watch the reactions of the legal world getting a little of its own medicine, justice by one of its peers.

He took out his notebook and began to write. He was going to play a game with this guy if he could, cat and mouse through the newspapers and the media. All he had to do was get the chief's approval to build a better mousetrap!

–16–

It had been eight weeks since the first body was found, and there had been two more murders since then. The entire department and the news media were waiting for the inevitable fourth. The department psychiatrist was trying to assemble a profile of the physician responsible for the deeds. Every legal convention was covered, every physician with recent major malpractice decisions was scrutinized, and still nothing had come up. The number of new malpractice suits filed in just the previous ten days had plummeted ninety percent.

The surgeon read *The New York Times* front page commentary and smiled to himself. He was having a bigger impact than he had hoped for and was looking forward to his next activity. This one, he was sure, would set a new precedent, although it might prove more difficult. But he always liked a challenge, and this was certainly going to be that. Anyway, he knew everyone was focusing on New York City, and his opportunity for detection would be low in the Boston area.

Dean Arthur Fieldman was professor of law at the Harvard Law School. He had specialized in personal injury and malpractice law for twenty years in a very lucrative private practice before a mild heart attack had curtailed his activities at the age of forty-seven. He had graduated *cum laude* from the Harvard school and was readily accepted back into a full-time teaching position, initially as an associate professor, elevated last year to full professorship and associate dean for admissions. He had written articles about the law as it concerned medical malpractice and had been deeply involved in the silicone breast implant fiasco, which lined his pockets with several millions before the settlements were finally reached. He was married for eighteen years and had one daughter, a junior in high school who had her heart set on Wellesley College in two years.

The surgeon had researched him well and started to compile a daily log of his comings and goings by driving to Cambridge, Massachusetts, whenever he could break away for a day. He found Fieldman an easy man to follow, a man of fairly strict routine. He lived in the outskirts of Cambridge and arose about six every morning. After a two mile run, he returned home for breakfast with his wife and daughter, then left for the campus on Tuesday, Thursday and Friday at about nine o'clock to make his two classes, one at 10 A.M. and a seminar at 1 P.M. On Mondays, he went to the library about midday to do paperwork and research. On Wednesday, he alternated lake fishing with one of his cronies and an afternoon of tennis with anyone he could find at the local tennis club, which had both indoor and outdoor courts. On the weekends, he and his wife drove to a small cottage on the ocean where he just relaxed, read, or walked up and down the beach.

The surgeon had it all written down in his notebook. All he had to do was devise a plan of action. Plan the case, plan the operation. The only problem was making enough time to complete the procedure he had planned, and that meant at least two hours. How could he get him alone for two hours? Then he thought about Marilyn and an idea came into his head.

–17–

Art Fieldman had laid out his running clothes for the morning. He was very organized and had the running shoes—cross trainers to be exact—in front of the chair where he had placed his shorts, jockstrap and tee shirt. He didn't need a jockstrap to go jogging, but it was part of the image he projected for himself, and he liked the sense of manliness it gave him. When he wore it, he was an athlete; in plain jockey briefs, he was just another amateur running for exercise. He always arose before Sandy, his wife, and leaned over to kiss her goodbye after he was fully dressed. He put a sweatband around his forehead and went out the front door, closing it softly behind him. He leaned against the door, stretching his hamstrings, then bent over to touch his toes and complete his stretches.

He attached the Walkman radio to his shorts, put the earphones into his ears and set off down the driveway to the street. He took a left onto the country road, facing traffic, and looked at his watch. It was just six fifteen; there was still a bit of moisture on the ground and glistening on the grass and trees as he increased his pace. He tried to get into a steady pattern, moving his arms the same way with each stride, like he had seen the professionals do. He imagined himself at the Olympics and tried to conjure up some great opponent, such as Roger Bannister breaking the four-minute mile or the great Finnish runner, Paavo Nurmi, or the Czech, Emil Zatopek. He closed his eyes for a few seconds as he continued down the road. He had been over this route a hundred times and knew every turn and tree.

The sun was just beginning to illuminate the roadway and, as usual, the road was deserted this early in the morning. It was almost a country setting—each house on fifteen to twenty acres of land. It had originally been farmland, now converted to large acreage lots for the wealthy Bostonians. The heavily wooded countryside came right up to the edge of the road, and it was not uncommon to see occasional deer and other wildlife. It was isolated and beautiful. He often thought how fortunate he was to have landed the job at Harvard. He had the best of the best without having to go the trial route anymore. He had liked the excitement and the challenge, but these had worn thin and he was glad to be out of the rat race. Most people here didn't arise until after eight or nine o'clock, and he enjoyed the solitude.

The object looked like a heap of clothing from a distance, until he was about fifty yards away. Then he could make out the curled-up figure of a person lying at the side of the road. He took the earphones off and shut off the radio as he jogged up to the motionless figure. There was a small amount blood on the ground and tire skid marks near the body. No car in sight and nobody around as he knelt down beside the inert figure. The eyes were closed and the breathing shallow as he turned the large man over and felt a strong carotid pulsation. The face and neck were warm, and the color was good, he thought to himself. *If he's been struck by a car, it must have been very recent*. He looked around several times, but there was no one.

"Can you hear me, sir?" he asked, careful not to move the man or cause any further injury. He remembered all the info about neck injuries and wanted to keep from causing any further harm. The man was over six feet tall and powerfully built, with large hands and broad shoulders visible beneath a thin sweater. At first there was no response, and then the eyes opened slowly and gazed up at him with a puzzled expression.

The man spoke faintly. "Was that your car that hit me? We got our differences but you didn't have to run me down, did ya?" Fieldman looked down at him. "Oh, no. It wasn't me. I was just running by and noticed you here."

The man looked at Fieldman. "Yeah, I guess that's right. The other guy was different." He took a few labored breaths and tried to raise his head up.

"Now, just hold on," called out the attorney. "Wait 'til I call the paramedics before you hurt yourself more." Fieldman pulled out a small pocket portable telephone and was about to punch in a number when a great arm reached out and grabbed his neck.

It was a commanding effort and forced him backwards as the *injured man* bolted upright and secured a second hand around the throat before Fieldman could understand what had happened. Then a knee came up and caught him firmly in the groin. The pain was excruciating, taking his breath away, shooting through his groin and causing him to fall backwards onto the side of the road.

Even semiconscious, he was aware of being dragged by two hands under his armpits. He was pulled powerfully and quickly off the side of the road into a dense section of the woods and twenty feet from the roadway he was propped up against a tree.

"Good morning, counselor," said a soft voice.

Fieldman was moaning from the terrible blow to his genitals, but the strange voice snapped him back to reality, and he looked up directly into the barrel of a small handgun.

"Wha—what's happening? Who are you? What do you want?" He was just getting his breath back. The deep, slow pain was agonizing.

"Just want to talk for a few moments."

The stranger grabbed him by the arm when he seemed capable of responding and helped him up. "We're going for a little walk, and then we'll talk before I leave you." He urged the puzzled attorney deeper into the woods with the revolver pressed against the side of his head.

The rapidity of the events prevented the usually alert and responsive Fieldman from doing anything but what he was told. Finally, they reached a small clearing, and Fieldman saw a backpack and some sheets over to one side. The thick underbrush had been cleared away, leaving just a bed of dirt and pine needles on a space about eight feet square.

As his mind cleared, Fieldman became more assertive. "What is all this? What do you want?" He started to turn towards his assailant, but the gun pressed more firmly, and he was shoved violently to the ground.

"Silence, counselor, if you want to stay alive!" The large man loomed over Fieldman, who was now lying on his back, propped up on one arm. His other hand was at his groin, trying to do something to allay the pulsating pain.

"Okay. Okay. Just take it easy, man." He brought a hand up towards the gun nozzle in a feeble attempt to ward off the threat.

"Attorney Arthur Fieldman," said the soft voice leaning down closer to him. "You have been found guilty by a jury of your peers. Do you have any comments before sentencing?"

"Hey, man. What the fuck are you talking about? What's going on here?"

"If you want to stay alive, you will do exactly as I say."

"Hey, wha—"

"Exactly!"

"Okay. Okay." He was sweating profusely as pre-knotted ropes were tied around his wrists and ankles, then secured to stakes already pounded into the earth. It went very quickly, and Fieldman was spread-eagle on the ground. It had been less than ten minutes since he had first seen the man lying by the roadside, and things were progressing so rapidly that he was dizzy with nausea and pain from his groin, combined with fear of his assailant.

The big man returned holding a scalpel blade, and suddenly Fieldman knew who he was facing, and a terror spread through him. It was the mass murderer who was killing off attorneys, and he was the next victim. "Oh, my God." The words were barely able to emerge from his mouth before a large hand came down over it.

"I'm afraid you won't be teaching malpractice law anymore, professor," said the calm voice.

Fieldman was pulling futilely against the tethers and moving his head from side to side, eyes dilated in terror, as the pistol was placed slowly up to his forehead. There was a dull "thud" as the silencer muted the blast. The body jerked forward, then settled back onto the ground.

The big man waited a full ten minutes before releasing the extremities and placing the sheet under the body. There was surprisingly little blood.

He draped the head and neck appropriately and made a collar incision in the neck just above the bony sternum. There was a small amount of oozing, and he quickly applied instruments to the vessels. Visibility was barely adequate, but he had done the procedure so many times that it was almost second nature to him. Down through the thin superficial neck muscle, then the strap muscles in front of the neck.

There it was. The thyroid. He made incisions on either side of the gland, removing it entirely. In a surprisingly swift movement, he dug deeper into the space between the trachea and the esophagus, found the nerves that went to the voice box, and divided them both. In a living patient this would paralyze the vocal cords so that an individual could not talk or breathe.

He looked down at the neck. He had never cut those nerves before. It was a new experience, and he smiled to himself. "Remind me never to do that, Marilyn," he said slowly, as he placed the thyroid in a plastic baggie and set it on the chest. He carefully sutured the muscles closed in the midline, then approximated the superficial muscle and the skin. He went over to his knapsack, replacing the instruments and taking a prewritten card with a string attached. He tied it to Fieldman's right big toe. It read:

The Defense rests.
The Prosecution is at a loss for words!

It took fifteen minutes to clean up the area and check the site. In all, the whole thing had lasted less than one hour. *A new record*, he thought. He changed into a woman's flat shoes and made his way through the woods to his car. He drove carefully to the Mass Turnpike, then to the New York State Thruway and on into Manhattan. He had tickets for *Die Zauberflote* at the Metropolitan Opera and didn't want to be late.

–18–

The diary was open on the desk.

Marilyn got her medical degree three years after I did. I was a fourth year surgical resident when she started her first year at the same institution. We decided to wait until she had the post-doctoral position before getting married. Since the residency year always starts July 1st, we were married in a small ceremony on my weekend off on June 28th. She had a mother whom she hadn't seen in six years, who didn't attend, and I had no one except old Martin. His wife had died two years before, and he was still seeing to the family business, me being the only family. There were six other friends—doctors and their wives—at the mini-affair and the delicatessen wedding meal. It was all we wanted, and it went over quite well.

I started into private surgical practice that year, and with the family money there was no financial concern. Marilyn and I saw very little of each other for those three years, but we were very much in love and cherished the few hours we had together. She was the light of my life, and we made plans for a family in the coming years. Marilyn came from a poor family. My affluence was new for her, and she bathed in the luxury of new clothes, a fine country home, and an apartment in the city near her work. I even had the occasionally embarrassing situation of serving as an attending on her surgical service throughout her training, and we avoided all personal conversation at those times, although everyone knew of our relationship.

She was sensitive, intense and very dedicated in a surgical field that, in those days, was often a rarity for women. She felt challenged to be the best of the best, since it was assumed by so many of the "old guard" that she would be only mediocre or just an out-and-out failure. When we had our few hours together on her evenings off, they were filled with quiet touching or intense love-making and acted as a foil for all the seriousness and stresses of her residency training. Having just completed the same program, I was aware of what she was undergoing, although we had no women in our training group. And, I must admit, many years ago the other surgical resident men, myself included, often had cast aspersions on the few women in the surgical programs, snickering about how they couldn't face the rigors of the residency. But Marilyn persevered and did well for her first three years and was appointed as a chief resident in surgery in her final year. It was a most strenuous period for her, and with her ever-present desire—not just to succeed, but to be the best—she often became testy, overly serious and nervous about her cases, and doggedly persistent about caring for her patients.

In May of her last year, six weeks before the end of her program, she first encountered Arnold Carstairs. He was a high-strung, thirty-year-old married accountant with one child and the only son of Matthew Carstairs, senior partner in the law firm of Kittings, Marshall and Carstairs. Arnold was admitted through the emergency room at two in the morning with excruciating abdominal pain and an elevated white blood count. The family physician had requested his personal surgeon, but that doctor was not available, and Marilyn was the well-respected senior surgical resident on call.

When Carstairs was seen, his temperature was 104 and his abdominal x-ray showed free air in the abdominal cavity, indicating there was a perforation or hole somewhere in one of the loops of intestine. This was usually from a perforated stomach ulcer or ruptured appendicitis or colon. Regardless of the cause, it was an indication for urgent surgery. Marilyn was well aware of this, after personally seeing to the situation along with her many more junior residents. It was one of those rare times when an attending surgeon was not available to come to the hospital and, as is often done in training programs—especially with a senior, well-trained resident such as Marilyn—the attending physician told her by telephone to go ahead with the surgery as she saw fit. No one knew the prominence of the family until several hours later.

Mr. Carstairs, who was alone at home, had been taken to the emergency room from his residence by ambulance. His wife and child were visiting relatives in another city, and apparently he could not reach them when he started having the severe pain. At any rate, Marilyn assessed the situation and decided he had a perforated ulcer and prepared for surgery as soon as possible.

Carstairs signed the consent and told a nurse to call his relatives when the opportunity arose. He was taken to the operating room at four o'clock in the morning, was anesthetized and prepared for the procedure. Marilyn and her team made an incision in the abdomen and indeed found a hole in the stomach through which food and acid were leaking into the abdomen. The procedure called for was an over-sewing of the hole with sutures, and using a piece of intra-abdominal fat, called omentum, to reinforce the closure. Then she washed out the contaminated fluid from the abdomen with a saline solution containing antibiotics. She told me that the procedure was uneventful and went well. She completed the case in less than an hour, an excellent time for even a seasoned surgeon.

The abdomen was closed, and Marilyn was met at the operating room door by the family physician and several of the patient's family members. The father was very upset that she had done the operation, even though it was explained to him that Marilyn was an excellent resident and that the urgency of the situation warranted she go ahead with the procedure. Marilyn told me that she stood there in her operating room green outfit and cap, her mask hanging down over her chest, and just stared at the angry man who was the patient's father. He glared at her and without a word of thanks said, "My son had better do well or your head will be on the chopping block, sister."

Marilyn couldn't restrain herself and calmly responded, "I am not a sister, sir, but a doctor, and your son is doing very well." She turned and went back into the operating room, where she sat down in the recovery area, wrote post-operative orders and dictated her operative report. Then she called me and explained the entire situation, almost breaking down in tears, she was so angry.

Within a half hour, the attending surgeon, who had been tied up elsewhere, was at the scene and, after speaking with the irate family and with Marilyn, began to berate her for going ahead with the surgery without his being present, even though she had been told to proceed by the family physician and had followed the usual protocol under emergency conditions. Marilyn was devastated, but felt confident she had done the right thing.

Shortly after eleven o'clock the following morning, she was called to the intensive care unit, where she was informed that her patient showed signs of internal bleeding with a falling blood pressure, rising pulse, and falling blood count. The family surgeon was called and, completely ignoring Marilyn, ordered the patient taken back to the operating room. Exploratory surgery was done and bleeding was found coming from the area of the ulcer, a very unusual circumstance and one that apparently had not been seen or anticipated in what had otherwise been a fairly routine surgery. The surgeon did not allow Marilyn into the room because of the family's anger towards her and, after controlling the bleeding with a few sutures, he reclosed the abdomen and went out to see the family. They were angry and again threatened everyone for the incompetence of the surgeons and wanted the patient transferred to another hospital. When it was explained that he was too sick to transfer, their ire was even more accentuated, but they made arrangements for transfer as soon as he would be more stable.

Marilyn was distraught and angry about the entire situation, but she had many other patients to care for, and I called her several times during her shift to give her support and encouragement. The following morning Mr. Carstairs was awake, alert and doing quite well. Marilyn was not allowed into the room because of the family's wishes, but she followed the case from the periphery and was happy to see that he was doing well. The next day he would be transferred to East Side Hospital, and everyone in the department would be happy to see him go. At three that afternoon, he got out of bed to sit in a bedside commode and suddenly collapsed onto the floor. An emergency resuscitation team was called, but he was dead within a few minutes.

A postmortem examination done the same day by the medical examiner showed that it was from a massive blood clot in the lungs, a pulmonary embolism.

Marilyn was terribly upset, but I assured her it was not her fault and was a complication that could occur after major surgery. She, of course, knew this, but could not be consoled. Nowadays, there are all kinds of preventative measures to decrease the incidence of pulmonary embolism, but this was more than twenty years ago, when such measures were not available.

The father, Mr. Matthew Carstairs, the fifty-one-year-old prominent attorney, was a powerful man in the city. He immediately demanded that Marilyn be fired, but the hospital initially defended her. After much political rambling, the chairman of the department of surgery called her into his office, where there were several other physicians present. He informed her he was going to put her on paid leave until there was an official hearing, although he was sorry to do this. He stated she was an excellent resident and was sure everything would work out satisfactorily.

Marilyn came home that day very despondent and, to make matters worse, that afternoon she received a letter from a malpractice attorney indicating the Carstairs family's intent to sue her for malpractice. The letter listed a long series of complaints including misrepresentation, incompetence, loss of consortium, failure to do the right procedure, etc., etc. It went on and on in the standard fashion of what I now know is attorney verbiage. But Marilyn and I had never seen such a letter before, and it instilled fear and depression in both of us.

"I'll never be allowed to practice surgery" she cried. "After all my work and all these years. It's so unfair. I did everything right. I'm sure of it."

I remember the way she cried in my arms that evening and became inconsolable. I went to the department chief the next day, and we had a long talk. He had been a friend for many years, and he told me that the Carstairs family was very powerful and had strong representation on the hospital board. He was being forced to do what he had done and was trying his best to correct the situation.

I could see from his facial expression that he was in a quandary. It was his job or my wife's position at stake, and I knew what was going to happen. As a young surgeon with limited influence, I had little chance of making any inroads in the situation and decided to hire an attorney. Marilyn and I went to see a Mr. Baumgartner the next day, and he basically stated it would take months before the case came to court and was eventually resolved. But he did tell us he couldn't guarantee that Marilyn would be exonerated.

She was becoming more silent and withdrawn by the day, and I felt uncomfortable going to work each day and leaving her at home.

It was on a Thursday, late afternoon, that I returned home to find her in bed asleep. Next to her was the formal court summons for malpractice with a long list of the terrible things she was supposed to have done. I sat down next to her and put my hand over her sleeping face, only to draw it back quickly. Her face was cold. I felt for a pulse. There was none. She was gone. My darling was gone. Next to her bed was a vial of sleeping pills and a note.

My darling,

I love you more than life itself, but I cannot go through the horror and shame of this lawsuit. Somehow, I am responsible for that man's death, and I don't understand why my God has brought me to this misery. I will not let my failure end your bright career and cannot see myself without the work that I love. You are young, handsome, and wonderful and will find someone in the years to come. I only tried to do my best, but these people have turned everyone against me. I could even handle the anger of the family, but the malpractice suit and the attorneys will hound my memory all my life. I have not had a peaceful

*moment since the death. I received this horrible
letter today and know that it spells the end for me.
Please forgive me. It is better for both of us. Know
that I have loved you and do this to keep my
memory an untarnished one. I am sure if I went
through the hearings and the trials, I would
become a bitter, angry person, and I am already
too depressed and sorrowful to live another
moment. Goodbye, my darling. I will always be
with you.*

Marilyn

*I put the letter down and sat on the floor. I was in
shock and stayed there for almost fifteen minutes before
calling the police and the chairman of the surgery
department.*

*Before they arrived, I took the letter, folded it into a
small square and hid it behind our wedding picture. I
never looked at it again until now. Something died in me
that day, and I have never felt the same since.*

*Oh yes, I took off for a full month after the burial, and
then came back to work. I became engrossed in my work.
Five years later, I met a charming lady and remarried.
She was good and loving, but soon after the wedding I
began hearing from Marilyn in my sleep. At first, it was
once a month, then weekly, and then almost every night. It
was as if I was having an affair with Marilyn, and it
drove me away from my new wife. She noticed the change
early on. Fortunately, we had no children.*

*We attended social events together and lived sepa-
rately in the same house as roommates, but there was
never any intimacy. We often traveled together with
friends, but we had given up all sexual relations several
months after the marriage. She led her life as an active
socialite and seemed satisfied to be the surgeon's wife.
On a hiking trip in the Alps one summer, she fell and
sustained*

a head injury from which she never recovered. After she was gone, I never had any desire to remarry, although I did socialize from time to time.

Life has never been quite the same as it was with you, Marilyn. I still miss you dearly.

I have had several minor lawsuits in the past twenty years, and they all start with the same vituperative, vicious language, which is devastating for the uninitiated. The legal battles are more emotional than real, and I have let the malpractice insurance companies handle my cases. Almost every surgeon gets sued at some time or other. But each time I hear from or about a malpractice attorney, I get a sense of nausea followed by great longing and sense of loss for my darling Marilyn.

Last year I was alone on a beach when I heard her voice again for the first time during my waking state. It was a shock, but I just closed my eyes and listened.

"I have missed you, my love," she said. "But I have come back and will be with you now and forever." I thought I must be crazy but found that I could carry on my normal activities better than before. I was much calmer and more understanding, and she even spoke to me about my having liaisons with other women. She knew we could never be together physically, so she would be with me in spirit when I was with others. And it was not unusual for me to whisper her name at times of physical passion with other women, not exactly a winning proposition.

Marilyn, I miss you so much, and we have talked about the malpractice attorneys that caused us this separation. It was you who asked me six months ago to help prevent the same thing from happening to others. Now, Marilyn, I have been fulfilling your wishes. I love you and I always will.

—19—

Mac hated leaving the city. The call had come in from the Cambridge P.D. at about eleven in the morning and been referred to him directly. He was surprised by the location from which the call originated, but not overly so. He'd been around long enough to expect the unexpected, and he just exhaled. "Who found the body?"

"The wife. She went out with the dog after he failed to return in two hours. The dog went right to him. Stretched out on a sheet with a hole in his forehead. The neck had been cut and then closed up with stitches. Tag on the toe says, 'Prosecution is at a loss for words.' Probably took out his voice box or something. Sounded like your guy. Oh, yeah. The victim's a professor of law at Harvard. Used to do malpractice law in St. Louis, but moved here a few years ago."

"Where's he going to be taken?"

"He's already down at Central morgue in Cambridge, and Doc Morrison's gonna wait 'til you get there before he gets started. We've been over the crime scene carefully, and I have good photos for you."

"Thanks," said Mac. "I'll be up there at Logan airport in about two hours. Can somebody meet me?"

"Sure, Mac. It's good to hear from you again. Been a few years, eh?"

"Yeah. A few." He hung up the phone and called the chief.

The phone rang a few times, and then he had to be connected. No one ever spoke directly to the chief.

"Mac here. We've got a bigger problem. Another dead attorney, this time in the Boston area."

"Are you sure?"

"Same deal. Attorney, operation, and note. I'm on my way up there now. Better get your PR people on this right away. The papers are gonna eat it up."

"Thanks a lot, Mac. I'm trying to simplify my life, and you never make it any easier."

The chief was a very laid-back guy. He knew how to delegate responsibility, and Mac was a chief's dream cop. You just assigned him a case, and eventually it got resolved. He liked Mac because he knew he was a *no bullshit* kind of guy who rarely caused waves and got the job done. But this serial killer case was a thorn in everyone's side, and he would be on the hot seat until it was resolved. He'd watched enough TV cop shows to know that the public expected the Chief to be some obnoxious asshole, and he made a conscious effort to avoid that kind of behavior. "Got anything yet?"

"Not a goddamned thing. No fibers, no prints, no clues. It's gonna be a tough one."

"You need some help?" He knew full well that Mac always worked alone, but he always made the offer, anyway. Mac didn't even bother to respond anymore. Mac left the office and went directly to the airport, where he caught the next shuttle up to Boston. A young cop picked him up in a black and white and drove him first to the murder scene. Mac spent an hour talking with the forensic team there, looked around a bit, then had the driver take him to the morgue. It was a small facility, but well-equipped, and the pathologist, Harry Momson, was a seasoned pathologist whom Mac had met twice before.

He was in surgical scrubs and had on a pair of rubber gloves. He was working on another case when Mac walked in.

"Hey, Mac. Been a while. Let me just put this case back in the cooler, and we'll get to your guy."

He spoke to the assistant, who quickly covered up the body he was working on and wheeled it back to one of the storage compartments. Then he took out the other body and moved it onto the dissecting table. It had been partially dissected, except for the neck and the note attached to the right big toe.

"We found the thyroid gland in a baggie, but no vocal cords. I have a feeling what we're going to find once we open him up."

Mac put on a smock and a pair of gloves and went over to the body.

"They've already gone over him, including the note for prints. Nothing."

Mac looked up. "Thanks Harry. The note paper is the same as we had in New York. We've been over it, and even the FBI lab can't pin it down. Just ordinary file cards you can pick up in any five and dime. Ink is ballpoint pen. String is common twine."

They moved to the neck, and the pathologist removed the skin sutures. Mac looked on as the small threads were placed in a specimen bag.

"They're Ethicon Prolene. We had them all analyzed. They supply thousands of hospitals, as well as private clinics and doctors. Impossible to trace."

The neck was opened until the trachea was visible. Then the pathologist closely examined the right and left sides of the neck in the tracheoesophageal grove. He picked up a small string of tissue on each side, showing them to Mac.

"This killer is a surgeon, no doubt about it. He's selectively divided the recurrent laryngeal nerve on either side of the neck. Those are the nerves that supply the larynx, the voice box. He didn't need to remove the voice box because he figured any pathologist knowing his modus operandi and reading the note would find the answers. Clever son of a bitch."

Mac looked at the tiny nerve endings. "Yeah. Real clever." After completing the dissection of the head and brain and retrieving the bullet, the body was re-wrapped and placed back in the cooler. Mac was sitting in a corner of the dissecting room waiting for Harry to finish. He was tapping his pen on the table as he thought about the case. "Tell me, Harry. Is there any way to distinguish one surgeon from another?"

Harry smiled. "Yeah. Surgeons who become medical examiners drive Chevys, and plastic surgeons drive Rolls Royces and Mercedes Benzes."

Mac didn't smile, so Harry changed his tone. "I suppose there are differences in the instruments and sutures they use. Of course, there are different techniques, and more experienced guys have fewer complications. But that's very difficult to put a finger on."

"Could you identify a specific surgeon by any particular things he does in surgery, like where he makes his cuts or how the stitches look?" asked Mac.

"Well," said the pathologist, "each surgeon has his own specific card in an operating room which lists what he particularly uses in each operation. Every operating room keeps a file of what a surgeon uses on, for example, an appendectomy, colon resection or thyroid case. But, for the most part, the instruments and sutures are pretty much the same. The only way you'd be able to distinguish one surgeon from another would be if he used some very unusual technique or instrument. From what I see on this case, I can't make any guesses."

Mac went through the police file, and Harry said he'd fax his final report in a few days. So much information and nothing solid to work with.

"Stay for dinner with me and the wife, Mac?"

"No, thanks. I've got to get back. Maybe next time."

Harry chuckled. "You mean in another five years? You take care of yourself, Mac. When you decide to take some time off, come on up, and we'll fix you up with one of Ethel's friends and spend a week in the Berkshires."

"Right, Harry. Just what I'm looking for." He gathered his things together and put them in his old leather briefcase. He'd had the same one for over thirty years, and it had an aged patina to it that only time can produce. The two men shook hands and Mac went back to the car, then to the airport. It was half an hour before his flight left, and he just sat in the departure lounge thinking about possibilities.

He was sure he could make this killer take some bait and make a mistake. He took out his pad and pen and began jotting down notes. He was going to create a malpractice attorney to beat all malpractice attorneys, someone so vicious and sneaky, so thoughtless and vituperative, so disgusting that anyone with a bent on vigilantism couldn't help but take the bait. He was indeed going to create a better mousetrap.

—20—

The doctor spent the afternoon in the public library. It had become a relaxing place to get away from the office and the hospital. He rarely met his patients there, and he wondered if his surgical patients were a separate breed who didn't read books. He had met one "gall bladder" lady a few months ago but, aside from that, almost no one. Maybe it was the hour of day that he went or the day of the week. Someday, he would have to make a study of who goes to the library.

At this time there were mostly younger people in their late teens and twenties doing school or university projects. Young people were not the mainstay of his surgical practice. After all, most cancer patients were over fifty, and those with gall bladder disease were usually the five F's: female, fatty, forty, flatulent, and fertile. At any rate, he was happy to have some anonymity when he spent his time in researching his extracurricular activities.

The papers and magazines were headlined with the law professor's murder, and the editorials ranged from commentaries on malpractice law to the psychological makeup of a surgeon who would do in an attorney. He was happy to see he had made a dent in the number of malpractice lawsuits filed and knew that Marilyn was smiling along with him. It gave him a tingling sensation, almost sexual, when he read the articles. He almost wished he could see his name in print.

Scalpel Murderer Strikes Again

was at the top of the Herald Star, and he rather liked the appellation. He read on:

> *Another body of a murdered malpractice attorney has turned up outside of Cambridge, Massachusetts, bringing to four the cases of the alleged surgeon who is apparently getting even with the law. The latest victim, and the first outside New York City, was prominent Harvard Law Professor Arthur Fieldman, noted for his lectures in medical malpractice. He moved to academia several years ago after a mild heart attack and has authored a major text on the subject. Early inquiries have turned up no clues to the murder and no relationships between Mr. Fieldman and the other murdered attorneys. Although the first two victims were apparently random, the last two have been carefully selected, yet no other pattern has been found or admitted to by the police.*
>
> *Law enforcement has been asking the public for help in any way with the solution of these serial murders. Phone lines all over the country are ringing with men and women claiming to be the perpetrator. So far, according to the chiefs of police in two cities, no serious clues have been found. However, the police have been very close-mouthed about the cases, only reassuring the general public that the killer has narrowed his list of victims to malpractice attorneys. Several surgeons have been interviewed, and most don't want to be quoted. The general tenor of their comments is, "It's a situation which has been long in coming." Suffice to say no surgeons seem to be remorseful about these ghoulish killings.*
>
> *Several malpractice attorneys with whom we have spoken refuse to allow their names to be used; the more affluent have hired personal bodyguards, and multiple*

young men who only recently started out in this field have changed direction and moved into corporate or other areas of the legal profession. The number of malpractice cases filed is down significantly, and many attorneys have stopped accepting contingency cases unless the action under consideration is gross malpractice, i.e., the wrong leg was removed or the surgeon was drunk while doing the cataract surgery and a complication of blindness resulted.

The surgeon read the articles. In spite of his controlled maturity in all other situations, he felt giddy with excitement. He spent a full three hours researching the reports from all over the country, then went to the legal section of the library and started looking up case law, personal injury, and malpractice attorneys.

Then it struck him. If it weren't for the patients or their families, there wouldn't be any malpractice suits. It reminded him of Marilyn and that vicious family. That damned family that caused all the problems. They should have been more understanding. He immediately closed the large reference book he had in his lap and went back to the cubicle where he had left his briefcase. He took out a sheet of paper and wrote PATIENTS on the top. He knew he would have to stay away from anyone he knew, certainly away from the Carstairs. It would be too easy to trace him. No. He had to find a really vindictive, vicious patient or family. But how could he go about finding a person outside of his hospital or sphere or activity? He could look up newspaper articles, but many of them were about injured or dead individuals from gross medical negligence. He didn't want to go near those. After all, there were probably some valid cases of medical malpractice. It would take more digging to find a case that appealed to him.

He went to the rack, picked up the previous weekend's Sunday New York Times and fingered through the pages. Nothing. Then the Boston Globe and USA Today. Nothing. Perhaps he should go to the grocery store tabloids. It was getting late, and he had had enough of the library. He got his coat and went out to his car. There was a 7-11 nearby. He drove up to the front, got out and looked at the line of newspapers in the rack. He took six different ones and went to the counter to pay. The clerk was watching a basketball game on a TV overhead and barely paid attention to him as he gave him change for a twenty dollar bill. The surgeon quickly turned back to his car and drove home with his stack of newspapers. Once in the den, he poured himself a long drink, sat back in a lounging chair with his shoes off and started reading from cover to cover.

"My God," he muttered. "Amazing, the trash some people will read." Then he chuckled. "Hey, I'm some people." After forty minutes, he found what he was looking for and cut the section out of the paper, throwing the rest in the trash. He read the article over several times.

MILLION DOLLAR BABY GOES HOME

Chicago, Ill.

Janice Fell, the twenty-three-year-old, supposed victim of an irate Indian shop owner, has returned home after six surgeries to reconstruct her face. The family was at her side, and her mother made the only comment to the gathering crowd of reporters and onlookers.

Ms. Fell was the lady who tried to hold up a liquor store two years ago, only to be rebuffed by an irate shop owner who threw acid in her face. The shop owner, Mr. Pandit Asham, had been robbed three times previously and had a gun and a bottle of hydrochloric acid at his disposal. Ms. Fell demanded money at knife point, and the frightened Mr. Asham had thrown the bottle of acid at her, destroying her left cheek, left eye and left neck, with minor acid burns to the other cheek. She had several procedures done, but lost the left eye and had severe scarring over the face and neck. She and her attorney sued the shop owner for excessive force and won a verdict of 2.3 million dollars.

Mr. Asham didn't have any money, and the verdict resulted in the loss of his store and bankruptcy. After the trial and verdict, the distraught Indian left the country and went back to his native India, impoverished.

Ms. Fell used as much as $30,000 of the $45,000 that she received for medicine and plastic surgery, and was apparently scarred but improved by the end of the reconstruction. Her attorney, Randolph Bevis, who had taken the case on a contingency basis, only received $30,000, which barely covered his costs. But the well was dry! The public outcry against her and her attorney was deafening because she had attacked the shopkeeper at his place of business. But the jury felt that the Indian shop owner's response to the threat was excessive and had scarred the young woman for life.

In one month, Miss Fell plans a three-week vacation in Aruba before returning to her home. She has no definite plans for the future.

The surgeon folded the article and placed it in his desk.

—21—

Mac knew he would need help in this. It would require a separate phone line, an office, and at least three staff. It was the first time he'd actually gone to the chief, hat in hand, yet he had no qualms about it. He knocked on the glass door to the boss's office and, seeing he was alone, just walked in.

"What's up?"

Mac sat on the edge of the desk and stared at him. "This guy has such a loathing for malpractice attorneys, I think we're going to have to manufacture one for him. Basically, we'll have to give him a past, credentials, an office, and some newspaper hype about a case so bad it would make any surgeon's blood boil. Our guy has to be so enraged that he makes a move towards our man."

"And I suppose you're going to be that attorney?"

"I would have liked to, but unfortunately my picture has been in the paper too much, and either the reporters would catch on or the doc would catch on. We have to use someone who hasn't been in the public eye, then keep surveillance on him twenty-four hours a day. We need to establish an office somewhere far away, so our guy won't physically check on him by visiting, but only by phone calls and computers. Then we'll give him headlines and a visit to New York and just wait to see if anything develops."

"Sounds simple, but complex, Mac. I'm surprised at you. It's not your style."

"You're right, it's not my style, but then this guy is not my style, either. You should have seen what he did in Boston. The medical examiner calls it a good thyroidectomy, except for cutting the nerves to the voice box! Definitely not a meat and potatoes axe murderer. This guy is a homicidal dilettante."

"Homicidal dilettante. I have to remember that one. Good enough for Yogi Berra." The chief had a plaque on his desk with a saying by Berra. *There comes a time in every man's life, and I've had many of them.*

He took out a pad and pen and wrote down some figures. He turned it back to Mac and tapped it with his pen. "Give this to my secretary and she'll get the authorization for the expenses. There's a fellow, Sam LaVere in BBL division, who hasn't been seen in public. He only does undercover work and would be a perfect candidate for your attorney. I'm sure he'll go along, but I'll call him personally and make him an offer he can't refuse."

The two policemen looked at each other, and there was a slight smile on the chief's face. "There won't be any contact with reporters except through your office, Mac. No written reports and no contact with other staff except through me."

"Sounds good." said Mac. He was happy that his boss was so supportive and knew he could count on him a hundred percent.

"Along with LaVere, you'll get two secretaries. One, Mary Carliss, used to be a legal secretary. We've used her before, and she's good and very independent. She has experience in making up false past histories and putting all the right information in the right places. The other one I'm thinking of, Beth Charles, is my own secretary. She knows all the legalese and jargon. I'll speak with both these women and have them sign confidentiality statements before starting."

"My God. I should have used you earlier."

The chief shook his head. "You're such a stubborn man, you would never give me the opportunity. This way, you'll be indebted to me. Something I've wanted from you for years."

They both laughed as Mac stood up and shook hands with his boss. He felt good because, for the first time in this case, he sensed it might be possible to catch the serial killer.

"I'll get the office set up and start developing a background with the secretaries tomorrow morning. Tell them to meet me in the office at eight, and we'll start the ball rolling." Mac turned and left the room more excited than he had been in years. So much of police work was tedious and boring that he reveled in the opportunity to approach something from a new perspective.

"I'm gonna get you, you son of a bitch," he said to himself as he walked back to the cubbyhole office he called his second home. "I'm definitely gonna get you."

He would never openly admit it, but Mac loved being a cop. He didn't want to be an administrator; he had no desire for further advancement and certainly had no desire to retire one day earlier than required. He thought highly of himself as a police officer and knew he did his job well. He couldn't understand people who wanted to retire. He worked hard to be a cop, had worked many years improving his abilities and was at the height of his expertise in a field that he loved. He had many friends who often spoke about retirement, but he frequently said, "You only live once; you better enjoy what you do. If not, get out of it and do something else."

Many of his fellow cops were burned out, disillusioned and angry with the system. Mac had fleeting moments of anger and sadness, but by and large he loved his job. He knew he could never be on an assembly line or in sales. He liked being deeply involved with real people in serious situations... making a difference in a life. At times he wondered if it were altruism or just the excitement of the chase that interested him most. Somewhere in the back of his mind he had a strong sense of right and wrong, but whether he had incentive from this or whether it was the lure of the game, he hadn't really decided. He had been in Viet Nam and knew well that ends do not justify the means. He also understood about history usually being written by the victor and could extrapolate that to his own work on the streets.

How would he feel if he were in Germany in 1942 and was assigned to capture a madman who was serially assassinating the Nazi leaders? Would the job take precedence over ethics, and would he feel justified in capturing that serial murderer?

Suppose this surgeon had legitimized the killings of these attorneys as justifiable homicide along ethical lines and felt strongly that he was doing a service for humanity. Mac thought about this for a few minutes and then dismissed it. He understood that agreeing with this kind of logic meant supporting anarchy. At what point should the soldier desert his comrades because of his philosophy of life? When is vigilantism acceptable, if ever?

He thought about the film industry and Charles Bronson in the *Death Wish* movies. How would he have reacted if he were the policeman in that film? His mind was wandering, as it often did in cases like this, and he began thinking about attorneys he had known. They were divided into prosecutors helping him get the bad guy into jail and defense attorneys attempting to find some way of keeping someone whom he considered a guilty client out of jail. He bore a deep resentment for many of the latter and often questioned their ethics. While he believed in justice, he tended to want immediate justice for the guilty. He saw a bit of himself in this assassin who was eliminating malpractice attorneys, yet he knew he could never justify those actions. The man had to be found and eliminated. Deep inside, he wanted there to be finality, like a death, rather than the usual long, drawn-out public trial with its eventual punishment.

—22—

The surgeon drove to Manhattan and went to a public telephone, where he placed a conference call to Miss Janice Fell and attorney Randolph Bevis. He informed them both that he was a representative of the United Civil Liberties Organization in New York City called *We Speak.* He informed them that his group was very small, but had several wealthy patrons who strongly supported their cause. They raised money to pay individuals who were harmed by others, awarded large sums, but who could never collect the judgment because there were no deep pockets. The doctor was very convincing, especially when he mentioned that $ 25,000 had been accumulated for the case, and he would like to present it to them in person. Bevis, usually a very wary man, was enticed and lured by the sound of the money in a case where he had received but a fraction of the settlement amount. The surgeon didn't give any more information, indicating that the group did not want any public notoriety, especially since there had been a negative public outcry. He emphasized the privacy of the matter and arranged to meet them in Mr. Bevis's Chicago office late in the day to avoid attracting any attention. Both Bevis and his client were very excited by his proposition.

He went into detail about certain release documents to sign, about keeping the source anonymous and a whole bunch of legalese jargon he had found in law books. They ate up the whole idea like two children waiting for milk and cookies.

The surgeon thought to himself, *Greed and money are great managers of men.* He had three days to get to Chicago and decided, again, to take the train to avoid recognition or leaving any record. This time he would dress as an overweight businessman. He thought about the television program he had seen as a child years ago, where a millionaire gave money to people on the understanding that they were not to reveal the source to anyone. The plan was so ridiculous, he thought, that it would probably work. He had never had a *double header* murder, but thought it would be a wonderful first. He had seen pictures of the diminutive girl and the mousy-looking attorney, and had no doubts he could easily control them, even in the worst of scenarios. The most important thing was to avoid falling into a trap, so he wanted to be there a day early to case out the offices and be sure there was no funny business. These people had their eyes only on money, and that often made the most cautious persons careless.

He designed the surgery and the notes and arranged the equipment in his carryall bag, along with additional makeup. Everything was standard supplies he had purchased over a long period of time in many small stores. The surgical equipment was taken from the hospital operating room without difficulty, often partially used or unused disposable instruments, suture or staples that would never be missed. He traveled without any article of identification that could be his undoing. He carried a couple hundred dollars in his pocket, but no credit cards or license. He had watched *Columbo* on TV for years and would not be caught because of some minor, careless error. He thought how useful the television programs had been and supposed that many perfect crimes probably had been designed by avid TV watchers. He had a slow week in surgery and decided to travel on Saturday in order to make the Tuesday appointment with his two *clients.*

His compartment in the train was almost deserted. He sat in a coach with only five other passengers scattered among the many empty seats. Even if he were seen, no one would recognize him, and he felt comfortable in his disguise. He slept a good deal of the way and got into the windy city at 9 A.M. He went to a small hotel and checked in, paying for three days up front. He walked to local fast food restaurants, frequently bringing a meal back to the room. He had been raised on gourmet meals, yet he was quite comfortable with the deli and hamburger menus. Having lost five pounds since he started his *activities*, he actually felt comfortable at the new weight. He had less appetite and found himself satisfied with several small meals a day instead of a multi-course dinner in the evening. He occasionally had what he felt were hunger pangs, but he chalked it up to nerves. Although he was very calm during the killings, the time before and a few hours afterward were often stressful, requiring him to take Tums for his occasional acid indigestion.

He slept all day and at seven in the evening got into his disguise and left the hotel. He walked the twenty blocks to the attorney's office and sat outside, across the street, for an hour. It was a middle-income type, five-story building. Obviously, the guy had not had many successful cases. There were no marble floors or huge glass windows reeking of opulence. He figured the place was at least forty years old. There wasn't even a doorman, and the lobby was an open rectangle with no receptionist.

He crossed the street and went into the lobby. On the side wall was a large directory. He glanced at the list of names.

Randolph Bevis, Esq., Attorney-at-Law
Suite 201

The surgeon thought for a minute. *What other kinds of attorneys are there?* He started smiling and began talking to himself. "Well, let's see, there's attorneys-in-law, attorneys-outlaw, attorneys-outside-the-law, and then this guy, soon to be attorney-in-a-box." He laughed aloud. No one heard. The place was deserted. He scanned the other names. There was a dentist, a coin seller-numismatist, a psychologist, a PJ Industries—whatever the hell that was—and several others. The guy was not a Melvin Belli.

There was an elevator, but instead the doctor went for the door that said *stairs* and walked up one flight. The landing door was unlocked, and he exited into a moldy-smelling hallway. The attorney's office was the second on the left. The lights were off. He stood for a few minutes. No sound. He went to the door and fiddled with the lock. He was inside the office in a few minutes and closed the door behind him. Nothing special. Basically, a waiting room with five chairs, a secretary's office, sliding window, and a larger back office looking out onto the alley beside the building. Everything said *cheap* and *used*. After looking around for a few minutes, he went back to the door, listened for a moment, then opened and left, down the stairway again. He'd have to see what time the secretary left. Otherwise, it was smooth sailing.

The following day he called the office at 7 A.M. No answer. He called every half hour until a soft voice answered at 10 A.M.

"Mr. Bevis's office. Can I be of assistance?"

He hung up immediately. Later in the day, at 3:30 P.M., he called again, heard the same voice and hung up. Again at 4:30. The voice gave the same inquisitive remarks. This time, however, he identified himself and wanted to confirm his meeting with Mr. Bevis the following day.

"I'll be there at about 5:30 P.M. tomorrow. Hope that's not too late."

He heard her talking in the background. He thought, *the cheap son of a bitch doesn't have an intercom.*

"That will be fine with Mr. Bevis, sir. He will be waiting here for you tomorrow at 5:30 P.M."

The surgeon hung up and went back to his hotel room. At 5:30 P.M. he returned to the pay phone and called the office again. No answer after ten rings. The secretary was gone and so was her employer. "Wonderful. Let's get ready for tomorrow's surgery, shall we, Marilyn?"

—23—

By midday Tuesday when he awoke, he was excited. He packed all his gear, put on his disguise and went for a late lunch. He took everything with him and went over the hotel room carefully to be sure he had not forgotten anything. After the procedures this evening, he would go directly to the station and take the 11:55 P.M. train. The half hour walk from Bevis's office to the train station would be refreshing after all the activity. He was
giving himself ample time to complete the work.

"Never rush. Never, never rush. That's when mistakes happen."

The restaurant was six blocks from the attorney's office, and he settled into a booth, putting the bag on the seat next to him. He looked like any other customer. He avoided looking directly at the waitress, ordered two eggs over easy and a side of home fries, toast and coffee, then went back to reading a local newspaper.

"No news today," he muttered softly. "Wait until tomorrow."

"What ya want?" the waitress asked.

He stared up at her, then back to the paper. Again, he had spoken out loud without realizing it. He would have to be more careful.

"Regular or decaf, sir?" she asked.

"Regular. And leave the check with the food," he said abruptly.

She stared at him and, turning to go, muttered, "Yesss sirrr."

He didn't want to attract attention, and he was angry that he had gotten upset with the waitress. He couldn't concentrate on the paper anymore. She brought the coffee and, soon after, the eggs and potatoes. He took his time finishing, then left a ten dollar bill to cover the meal, along with a meager tip. It was almost 5 P.M. There was a pay phone in the restaurant. He went over and deposited a quarter and dialed the attorney's office.

Bevis answered. "Bevis here."

"Oh, yes, Mr. Bevis. I'm the fellow from *We Speak*."

"Yessir. We'll be waiting for you."

"Yes. I spoke to your secretary yesterday and told her I'd be there at 5:30, but I'm running a bit late. I'm sure I can make it by 6:00, if that's okay. I won't take much time."

"Of course, that's okay," puffed Bevis. "We'll see you then." The doctor hung up the phone and walked out into the street with his bag at his side. The disguise made him look at least fifty pounds heavier. He had donned a brown wig and put cotton balls in his cheeks to puff them out a bit. He wore narrow-rimmed glasses to further alter his looks. He had picked up the glasses at Target in Chicago the previous day along with some candy bars for energy and a black, woolen, Greek fisherman's hat that was a special on sale. He seemed to fit in with the neighborhood as he continued walking slowly, street after street, arriving across from Bevis's office shortly after 5:30 P.M. Sitting on the edge of a garbage can in the adjacent alley, he had a good look at the building and saw one person leave at 5:40 P.M., then no activity for the next twenty minutes.

He crossed the street and went into the empty lobby, turned to his right entering the stairway and walked up the single flight. Before opening the hallway door, he took out the 22 caliber pistol with a silencer. He removed the clip, checked that it was full, then popped it back into place. He pulled the magazine back and replaced his right hand and the gun in his coat pocket. He let the gun fall into the pocket and, holding the equipment bag in his left hand, he reached for the hallway door knob, then stepped across to Bevis's office. He knocked twice and a voice called, "Come in, come in. The door's open."

Entering the room, he could look directly past the secretary's desk into the back office, where Bevis had ensconced himself at his desk, trying to look as professional as possible in this flea-trap. The surgeon walked directly into the room, and the small man rose from the desk with a somewhat surprised look on his face. Bevis had expected someone more formal than this pudgy, tall man in a Greek fisherman's hat and glasses. However, he maintained his composure and extended his hand towards him.

"Randy Bevis." He motioned to the woman sitting in the chair to his right. "And this is my client, Janice Fell."

The surgeon let go of Bevis' hand and, putting his own hand into his coat, withdrew the revolver, aimed it directly at the woman and fired into her forehead before Bevis had any idea what was happening. She fell to the floor with a thud. The surgeon dropped his handbag, took two steps forward, leaned across the attorney's desk, grabbed him by the front of his shirt and pulled him across the desk.

Bevis was muttering, but tongue-tied, staring at the blood pouring from the girl's body on the floor in front of him. He was a small man, barely five foot three inches, and very thin. He posed no threat to the physician, who literally dragged him across the desk until he was standing in front of him.

"If you want the same thing, just open your mouth."

Bevis's eyes were dilated and his mouth open, but nothing came out. He peed in his pants as the surgeon stared at him.

The doctor towered over him. "Mr. Bevis, attorney-at-law. I'm your doctor, and I'm here to ask you a few questions."

Bevis was beginning to regain some of his composure, but then a scream emitted from his lips, and he stuttered, "Y—you're the guy that's been killing malpractice attorneys in New York."

The surgeon reached up to cover Bevis' mouth with his left hand, then heard a noise behind him.

"Hey, Randy, what's up?" A huge man walked into the office and saw the woman on the floor and Bevis in front of him. The physician turned to face the intruder, pushing Bevis onto the floor like a rag doll. He raised the gun and shot the man in the chest. It didn't seem to stop the huge fellow, and he fired another directly into his head. The man crumpled to the floor. Then the physician looked down at Bevis, who was cowering and trying to back away under his desk. He grabbed him by the hair and fired a shot through his left eye, causing the man to jerk backwards on the floor.

The surgeon picked up his bag to prevent any blood getting onto it and backed away from the carnage.

"Oh, shit." He felt himself getting very hot and sweaty as he looked from one body to the next. He could feel his heart pounding. This was definitely not in his planned scenario. He didn't mind killing the attorney and the woman, but who the hell was the big ape? He went over to him. He was lying on his side. The surgeon reached into the man's back pocket and pulled out a wallet. A business card fell out.

Will Forseman, Esq., Personal Injury Law

The surgeon heaved a sigh of relief and looked towards the ceiling. "Thanks, Lord. Now I feel better." He stepped back for a moment, pondering whether to complete the situation. *No,* he thought. *I'm too upset and nervous. Leave the case for another day. If you can't do it right, don't do it at all.*

Blood was a starting to flow all over, and he had to be careful not to get any on his shoes as he made his way around the bodies towards the door. It was only 6:15. The whole affair had taken about ten minutes.

"What a mess. What a goddamned mess. I'm supposed to be getting better, not worse." He took a deep breath as if to clear his mind and relax. "Damn. I'm sorry, Marilyn. I'm really sorry. But at least the other guy's an attorney."

He reached the office door and heard no sounds. He opened it first a little, then all the way and stepped into the hall. He went to the stairwell, opened the door and heard some footsteps coming down from above. He ducked back into the hallway. There was another set of stairs at the other end of the hall and the elevator in between. He raced towards the other stairs and took them down one flight to another door, opened it and found himself at the alley between the buildings. He went out quickly, then walked slowly to the street and started moving away from the building in the direction of the train station. There was a train at 8:17 that he'd be able to make without any trouble. He didn't feel good. Everything was wrong. It was not well done. It was the way any two-bit hoodlum would have done it. He kept shaking his head from side to side as he made his way down the block.

—24—

Evelyn Carter had been Randolph Bevis's secretary and part-time lover for three years. She was supposed to work from nine to five, four days a week, but at the salary he paid her and the favors she gave him, her hours were quite variable. On this Wednesday she came into work at ten in the morning. When she opened the office door the lights were on, and it took only a few moments for her to see the three bodies. She began screaming at the top of her lungs until someone from another office came to her assistance. The police were called and arrived within five minutes. As the first officer came into the room, he heard a few gasping breaths and a voice calling, "Help me. For God's sake, help me." It was Forseman. He was still alive. The other two were dead.

The officer radioed for help, and the paramedics arrived shortly and took Forseman to the nearest receiving hospital, where he remained in the emergency room while the physician evaluated him.

The emergency doctor came out and spoke to the detective. "The chest wound penetrated a lung and caused bleeding into the lungs and chest. We placed a tube that re-expanded the lung and stopped the bleeding. The head wound is another matter. We took x-rays and found the .22 slug at the back of the skull, under the skin. Being a small caliber and fired at an oblique angle, the bullet apparently went into the front of his forehead and hit the skull at such an angle that it just coursed around the top of the head and lodged beneath the skin." He pointed to the path on his own head and indicated where the bullet was. "The skull received a tremendous jarring, enough to knock him unconscious, but the bone was not penetrated, and the brain is intact. One of those peculiarities we see in the emergency room once in a while."

"Can we talk to the guy?" pressed homicide detective Cavendish.

The ER physician looked at him. "Yeah, sure. In a few minutes, after we finish examining him. The guy's lucky to be alive."

"Call me when I can speak to him. I'll be in the lobby." He pointed to a uniformed policeman. "Officer Davis here is going to be with him all the time in the hospital, since the guy who did it may want to finish the job."

Davis was a huge man, six foot four, looking as if he could take care of anyone with his bare hands, much less his service revolver, a Smith and Wesson 40 caliber that most men would have trouble holding steady. Davis handled it easily with one hand and could hit a moving target at fifty yards. The ER physician looked at him, then went back to his patient.

Forseman had a terrible headache and was having difficulty remembering anything. Aside from the memory loss, he was neurologically intact. A thoracic surgeon had been called in to evaluate the chest wound and felt that the bullet, lodged in the back, did not need to be removed. The lung would heal on its own with the chest tube in place, as long as there was suction on the tube. He was kept on antibiotics to prevent infection. Forseman said he felt as if he had been hit in the chest and head by two-by-fours, but was able to talk in spite of the medication he was given.

In the meantime, Cavendish made a call to the precinct and was referred to New York and Septimus McClymonds. He was contacted on his cell phone almost immediately.

"McClymonds, this is Lieutenant Cavendish, Chicago PD. I think we've got a break for you on that attorney serial murder case."

"Great." said Mac. "We've been hitting a brick wall here. What have you got?"

"Seems your man was in the process of doing in an attorney and his client when a third person walked in on him. He was shot in the chest and head, but was very lucky. The bullet didn't enter the brain, and the guy's alert. I'll be talking with him soon and thought you'd want to get out here and question him. The ER Doc says he has no memory of the shootings, but that may clear in time. I'll go over it with him until he remembers."

"Any messages left on the bodies?"

"No. And no operations like the ones you saw. The only thing that's similar is the fact that they're malpractice and personal injury attorneys. The woman is that lady who tried to rob a store and got a judgment against the store owner."

"Yeah. I know the case. She just got out of the hospital. That's the only part that doesn't figure. My guy hasn't been doing clients, only attorneys. And the other guy, he's an attorney, too?"

"Yes. But from what we gather he just happened on the scene. Maybe that's why the guy didn't do his usual operations on the bodies and leave the tags? He's also an attorney; personal injury, malpractice stuff. Apparently, according to the secretary who found them this morning, these two guys were best friends."

"Secretary know anything?"

"Says her boss was expecting a man from New York who was from some organization called *We Speak*. Some kind of nutty arrangement to pay her boss and the client money they couldn't collect from the store owner. Sounds very fishy to me. There is no such organization. It was just a setup."

"Can we get a trace on the calls?"

"We did already. The first call was from a pay phone in Manhattan, and the second from a pay phone across the street from the victim's office here in Chicago. No prints here and probably no prints in New York, but you can try if you want."

Mac was writing everything down as he listened. "Can I talk to the survivor if I get out there tomorrow?"

"According to the ER Doc, I'll be able to talk with him today," said Cavendish. "So I'm sure he'll be up to seeing you tomorrow. I have him under protective guard."

"I don't think our guy will come back for him."

"Okay. Well, we'll keep the guard, anyway." Cavendish gave Mac some more details about the scene and told him where to go when he arrived.

Just about the time he hung up the phone, the ER doctor came back and told him the patient would be moved into the intensive care unit and that the policeman could talk to him there in about half an hour.

Cavendish went down to the coffee shop, had a snack with another officer and wrote down everything he had witnessed. A short while later, he got a call from the Intensive Care Unit, and he went back up to see the patient/victim.

Forseman was in a semi-sitting position in bed with a rubber tube coming from his right chest. The tube was attached to a large plastic container on the floor at the foot of the bed. This was connected by another tube to a wall suction machine, which caused the fluid in the plastic container to bubble slightly. He was wearing a hospital gown and had a tube coming from his nose, connected by another tube to another wall suction device. Near the bed was a third tube siphoning urine from a bladder catheter. An intravenous line was in his left arm with clear fluids dripping. The guy had a total of four tubes and was wired for electrocardiogram and blood oxygenation, as well as having a two-pronged oxygen cannula in his nose. Cavendish looked at him a moment as he entered the room. He thought, *Just about every inch of this guy has a tube or something.*

He walked up to the side of the bed. Forseman opened his eyes and turned his head towards the policeman. His eyelids were droopy from narcotic analgesics, and he was so drowsy that he could barely focus on the man who was leaning over him.

"Mr. Forseman. I'm detective Cavendish of the police department. I'm happy to see you're going to pull through. The doc gives you a good prognosis, says you were very lucky."

"Yeah" he mumbled. "Very lucky."

"Can you tell me anything about the man who did this?"

"Not really. It's all pretty blurry to me right now. Big guy with a little gun, I think. Just can't seem to focus yet, ya know."

"Okay. Well, I just wanted to say hello. I'll be back tomorrow with another officer, and perhaps you'll be able to give us a little more information."

"Yeah. Whatever." He turned his head and closed his eyes. Cavendish stared at him for a few minutes, then left the room.

—25—

 The surgeon got off the train at Grand Central and went directly to his own car. It was getting cool with the late October wind in the evening, and he had parked in a private lot several blocks from the station. His clothing and the extra abdominal girth kept him warm, but the occasional winds gusting around the corners hit his face like a slapping hand. When he got to the car, he unlocked the door and tossed the bag inside.

After settling into the driver's seat, he turned on the engine and heater, drove to the cashier, paid the fee and gunned the engine to warm up the car. He was still angry and upset, going over the incident in his head. As he pulled out onto the street, he was met with a loud honking and almost sideswiped another car. His mind was wandering. He thought about the meeting in Chicago again. *Did I leave anything in the office? Is there any way I can be traced? I had my gloves on. Thank God for that. Damn shit attorney had to walk in on us.*

There was another horn and loud yelling as he pulled up to a red light. The man in the car next to him was yelling obscenities. He had cut him off, narrowly missing a collision. He pulled the car over to the side of the street into a parking space and stopped.

Can't concentrate. Can't drive. I'll stop for a few minutes and regain my composure.

The last time he had felt like this was when he inadvertently cut the common bile duct during a gall bladder surgery. He had to repair the damn duct. Fortunately, there were no adverse complications or side effects. But he had that same feeling of indigestion and a cold clamminess shooting through him.

That feeling had come and gone during the train trip, but he didn't have to concentrate on driving then. He took several deep breaths and finally felt himself warming up and relaxing. He took off the abdominal padding and the wig and threw them into the back seat of the car. That gave him some relief, and he sat back in his seat. He drove out into traffic and took the highway south towards home.

He had felt very comfortable after his other activities, and he didn't like the way he felt this time. That third victim might not have turned out to be an attorney, and he shuddered to think that he might have killed an innocent bystander; he was disturbed by his mindset. He had fired the gun without thinking, a stimulus and response thing. He was just like the guy who goes into a store to steal a few bucks and ends up shooting and killing the clerk. "Marilyn, I hope you'll understand. But I was lucky. God sent in another attorney. Please forgive me for being so impulsive. The plans were good, but not good enough. I can't leave anything to chance or another accident could happen."

There was honking behind him. He had slowed down too much, and there was a line of cars behind him. He sped up and pulled to the right side into the slower lane. "I'm okay, Marilyn. It won't happen again. I love you."

"It's okay, darling. It's okay." He seemed to hear the words whistling from outside the car as he drove. Now he felt reassured and relaxed. It was all going to be okay.

—26—

Mac felt as if he hadn't sat down for twenty-four hours. The last thing he wanted was to get back on a plane to Chicago. He didn't like leaving Manhattan, and Chicago was not one of his favorite places. He had spent several years there and, between an ex-wife and unpleasant memories, it seemed the past was coming back at him as the miles outside the plane raced by. He stared out the window, and his memories inundated him. At least now he didn't have to tell someone where he was going, didn't have to hear the complaints from his wife. His life was his own. Well, not completely, but he had his work, and he was satisfied with that. His life was like a never-ending book, one adventure after another, and he liked it that way.

He started jotting down questions he would ask. Probably would do just as well without it, but he wanted to make sure he would remember everything. No mistakes, no errors in questioning. He knew he was good and prided himself on his attention to detail.

That surgeon probably was shaken up by the events in Chicago. Mac pictured him as he imagined himself in the same circumstance.

Pissed off. That's what he is. That's what I'd be. You're not such a smart asshole, after all. I'll bet this shook you up.

He leaned back in the uncomfortable seat and dozed off. He was awakened by the stewardess serving dinner, then fell back to sleep until he arrived. Cavendish met him at the airport, and the two of them drove into the city.

He felt tired when he got to the hospital, but was eager to talk with the victim. This might be the only opportunity they would get to identify the surgeon. There was also the possibility the surgeon might be so put off by what happened that he would call it quits.

But the police shrink had told him that wouldn't happen. It might put the killer off for a few weeks, or even months, but the seed had been planted and would grow; he would kill again and again until he was stopped.

A uniformed officer sat in a chair near the door as McClymonds and Cavendish went into the room. Forseman was more alert, nodded hello to Cavendish, and raised his right arm, the one that didn't have the intravenous. Cavendish walked up to the bedside.

"Mr. Forseman. This is detective McClymonds from New York. He's been covering the attorney killings, and he just arrived here to speak with you. I hope you're not too exhausted to give us a few minutes."

"No. Actually, I'm feeling a lot better now. That tube in the chest hurt, and they took that tube out of my nose. It gave me a god-awful sore throat."

"I take it the doctor and detective Cavendish have filled you in on what happened?"

"Well, a lot of it's a fog, but I understand Bevis and his client are dead. I knew the guy real well. I often stopped in for a few minutes to shoot the breeze. No pun intended."

"Can you tell me anything about the man who shot you?"

"Didn't have much time to look at him. He turned around and started firing. Then I went out like a light. Really can't recall very much except that he was a stocky guy, big gut, and probably in his fifties or so. I think the hair was brown. He had funny glasses, and—oh, yeah, the eyes. I recall those eyes. Very blue. I mean, unless he was wearing contacts, those blue eyes were really something. They sort of looked right through ya. And the guy was about as surprised to see me as I was to see him."

"What about the face? Can you recall anything about his face? Beard, mustache, long or short hair, acne, anything particular?

"Sorry. I just didn't get that much of a chance to look at him. Just those eyes…and maybe a mustache."

"Just close your eyes and try to visualize him. Anything else. *Anything at all*."

Forseman closed his eyes for a few seconds, and at first it looked as if he was going to sleep. Then he opened his eyes quickly and stared at the two policemen. "Oh, yeah. I remember now. That hand. He had a huge hand. It made that gun seem so small. He had a white glove on. Real tight, white glove."

The two officers continued to question him for a few more minutes, but no further information was forthcoming.

"Mr. Forseman, you have been very helpful, and we appreciate your talking to us in this condition. We'll leave our cards here on your side table, and if you think of anything else, give a call. Tomorrow I'm going to have a police artist come in and see if you can help him draw a sketch of the guy. Sometimes it can be very helpful."

The two investigators left the room together. Mac looked at Cavendish. "Thanks for the call. No surgery on the victims; he must have been rattled by Forseman coming in."

"He probably thinks Forseman is dead. When the killer discovers Forseman's alive he'll be wondering how much information he can supply."

Mac nodded.

Cavendish continued. "The reporters already have the basic police reports, so it'll be in the morning papers. I gave a brief interview, but I didn't want to comment on Forseman's condition until I spoke with you. However, knowing the departmental leaks in any big city, I'm sure they know he's alive and talking."

Mac thought a moment, and then said, "It's always harder if the criminal thinks you know more than you do. He becomes more cautious. I think we should say that nothing was learned, and the man has total amnesia about the incident."

"Sounds reasonable. I'll report that to the other officers and let it filter out to the reporters. Non-information becomes information very quickly in a police department."

Mac went to a hotel that evening and returned early in the morning to speak with Forseman while the forensic artist was present. They couldn't come up with a very good drawing, and no other information was gathered. Mac took the next flight back to New York.

—27—

Two weeks had passed, and he was back into his usual surgery schedule. He hadn't seen any women and had kept pretty much to himself in the evenings. He had read the Chicago newspapers and found out about Forseman. After reviewing the situation in his mind several times, he felt sure that, even if the guy survived, he couldn't be in very good condition with a bullet in the brain. *Even if he were alert, how much could he describe, since I was fairly well disguised, and the exposure couldn't have been more than a second with the man totally surprised and emotionally off-balance. Nah. He wouldn't know me if we sat across from one another in a bar.* He reassured himself several times until he felt convinced.

"Time to take a rest for a while, huh, Marilyn?" He could hear the wind rustling in the trees outside the house. The leaves were red and yellow from the autumn weather, and the breeze always blew some up against the window in the study where he was sitting. He thought about death and murder, and justified his actions once again. He would keep some notes for a day or two, then run them through a shredder. His housekeeper came to work each morning, but his study was strictly off limits, and he kept the door closed and locked whether or not he was at home.

On Wednesday evening, after a light day of surgery, he fingered through his phone directory and decided to have a dinner liaison for the coming weekend. He spoke to Marilyn, and she seemed to agree that he needed some release. He was happy

131

she understood him so well.

He called Cynthia, one of the women he had known over a year ago and found her at home. They spoke for a while, and then he asked her for dinner and the theatre for Saturday evening. She was a business woman, twenty years his junior, and he had been told by several of her male co-workers that she was very enamored of him. But, somehow, after she assented to his invitation and after he had hung up the phone, he was no longer interested. He was going to call her back, but decided to wait a few days before making that decision. Being a surgeon, the women always accepted the sick patient or surgery excuse without question. He decided to wait until Saturday before making a final decision. Part of the problem was his upset stomach and his progressive loss of appetite. He had become nauseated after the failed experience in Chicago and began taking some Valium to settle his nerves. He knew well the effects of stress and worry on the human body, since he had seen it in his patients over the past twenty-five years.

"I have to watch my behavior in the operating room. I was a bit terse with the scrub nurse today. At least, I haven't been talking to myself out loud recently."

On Saturday, he decided to go ahead with his date and arranged for dinner at a Japanese restaurant that had a Teppan stove. He picked up Cynthia and found her very attractive in a tight woolen dress that was obviously meant to entice him sensually as well as stylistically. She immediately took his hand on getting into the car.

"It's been a long time. I thought you'd forgotten about me."

"No. Just been busy with work. Time seems to fly by, and I tend to isolate."

"I know that. Let's have a good reunion tonight." She squeezed his hand and smiled at him. She was aware of her body language, and he was aware of her forwardness. He liked it. He needed it. He even acknowledged to himself that he wanted someone to hold onto, someone to love, if even for a few hours.

A deep loneliness occasionally overcame him, and it had been more frequent since his Chicago activities. He felt the work was incomplete, and it bothered him. It was as if he needed to finish his work. He had a sense of closure each day with his surgery, but the last three—no, two—murders were a botched mess, and it left a hollow space in him.

They arrived at the restaurant and were shown to a table for six with a Japanese chef cooking the food in front of them. When the chef started cutting the shrimp, steak and chicken with his knife, it caused a strange nausea in him. He got up from the table and excused himself for a moment to go to the men's room. He just stood in there for a few minutes until the nausea passed spontaneously, and then he felt fine. When he returned to the table, the dishes had been prepared, and he found that his appetite had returned. He had a pleasant dinner and actually enjoyed talking with Cynthia. She was interesting and intense and looked directly into his eyes when he spoke, as if she savored every word. It reminded him a bit of Marilyn, and he knew that her body would be Marilyn's body, her mouth would be Marilyn's mouth, and her breasts would be Marilyn's breasts.

He sat back, ate the dessert and had some after-dinner drinks. Cynthia was a bit drunk, but more relaxed and happy than obnoxious. He drank so little that he never got drunk and was always in control. He did not savor the idea of ever losing control because of alcohol or drugs.

He paid the bill and escorted her out in front of the restaurant where the valet got his car. He led her around to the passenger side. She leaned against him and kissed him deeply as the valet opened the door. She smiled up at him as he helped her into her seat. He went around to his side, got in and drove off.

When he arrived home, he left the car in the circular driveway in front of the house and escorted her in. They hadn't spoken, and it was understood she would be staying the night. He led her directly into the bedroom.

She put her arms around his neck and pressed herself against him. "I've thought a lot about you over the past months. I wanted to call, but when we spoke on the phone last time you seemed very distant."

"Am I better tonight?"

"Much better. We do have so much in common."

They embraced and kissed; he felt her body and became aroused. He thought of Marilyn and almost said her name, but Cynthia broke the silence.

"I don't want to talk about anything. I just want to make love to you." She kissed him with an urgency, and he responded.

But it was not Cynthia he was kissing, it was Marilyn. His eyes were closed, and the room was dark as he lifted her onto the bed and removed her clothing. She was lying nude beneath him as he undressed. Somehow, he knew he should not open his eyes to dispel the magic of the moment, and he began kissing her from face to breasts to belly, mumbling, "My darling, my love. I have missed you so much."

Cynthia responded by encircling him with her arms and legs and pulling him into her with rapid breaths and sighs until they both climaxed. Then he opened his eyes and looked upon her. At first, there was confusion. Then his mouth opened as he realized who she was. He looked around the moonlit room and spoke softly into the semi-darkness. "Thank you, my darling. I know it was you."

Cynthia was lying supine with her legs bent to one side, and didn't understand the words. She looked at him, and he seemed far away again. She reached up to kiss him and draw him back into an embrace, but he had started to rise from the bed.

His mind was clearing as he turned to her and said, "Please understand that this has been wonderful for me, but you must allow me more time. We'll see each other again, soon, but now I must be alone. I hope you understand."

She didn't, but hoped he was actually becoming enamored of her. She sat up, watching his dark figure across the room. "I do understand, and I'll give you as much time as you need. This has been a wonderful evening for me. I'm glad we'll be seeing each other again."

She got up and dressed quickly. He wanted her gone, but had to take her home, so he tried his best to accommodate her as they went to his car. She wanted to kiss him again and even that was difficult, but he managed to give her a goodbye caress and kiss as he left her at her apartment.

When he got back in the car alone, he closed the door and sat for a moment with his eyes closed. "It was you, Marilyn, wasn't it? You have come to me through her body, and I felt your voice and your hands and your body. I miss you terribly, darling, but we will always be together." He accelerated the car and drove home with a peace and relaxation that he had not known for over a month.

–28–

Mac sat in the office with Peter Davidson. He was a gray-haired man of forty-eight who had moved to New York from Phoenix one year ago. Davidson had been a lieutenant in the Phoenix PD and hadn't wanted to move, except that his three grown children were in New York, and his wife had died of breast cancer two years ago. His boss had worked a deal with the NYPD, and he was able to transfer to Manhattan. Davidson had agreed to spend two years in basics getting to know the city before taking on any major cases. He was the perfect guy for Mac's plan, and the two of them sat down on a Saturday morning to review the cases and go over Mac's notes. Davidson was a handsome man who looked more like a movie star than a policeman. He had a casual way about him that attracted attention, and he made friends easily. Peter Davidson was going to be Harvey Dollworth, attorney-at-law, and one of the sharpest up-and-coming personal injury lawyers in Montana. Before they finished the morning session, he had a computer history of cases dating back seven years that were accessible to anyone with the most minimal computer expertise. Being a single man, it would be easy to keep him single in his new role, and his life would be slightly less complicated to manufacture.

According to the records, he would be a graduate of Columbia University and Columbia Law School. A few key professors were pulled into the ring to supply any missing information. His office was in Butte, Montana, but the phone rang in a Manhattan apartment set up for the purpose. Shelley Marshall, a six-year female officer, would be playing the undercover secretary to field all calls, and a complex case of medical malpractice was already being played out in the local Butte newspaper and a few key national papers. Mac didn't like the fact that he had to involve several people, but he knew all of them well and could trust them.

He felt as if he were writing a script for a new version of the movie *The Sting*. The entire setup had to be believable with no loose ends, and it had to be done quietly, quickly and efficiently. He had to develop a plot with an injured patient, a likable surgeon and a believable miscarriage of justice that would devastate the surgeon and generate an outcry of vengeance from the medical community. Harvey Dollworth had to become the man whom everyone loved to hate! Mac had to make his behavior and attitude so offensive, and his actions so repulsive, that it would be easy to justify doing him in. At least, he hoped he could lure his surgeon into taking a chance. Mac saw the plusses, but he also saw the many problems and didn't want to get anyone accidentally killed.

The two men sat for three hours designing the situation before they were satisfied. That afternoon they had a full-on meeting with the other individuals involved. All they had to do was plant the first seed and let the weed start to grow. Richard Demarest from the city attorney's office sat in and helped with the legal aspects, and Mike Persons, an older doctor and friend of Mac's, put in his two cents from the physician's point of view.

The case was worked out. The patient would be a thirty-eight-year-old woman, Molly Glenn, who came to the surgeon, Dr. Peter Nemeroff, for management of a problem with her gall bladder. She had stones and was experiencing abdominal pain every few days just below her right rib cage. She was nauseated and vomited several times before she first saw her general practitioner. She was sent to the surgeon for definitive treatment, which meant removal of the gall bladder. Dr. Nemeroff was a forty-two-year-old surgeon who was, according to the script, well-respected in the community. He planned to remove the gall bladder laparoscopically and explained the nature and risks of the procedure to the patient when he saw her in his office.

According to the plan, she had a complete workup prior to surgery by her own physician, as well as Dr. Nemeroff. This included the ultrasound, which indicated gallstones and, therefore, a diseased gall bladder. The surgeon was supposed to have done many of these procedures and had an excellent reputation.

Mac felt that the killer surgeon would not be interested in a lot of detail about the surgeon and felt it would not be necessary to build up a whole background on him. The killer was apparently focused primarily on the attorney and, in one instance, on the patient. This made the job a bit easier by eliminating one of the fake identities.

The patient was to have gone to surgery, had the laparoscopic procedure with removal of the gall bladder, and done well post-operatively. However, four months later she presented to her physician with a swollen abdomen, and a complete workup revealed a cancer of the ovary, which had already spread throughout the abdomen. Although she could be treated, she could not be cured, and the gall bladder surgeon was sued for not recognizing the cancer at what would have been an earlier stage.

The surgeon said he had explored the abdomen with the scope and had seen the ovaries, and that they looked normal. The patient and her family sued the surgeon, and Harvey Dollworth was the malpractice attorney. Rather than have a long, drawn-out case, only the final result was reported in the newspaper and throughout the nation, in whatever yellow journals could be safely approached to run the article. The headline read, *Attorney Gets Another Big Judgment*, and was followed with a scathing article.

Attorney Harvey Dollworth, representing a local client [they left the patient's name out of the article to protect her anonymity, since she was supposed to be dying of cancer], *won a malpractice case for twenty million dollars*

*for negligence against Dr. Peter Nemeroff. The patient,
now dying of cancer, underwent a routine gall bladder
surgery by Nemeroff, who apparently did not identify a
concurrently existing cancer. By the time it was finally
diagnosed, it was too late to cure. The jury was
mesmerized by Dollworth and didn't accept the defense
arguments that the tumor was too small to be seen by the
operating surgeon. Several experts supported the surgeon.
However, when the patient was wheeled into the
courtroom to testify, several jury members began to weep.
The closing arguments by Dollworth depicted Nemeroff
as an uncaring, money-hungry man in a hurry to get
through the case and out to the golf course. The surgeon,
according to our records, has been in practice for six
years and was left financially destitute. He has left the
practice of surgery. Mr. Dollworth, when approached by
this reporter, said it was a good thing that the surgeon
had left the profession and made it safer for society.*

*In follow-up on the case, this reporter has found that
Dr. Nemeroff was actually noted for his community
activities, including a practice dedicated to taking care of
many of the indigent patients of the area. Speaking with
several experts in the field, they felt that it was extremely
difficult to make an early diagnosis in such cases, and
that the surgeon's performance was well within the usual
and acceptable standards of the community. We are sorry
to lose this excellent young surgeon, as well as sad about
the serious nature of the patient's cancer. In this writer's
opinion, a great disservice has been done that cannot be
righted.*

This article was followed by several angry letters to the editor.
When approached by another writer, Mr. Dollworth apparently
used obscenities and several crass expressions, including some
demeaning Dr. Nemeroff. Mac crowned the article with a picture
of a surgeon in cap and gown sitting, bent over and crying with
his face in his hands and a heading,

Surgeon devastated by malpractice loss. Next to him was a picture of Mr. Dollworth, grinning ear to ear and holding a check for $3,000,000 from the surgeon's malpractice company.

Mac sat with the team and reviewed all the information. Then they waited. The first call came in one day after the article hit the Times. The phone rang twice, and the secretary answered. "Mr. Dollworth's office."

"Hello. I'd like to speak to Mr. Dollworth."

"Who's calling, please?"

"Tell your boss he's an asshole." Then the phone slammed down.

The team looked at each other and smiled. Then the phone started ringing with crank calls from all over the country, a total of seventeen in all, eight from pay phones in Manhattan.

Mac said, "We just keep answering and, if anyone wants to see Dollworth, we just say he's on business in New York City. If it's urgent, we can reach him there. One of those calls could have been from our guy just as a preliminary, so we have to be very careful."

They checked the calls from Manhattan, and they were from all over, in three instances from phones outside large hospitals.

"Pissed-off surgeons or surgical residents," thought Mac. For five days they came to the office and waited. Then Mac ran another follow-up article in three newspapers. He was concerned. "Maybe the bait won't work!"

—29—

He had settled down. It was time to begin again, and he had returned to the library. Over a month had gone by, and the stories about the serial attorney killings were still front page. The malpractice cases filed had dropped to five per cent of their usual frequency, and several attorneys made public announcements of changing their business to personal injury with no more medical malpractice.

It was therefore interesting to him when he came across the article in two papers about Mr. Dollworth and the large award malpractice suit. At first, he started taking notes very eagerly, then suddenly stopped.

"Son of a bitch. It's too good. Rather, it's too bad. The case is so enticing, it bothers my sense of reality. Something about it smells."

He called information and asked for the phone number of the surgeon. He made a quick call and found that the office was now closed and to leave a message. Dr. Hogan would be covering for Dr. Nemeroff in his absence. Still didn't sound right. He went to the directory of surgeons and looked up Dr. Peter Nemeroff. No such physician was listed.

"Hah. They're trying to set me up and thought I'd only look for the attorney."

He was both amused and angry. Amused that such a simple plan was tried and annoyed to think it might have worked had he not been so cautious. He decided he would play along with them. The following day, he drove up to Manhattan and placed a call to the supposed attorney from a pay phone on the street across from Samaritan Hospital. He placed a washcloth over the speaker and spoke in a low, slow voice after the secretary answered.

"May I speak to Mr. Dollworth, please?"

"I'm sorry sir, he's not in. May I ask what this is in regard to?"

"I'm afraid it's personal and rather important. Is there any way I can reach him by phone?"

There was a pause. "Mr. Dollworth is out of town, but I could have him call you if it's urgent."

"It is urgent, but he won't be able to reach me. Is there a number where I can call him? It's really quite important that I get in touch as soon as possible."

"I see. Well, I'll get in touch with him and ask if it's all right to give out his hotel number. Will you call back in about thirty minutes?"

"That would be fine. I'll call back in thirty." He hung up and went across the street into the hospital, taking a seat in the lobby where he could look across the street and see the pay phone.

Mac called over to his assistant. "It's a pay phone in Manhattan. We've got a location. Right across from Samaritan Hospital. Get a couple plain clothes officers over there, but don't go near the phone. Just get shots. We've got to see if we can identify him. It may not be our guy. I'm going there alone, and I'll be looking around the area."

The girl at the phone nodded. She knew what to do and would give the caller a second number at the Sheraton Hotel, prearranged to ring back at headquarters.

The surgeon looked at his watch. Five minutes passed, then ten. Then he saw the two men drive by twice. He smiled to himself and went out of the lobby with a large group exiting the hospital. He walked down three blocks and turned down a side street until he reached the next avenue. There was another pay phone four blocks up near the place he had found to park his car. At exactly thirty minutes, he called the number.

"Hello. I'm calling back to see if you have a number for Mr. Dollworth?"

"Oh, yes, sir. I just got off the phone with him. He's at the Sheraton in New York and can be reached at the following number." She rattled off the area code and the number and hung up the phone.

Mac called in just a few seconds later. "Anything?"

"He just called. I gave him the number." She looked back at the other officer, who was shaking his head. "Apparently, he called from a different phone. About eight blocks away. Probably gone by now."

Mac got the address. "I'll check it out, anyway." He hung up quickly, called the two plain clothes officers and went to the next pay phone. It was being used by an elderly woman who had not seen anyone. There were several people milling around. It was a dead end. Mac got in his car and drove back down to headquarters.

They just waited. One hour, two hours. It was almost 10 P.M. when the hotel line rang. "Hotel Sheraton. Can I help you?"

"Mr. Dollworth, please." It was a low muffled voice. The operator switched the call to the next phone, and the lieutenant, Peter Davidson, answered. "Dollworth here. With whom am I speaking?"

"Oh, great. Mr. Harvey Dollworth?"

"Yes. And who is this?"

"My name's Laver Billwig, and I'm in a lot of trouble. I was told you could probably help me out. I mean, I've got lots of cash, and I know you're a big-shot attorney and all, but money is no object."

Davidson tried to sound uninterested. "Well, I'm sorry, Mr. Billwig, but I'm in New York on business, and I won't be back for about a week. Can it hold until then?"

"Well, I dunno. It has to do with my wife, and I can't stay on the phone long. Can I call you back tomorrow evening?"

Davidson couldn't keep him on the phone much longer, and they were having a hard time getting a trace. "Well, just call me here at the same number and ask for extension 1235. I'll be in after 9 P.M."

"Thank you. I'll do that."

The phone clicked, and Mac and Davidson looked at one another. Davidson finally spoke: "We may just get this guy."

They made the arrangements to be at the hotel the following evening. They would have at least sixteen undercover police watching all the exits and elevators and room 1235.

—30—

It was a dangerous game, but he was going to enjoy playing it. He had no basic animosity towards law enforcement and actually considered himself a respectful, law-abiding citizen. His only problem was with malpractice attorneys. So he had no desire to harm the gentleman posing as an attorney in an attempt to discover who he was. His first thought was just to do nothing, but his sense of curiosity about what they would do got the better of him. His rational side struggled with his playful side, and the latter won out. He had a plan which would not expose him and would let the police know he was a bit more careful than they had estimated. He knew they would not stop searching for him, yet he felt a compulsion to continue.

He thought about the case of Nathan Leopold and Richard Loeb, the two sons of wealthy Chicagoans, brilliant, but misled by a strong compulsion to murder a fourteen-year-old boy, Bobbie Franks. They were eventually convicted and sentenced to life in prison. One of them dropped his eyeglasses at the site of the supposed perfect murder, and the glasses were traced to the murderer.

But what the surgeon was interested in was the nature of the compulsion. Deep inside, he recognized his own behavior was spurred on by his strange relationship with a deceased wife. He had a compulsion to get rid of malpractice attorneys. He was an intelligent man and had studied the nature of compulsive behavior, yet he did not want to change himself. He had thoroughly examined his motives and justified his actions. He knew well that his behavior was illegal and, in the minds of many, unethical. But then he knew that society determined the acceptability of behavior, and he disagreed with society on this matter. Malpractice attorneys were evil and needed to be eliminated. He compared himself to the few Germans in 1944 who disobeyed the law because they felt the Nazi regime was illegal and unethical. In his mind, he equated malpractice attorneys with Nazis, and that gave him the right and responsibility to fight the system and assassinate them.

You are my knight in shining armor, Marilyn would say to him in the deepest recesses of his mind. *You are cleansing society of a group of people who have stepped beyond the limits of ethical activity. You are standing up where others have sat down. You are fulfilling your destiny by doing what you are doing.*

If he could have spoken with someone in confidence, he might have acknowledged that there were ethical flaws in his reasoning. But he was isolated within himself, and his reasoning was flawed. Or was it?

Was there somewhere a society that would not tolerate the behavior of attorneys? Do I have an obsessive-compulsive disorder? I have recurring obsessions and persistent impulses that invade my thoughts. I'm not crazy, because I understand that I have the compulsion. Crazy, psychotic people may have urges and act strange, but they are often not aware that they are doing so. I understand that I have compulsions, but I'm not like the usual obsessive-compulsive person who does meaningless, repetitious things. I have an obsession. That's all. And it goes against the grain of usual morality. But I have thought about it and firmly believe my motivation is justified.

The surgeon was correct. He did not have the behavior of the obsessive-compulsive individual. He was not psychotic, because he understood his actions and gave a rational reason for them. In effect, then, he figured he was a rational, healthy person driven by his own moral and ethical code to right a wrong in society.

And for that reason, he would continue his activity as long as he could, with no sense of guilt or remorse. He was stepping on termites that were eating away at the basis of good medical practice. He was an avenging angel. God was on his side, and he knew he was right.

He arranged to have a bottle of Dom Perignon champagne sent to room 1235 at the Sheraton later that day. He had gone to a busy liquor store in full disguise and paid cash. He also sent a box of chocolates from the same store. He smiled as he envisioned the police analyzing each piece of candy for poison and wasting the good champagne on clinical tests for toxic agents. With these, he sent along one of his note papers with the statement:

The defense rests again.
You can't practice law if you don't have a law degree.
PS: Try again, officers.

He went to the hotel early the following morning in a new disguise. Now he had very long hair tied in a ponytail, a large nose and severe acne. He wore dark glasses and kept his normal figure, without any padding, but wore a baggy outfit that would not emphasize his muscular build. He had breakfast and lunch in the hotel and spent several hours in the lobby, talking with everyone. It was remarkable how easy it was to find out what a person did for a living. He was hoping that, among the several dozen people he met, one attorney would pop up. He was willing to accept any personal injury attorney at this point just to play his little game. He was about to give up on this aspect of the game when he had a beer with three men at four o'clock.

One came right out and said, "I'm surprised you even come out in public these days, Murray."

"Why's that?" asked the surgeon.

"Ho, ho! Murray is a malpractice attorney in Pittsburgh, and you've probably read about that serial killer."

"Oh yes," said the surgeon. "I did read a bit about that. I thought those murders stopped a couple of months ago."

"Actually, they did. But I still like to tease Murray about it."

Murray had had a few beers and laughed loudly. "I'm too mean an SOB for even that killer."

They all laughed, and the surgeon felt a tingling inside. *Jackpot!* After a few minutes, he left the group and went over to another table and started up a conversation with several others, keeping an eye on Murray. *God is surely in my corner to deliver this man so easily.*

He noticed a few extra people eyeing all the doors and was convinced they were plainclothes police. He kept out of sight until Murray went to the elevator, at which point he followed him and got in, smiling as the door closed. Murray got off at the fifth floor, and the surgeon followed, making small talk until he saw him go to room 507. He waved goodbye.

"Have a drink later, maybe?" asked the surgeon. "I see you're in room 507. I'll give you a call."

"Sounds good. Gimme a call later."

When the room door closed, the surgeon went back to the elevator, took the car down and exited the hotel. He went back to his hotel, where he changed into a completely different outfit and waited until about 7 P.M. He dialed the hotel.

"Sheraton. Can I help you?"

"Room 507, please."

There was a momentary silence, then the phone rang.

"Hello."

"Murray? It's me. Still up for that drink?"

"Oh. It's you. Sure. Sure."

"Say. I've got a bottle of champagne. Why don't I just bring it over to your room at about 8:30 and we can shoot the breeze? Lakers are playing, and I was hoping to watch."

"Yeah, sure. I was going to watch the game myself. I'll supply the glasses."

"You're a real sport, Murray," the doctor replied. The two men laughed and hung up the phone.

—31–

Mac had all his people in place, and the acting attorney, Dollworth, was in room 1235 with Mac and another policeman. The exits were all watched.

At 7:30 P.M. a young man with a delivery uniform and a basket entered the hotel and went to the front desk. He asked the clerk to call room 1235 and announce a delivery for Mr. Dollworth. After this was done, he went to the elevators. He rode up to the twelfth floor, exited and went directly to room 1235.

The three men inside, having been alerted, were ready for the visitor. There was a knock on the door.

"Who is it?" asked the substitute Dollworth/Peter Davidson.

"Delivery for Mr. Dollworth," answered a young voice.

The three cops looked at each other. This was not what they were expecting. Dollworth/Davidson went to the door and peered through the peephole. A young man, no older than twenty at the outside, stood in front of the door with a basket. He was about five foot eight, slightly built with small arms. The policeman could see the hands. They were thin and wiry, and when he looked up he could also see the eyes. They were brown.

"This isn't the guy," he whispered to the other two.

The boy knocked again and Dollworth asked, "What do you have for me?"

"It's a bottle of champagne and some candy for a Mr. Dollworth."

The policemen looked at each other, and Mac nodded to open the door. The door was unlocked, and the delivery boy was pulled into the room. He found himself looking down the barrel of a police 45 caliber pistol.

"Put the basket down and get down on your hands and knees. I'm a policeman, and I'm not going to harm you." The boy let the basket drop and fell on the floor. The three policemen circled him, two examining the basket, the other two carefully going over the boy.

"He's clean, Mac. There's nothing in the basket except an unopened bottle of champagne and a sealed box of chocolates."

"You can get up, son," said one of the officers. "Sorry for the inconvenience, but we were expecting someone else."

The boy was visibly shaken, but regained his composure after a moment.

"What's your name, fella?"

"Ralph Wiggins, sir."

"Where did you get these items?"

"From the store. Marshall's on 58th Street. I do their deliveries…"

"I see. Do you know who sent them?"

"No. But there's a card included. I saw the saleslady put it in before I left."

They opened the card and Mac sat down. He read it aloud and at first was angry, then laughed aloud. "Well. This guy has a sense of humor. Son of a bitch has us pegged." He shook his head and called the other men watching the hotel.

"He's onto us. Call off the watch. Everybody can go home. I'll see you all in the office tomorrow morning. We'll have to think of another tack. This guy's obviously smarter than we are for the present." He left with the delivery boy and went back to the store.

The owner was at first upset with the boy when she saw him returning with the police, but the situation was quickly explained. She vaguely remembered the man who came in to buy the champagne and chocolates.

152

"He was tall and heavyset. Kept his face down and sort of turned away. I didn't see the face. It was a busy time, lots of customers. Oh, yeah. I do remember he had real big hands. When he handed me the cash, he was wearing white gloves, and they made the cash look tiny. Never said much. Just pushed the cash across the counter along with the bottles and gave me the address and the note in an envelope to go with it."

"Anything else?"

"Sorry, officer. That's about it. Gets busy this time of year, ya know?"

Mac gave her his card and thanked the boy and the woman for their help. He was about to leave, then turned to the delivery boy. He held out a ten dollar bill. "Here's a tip for the delivery." The kid smiled and took the money. "If you can remember anything else, give us a call."

Mac turned to his assistant. "I doubt whether the champagne or candy are contaminated, but you better run 'em through the lab, anyway. And remember, that means run 'em through the lab. I don't want anyone drinking even a drop of that stuff. This guy is too clever, and he might have injected something into them with a syringe and needle before bringing them up to the saleslady at the counter. If I find anyone poisoned or dead tomorrow, there'll be hell to pay!"

Mac went home.

—32—

The surgeon walked into the Sheraton Hotel with a sense of accomplishment and self-assurance. He noted that all of the suspicious-looking plainclothes policemen were gone, and there was only the usual bustle of activity.

He hunched over slightly and kept his head towards the floor, avoiding eye contact with staff or hotel guests. There was nothing strange about him. No one noticed anything out of the ordinary. He went to the elevator and rode alone to the fifth floor.

He carried a small traveling bag that held the champagne and the tools of his trade. Murray answered the knock on his door almost immediately, and they walked into the small suite where the TV was blaring the basketball game. Murray had already gotten out two fluted champagne glasses and had a plate of snacks he'd ordered up from the kitchen.

"Thanks for coming over. Always good to have some company when I'm away from home."

"Married?"

"Yep. Twenty-two years. Three kids. The usual. One seventeen-year-old know-it-all who's a pain in the ass. What about you?"

"Single. Wife died a while ago."

"Sorry."

"No. It's been a while."

Murray gave a leer. "Still fool around?" he winked.

The surgeon countered. "You're a married man, Murray."

"Cat's away, mouse will play. Heh, heh!"

"Shame on you."

"Yeah. Shame on me."

They sat down, and the surgeon poured some champagne.

Murray took a sip. "Pretty snazzy. Usually, all I get is a six-pack for the ball games."

"Yeah. You in town long?"

"Just wrapping up some information on a case."

"Oh, yeah. You're a malpractice attorney."

"I call it Personal Injury. It sounds better." He pulled out a business card and handed it to the surgeon. "What's your line?"

"Oh. I'm in the health line—supply and demand."

"Sounds interesting. You deal much with doctors?"

"Occasionally."

Murray glanced at the surgeon. "I'm really socking it to a surgeon this time."

"Medical malpractice case, eh?"

"Yep. It's easy to sue doctors. They're so arrogant. They always say more than they should when they're on the stand. They usually hang themselves out to dry."

"You get lots of money in those cases, eh?"

"Well, sometimes we hit pay dirt, but lots of times we have to put in our own cash for no return. Sort of like that old saying, *got to kiss a lot of frogs before you find a prince.* But when ya do, it's payday. Do ya get my drift?"

"Sure do. Do you like the work?"

"Love it. Must say it's a lot like a hunt. The planning, the shooting, and the prize. Great satisfaction. Not just the money, but I love to cut those M.D.'s down a notch. They always say they did nothing wrong. Always innocent of any guilt or responsibility. Like the prisons…full of innocent men." Murray sat back and put his legs up on the table.

The surgeon asked, "Do you think any of those docs are innocent, as you call it?"

"Probably most are. But my job is to get as much money as possible for my client."

"And for you?"

"Oh, yes. We do manage our percentage." He laughed. "Love to see those surgeons wrung out...such arrogant sons of bitches." He took another swig of the champagne.

The surgeon also took another sip of the drink and ate a canapé. He was smiling at Murray as he got up. "Excuse me while I use the bathroom."

"Yeah, sure." He waved him towards the bathroom door and looked back toward the TV as someone made a lay-up shot in the basketball game.

The surgeon took his bag with him into the bathroom. Murray didn't notice. The surgeon went inside, locked the door and sat down on the toilet for a moment. He bent over, unzipped the bag and pulled out his 22 caliber pistol. He passed it from hand to hand. "Love to see those surgeons wrung out, eh? Well, I love to see those attorneys wrung out." He tucked the gun into his pocket and flushed the toilet. When he exited the bathroom, Murray glanced up at him while holding a champagne glass and went back to looking at the TV. The surgeon walked directly up to him and stood in front, looking down, blocking his view of the television.

Murray was a small man, and the surgeon's body was over-powering in his presence.

"What's up, guy?" Murray asked.

The surgeon took the revolver out of his pocket and shoved it forcibly into Murray's open mouth. "One peep and I'll blow your head off."

Murray at first recoiled, but then tensed as the metal gun barrel scraped against his teeth.

The surgeon looked down at the man and smiled. "Counselor. Did I overlook telling you that I'm a surgeon?"

Murray tried to pull back a bit, but the surgeon grabbed him by the collar and forced the gun barrel further into his throat. Murray was having trouble breathing and had begun to sweat, making little gurgling noises and flailing with his arms against the overpowering strength of the man standing over him.

"You know, Murray, it's not nice to say such denigrating things about the medical profession. You never know when someone might not like it. I'm afraid this is one of the cases you're going to lose."

Murray started to struggle, and the surgeon pulled the trigger twice, sending the small man backwards into the cushioned chair. There was surprisingly little blood.

The surgeon went over to the bed and stripped off the blankets, leaving only the sheet. He then removed all of Murray's clothes. He carried the man over to the bed and left him lying on his back with his arms out to the sides. Next, he went to his bag and took out a pair of white cotton gloves and carefully wiped all the surfaces he had touched, including the glasses and bottle. He went around the room and the bathroom, wiping off all prints. Then he repeated the process, examining both rooms until he was sure they were clean.

Murray had a dinner tray from earlier that evening and apparently had eaten half a grapefruit. *Good for you,* he thought. *Vitamin C. You won't die of cancer, you lucky stiff.* The surgeon looked at Murray, then reached into his bag and took out the label he had written and tore it up. "I've got a better idea for you, Murray." He took out a clean piece of paper and, writing with his left hand, made a new note. Then he went over to the dinner plate and picked up the grapefruit spoon. He walked over to the body and, leaning over the head, held each eyelid apart and scooped out the eyeballs with the grapefruit spoon, placing them in a baggy. The face appeared strangely blank, looking out from empty eye-sockets. He pinned the note on Murray's left big toe. It read,

The defense rests.
The prosecution won't be able to see his way
to a decent conclusion.
Justice is definitely blind.

The surgeon called the main desk after he had cleaned up and was ready to leave.

"Main desk. May I help you?"

The surgeon spoke through a towel. "This is room 507. Something's wrong up here. Maybe you should send someone up to check out the lights. Can't see a thing."

"Yes, sir. Someone will be right up."

He hung up the phone and went to the door. The corridor was empty, and he went directly to the stairs and practically hopped down the five flights to the lobby. He mingled with the clientele, made his way to the revolving door and found himself outside in the cold evening air.

The doorman was occupied getting someone a cab and didn't notice him as he exited and turned left. He went to the corner, crossed the street and walked eight blocks before hailing a cab back to his hotel. He picked up his clothes, cleaned the room, then left in another disguise. He had parked in a twenty-four-hour garage down the block. He got in his car and drove off, arriving at home early in the morning. He sat back in the car after he pulled into the garage and said, "I feel *good*!"

—33—

"Murray Lutz. His name is Murray Lutz, and he was in New York for five days on business. And yes. He was a malpractice attorney. We already called the next of kin, and his wife acted like she couldn't care less. Said they were basically roommates and didn't have much of a relationship. They stayed together for the kids. Yes. Yes. No. Okay. No. He apparently saw through that plan."

Mac listened to his chief for a few more minutes. It was one of the low moments of his life. He was standing over the eyeless corpse.

He looked over at Dr. Norman Birdwell, the medical examiner. "You're an M.D.. Do you understand this guy?"

"If you mean do I understand his motives? Yes. Sort of. He has a strange hatred of attorneys and a playful macabre sense of justice. These notes and the body parts. He sees himself as some sort of avenging angel for the medical profession and gets a great joy out of the murders."

"But how can he do this kind of thing and still be functional? How can he justify these horrible mutilations?"

"You know, those are the same questions they asked the Nazis back in Nuremberg. The human mind has the ability to dehumanize certain people whom they fear or hate. Then they can treat them as less than human. This guy sees attorneys as less than human and therefore can treat them as a sportsman might a fish or a deer."

"The difficulty with catching this guy is that he has no remorse or guilt about his actions," said Mac. "He can approach them coolly, yes, like a surgeon approaching a case or a big game hunter planning an expedition."

"I agree. Think of the commando in a war who kills the enemy. Most of those men don't give it two thoughts after the fact because they're convinced the enemy is real and expendable for the cause. I'm sure this guy would defend his actions in a very sober and rational way. He probably sees himself as cleansing society of an evil."

Mac turned to one of his associates with whom he had worked for many years. "Any ideas?" The man looked back at him, pursing his lips, saying nothing, but shaking his head as he looked at the empty eye sockets below.

"I mean, we know who's gonna get murdered each time, except that only limits it to several thousand people, and we can't guard every malpractice attorney in the United States."

Another police officer entered the room and swallowed twice as he looked at the corpse. "We've interviewed just about every-one. Apparently, the killer was circulating through the hotel yesterday making small talk until he found a malpractice attorney. This unlucky guy just happened to be here and opened his mouth a bit too much."

Mac perked up. "So we have a description of the man?"

"Yes and no. He's tall, stocky, and overweight. Yet no one seems to give the same description of his face. Some say he has brown hair, others gray or black. We've had four composite pictures drawn, and they all look different. It's almost as if he's some kind of makeup expert. One definitely described a mustache, another a small goatee, and still another said he was tall and thin and had severe acne scarring on his left cheek. The last man I spoke to said there was definitely no scarring. The guy's very clever and very quick at changing disguises. Oh, and they all say he's Caucasian."

Mac shrugged. "Great. We have a big, blue-eyed, husky, thin, fat man with a smooth, acne-scarred face, a goatee and a mustache. At least he's not in blackface some of the time."

Birdwell interrupted. "You know, Mac, you might just want to get in touch with a surgeon. You may get a different slant on the guy. Who knows, maybe some helpful ideas about the case?"

Mac looked at him. "Of course. Why didn't I think of that? It

takes one to know one."

Birdwell raised his eyebrows.

Mac retorted, "I mean it takes a surgeon to know a surgeon. I'm not casting aspersions on doctors, even if my own Dr. Smithen makes me wait an hour and is an arrogant asshole." He paused. "Just a joke, just a joke. He's actually a nice guy for a proctologist."

Birdwell smiled, "Is he the one who called you last week to tell you he'd found your head?"

"Very funny. Can you give me the name of a surgeon I can call?"

"Yes. That is, if you don't insult him and embarrass me."

"Well?"

"Dr. Sam Fishberg. He's even written two books, one on breast disease and another on operations, called *Understanding Surgery*. He's in California, but if you want I can try to find someone in New York."

"How do you know the guy?"

"I don't. My wife read the breast book and bought me the one on surgery. They're full of humorous verses and facts. The guy has a sense of humor and seems to know a bit about human nature. Mixes serious science with puns and poems."

"Oh, great. A wise-ass surgeon. Just what we need."

"It doesn't look like you're doing so well on your own, smart guy."

Mac looked over at him with a sneer. "All right. How do I get in touch with the guy?"

"He's got a website listed on the back of his books. I'll call my wife and get it for you."

"Thanks." Birdwell went over to the phone and dialed his home number. He spoke for a few moments, waited, then took out a pen and wrote down some information on a sheet of paper.

"Here it is: *www.webmd.com/care/~samfishberg~md.* As I said, that's for Dr. Sam Fishberg."

"Great. I'll give him a call. May even fly him out here if it'll help."

Birdwell went back to his forensics. The photographers had finished, and the rest of the forensic team was going over the site for prints and anything else. But it was clean.

The guy's good! thought Birdwell.

—34—

The meeting was held in the mayor's office with two representatives of the Bar Association, two reporters, McClymonds, his boss, and a man and woman from the City District Attorney's office. The mayor was in a foul mood and sat quietly scowling from behind a huge mahogany desk with nothing on it except a phone and a computer terminal. The room had a small library with book shelves lining the walls, as well as diplomas and photographs of the mayor with diverse dignitaries: some political, some theatrical, some just important businessmen.

One of the men from the Bar Association spoke. "The Bar Association is of course concerned with the turn of events over the past several months, and we need to know what's being done at present. We understand this is a difficult problem, but if you can't get a handle on it, we'll bring in our own investigators."

The mayor looked over at the Chief who looked over to Mac. He sat up a little straighter in his chair and took out the folder marked SCALPEL.

"I'll give you a rundown on what we have so far, but I must admit that at this point we're pretty much stymied." He looked at the two attorneys. "I can tell you that I personally welcome any assistance you can give us."

Mac went over all the cases and the facts to date. "We've struck out with fingerprints, voice prints, identifications, surgical objects and writing. He's left no apparent clues which would indicate

165

where he comes from, and there have been no specific leads about who his next victim will be. All the victims were attorneys except the one case where the client was also shot. And at that time an intruder, another attorney, was shot and wounded, the only survivor. The attorney survivor can't help us except for the blue eyes, generally stocky build, and large hands. It would take us years to trace every malpractice case in the country. I am in the process of getting in touch with a practicing surgeon in California to see if he can give me any insights into the case."

He looked at the rest of the people in the room. "The California surgeon may have some fresh ideas. I want to get his opinion on a profile of the guy—what makes him tick and how we might be able to pick out who he's gonna choose next. Also, we're hoping he may have some ideas as to how we can identify him from the procedures he's done or something peculiar about his technique."

The mayor spoke up. "The public is reacting strangely to this whole serial killer bit. It's the first time where there's less fear than pure interest. People seem almost delighted that attorneys are getting theirs. It's almost as if they have been a privileged group who make their money whether they win or lose. There are a lot of people out there who can't stand attorneys. I feel very anxious about this, since you all know I practiced corporate law for twenty years before getting this job."

Mac spoke up. "Well, I'm well aware you're getting pressure from the public and from the news media. I'm doing the best I can. I feel our police department has let you down, yet I don't know what to say. The last thing we should do is to acknowledge that we're stumped. That's like holding up a green flag for the guy."

The district attorney looked over his notes and shook his head. "One of the big problems is that this guy apparently can carry out his activities anywhere and be gone in a few hours. He probably takes a train or drives, because we have thoroughly checked the buses and airlines without any consistent clues or paths."

The two lawyers looked at each other. "So you're saying you really don't have a handle on him at all?"

"I'm afraid that's correct," said Mac. "You'll have to issue a warning to the attorneys to hire their own bodyguards and to be sure they know whom they're meeting. Don't open doors for anyone they don't know, especially when traveling. I would list Manhattan as the key city, but it could occur anywhere and at any time. In the meantime, I'll check with this surgeon in California and keep you apprised of the situation. We're not trying to hide anything and are as discouraged by the whole set of events as you are."

"We appreciate your honesty, and we'll certainly try to work with you. I only hope that the press," and he looked at the two reporters, "can be relied upon to be responsible in this situation?"

One of the reporters chimed in. "I understand your situation, but we do have a responsibility to the public. The best we can do is to indicate that everything is being done. I don't mean to sound crass, but what I've gathered from talking to the public is that a lot of people are actually happy to see the attorneys getting knocked off. I've never seen a public response to a series of murders like this one. There's some remorse and sadness about the families but, as far as we can tell, out of six corpses only one wife was unhappy about her husband's death, and even she was not terribly torn up about it. The children are a different matter, and we will try to present the family side to instill more public sympathy for the victims. But I do want to emphasize that most of the response is either in the form of sick attorney jokes or an *I don't give a damn* attitude. I thought it would change after the first one or two, but it hasn't. Of course, there are many who feel that any murder is a terrible thing. But I'm surprised by the lack of concern about this one particular segment of society."

The two attorneys fumed. "That's the dumbest thing I've heard. We're talking serial killer, and you're saying people aren't upset about it?"

"Look. I'm not telling you what I think or feel. I'm giving you an insight into what I hear on the streets. True, what I hear may be very biased and one-sided, but I have never heard this type of response before, and I think it will cause you to have more difficulty in tracing this guy."

"What do the police feel?" asked the attorney.

"That's meant to be a loaded question, I know." Mac voiced, "but I want to assure you that every man in this department wants to see this guy caught. In the same way that every attorney wants to do the best for his client, we feel we want to do the best for our client, and our client is the public and the laws of this state and this country."

"Sounds very noble. We're here to assure ourselves that the police are actually doing their best in this case."

The mayor jumped into that one. "Now, look here. I'm not going to tolerate that kind of verbiage in this office. I assure you our police and investigative arms are working as hard on this case as humanly possible. Let's not muddy up the waters with accusations which will only cause more animosity between the public, the attorneys, and law enforcement." He looked directly at the two reporters. "I know I can't muzzle the press, and I won't even attempt it. But please don't create a public outrage and uproar because of what you have heard here today."

One of the reporters asked, "Has there been any joking among the police about the fact that these victims are attorneys?"

Mac answered immediately. "I haven't heard a single word. In fact, today's the first I heard of a negative public response, and that's from reporters and attorneys. If you think we're not professional enough to handle this kind of case, tell me right now, and I'll hand in my resignation immediately." He reached for his shield and held it out towards the attorneys.

They looked at one another and realized they had over-stepped their bounds. They knew McClymonds very well from his past cases, and the last thing they wanted was his resignation. And from the look of anger in his eyes, they knew he was not bluffing.

The attorney who had originally spoken up held up his right hand. "Mac. I'm sorry. I guess I overstepped a bit. I know you well enough. It's just that I want to make sure there's no prevailing attitude in the department."

Mac glared at him. "There's not!"

"Okay. We'll take that at face value."

The mayor looked at Mac. "Put your goddamned shield back in your pocket, Mac. Let's not get carried away here. We've got enough problems to work out without getting on each other's nerves."

The mayor stood up and looked around at all the men and the one woman. "I had you here so we could air our dirty linen and resolve this petty crap. That's why I took the chance and invited you two from the press." He looked at the two reporters. "Reynolds. Parton. I chose you because you've got enough common sense not to let this get blown out of all proportion. I hope you'll live up to my expectations. I think we bared our souls. The main objective is to catch this nut before he can do any more harm. I know it's a big order, but I'm going to need everyone's cooperation and no more friction. So if you have any problems with the way it's being handled or any suggestions, let's hear them now or only through channels. I don't want to read about it in the papers, and I don't want every goddamned attorney organization breathing down my back. You all know McClymonds and respect his work as much as I do. I trust he'll do the best job possible." He sat back down and looked around the room. There were no questions.

After a few moments, he stood up and said, "Thank you, all. This meeting is over."

—35—

It was Sunday morning, and the surgeon had just finished seeing two patients in the hospital. He went to the cafeteria, got a blueberry muffin and cup of coffee and took them across the alleyway from the hospital to the office building. It was deserted, being Sunday, and he went down the hall to his own office, unlocked and opened the door, then locked it behind him. He went into his small private room at the end of the corridor, set the food and drink on the edge of his desk, then went back out to his car, where he retrieved the Sunday Times to take back to the office. He felt peaceful and relaxed as he sat back in his lounging chair and put his feet up on the edge of the desk. The coffee was just right with two sweeteners, and the muffin looked perfect. He tore the baking paper from beneath it, threw it in the wastepaper basket, and took a bite out of it. He loved being alone there to think and ponder over his activities. He often glanced around the room at the many framed certificates on the walls. He was pleased with himself.

He took the wrapping off the newspaper and quickly saw the headline.

Serial Killings Continue

The article went on to describe the latest death in the series of attorney murders and referred the readers to three other articles relating to the matter, including letters to the editor.

He turned to page 34 where there was a column entitled,

Vigilantism—The Poor Excuse for Justice

He smiled as he read on. It was a review of the life of Lafayette Curry Baker.

> *A Northerner in the American Civil War who was the director of the Union's intelligence and counterintelligence organizations, he had the infamous distinction of having been one of the active members of the San Francisco Vigilance Command, called the Vigilantes in the 1850's. They prided themselves on their success in wiping out criminal elements, although it was done without due process of law and in an arbitrary and totally illegal manner. Their results were so good that Baker was commended by General Winfield Scott, and later, in the Civil War, he succeeded the famous Allan Pinkerton (founder of the Pinkerton Detective Agency) as director of the secret service. He was the man responsible for the apprehension of John Wilkes Booth after the assassination of President Lincoln and was later promoted to Brigadier General. His methods were both praised and damned, yet he was known as a man who got the job done. His motto* Death to Traitors *was used for years.*
>
> *Vigilantism is raising its ugly head in the United States today with the serial killings of malpractice attorneys by a deranged physician, yet the public outcry is far less than might be expected….*

The article went on to castigate vigilantes and undermine the philosophy of self-appointed wielders of justice. The surgeon read the article, then went on to the article in the next column, which was headed *Serial Murder and Malpractice.*

Malpractice cases, settlements, and physicians' insurance rates dropped precipitously throughout the country in the aftermath of the serial killings of attorneys. Fear has spread throughout the litigation community, specifically in the area of medical malpractice, where the case incidence has dropped a staggering 86% in the past eleven months, since the first serial murders of several malpractice and personal injury attorneys. Conversely, the number of settlements and the settlement amounts have taken a significant decrease during the same period of time. National Medical Malpractice Insurance Company (commonly known as NaMMIC), has seen a reduction in claims payments of over 90% in the past several months, and has begun to pass this improvement on to their customers: thirteen thousand physicians and surgeons throughout the country.

The rates for general surgeons alone has dropped from an average of $2000 per month to $425 per month. The company has emphasized that this may well be a temporary reduction in costs, but states they will monitor the situation on a monthly basis to give their clients the best rates possible. Many other malpractice insurance companies are following suit although most major insurers feel that the downturn in malpractice cases is just a temporary response to the serial killings seen over the past year. Needless to say, surgeons are very pleased with this turn of events, and their reactions to the slayings are usually viewed from two sides. Most are sad to see that one of their physician compatriots has resorted to this extreme measure and have expressed sympathy to the families of the deceased. The major medical groups in the country have deplored the killings, and a spokesman for National Medical Group (NMG) emphasized that the *vigilantism is the action of a sick and deranged person. To quote Dr. Herbert Fonderdorf, "...this man has forsaken the basic tenets of the Hippocratic Oath, that time-worn pledge read to every physician at the time he graduates from medical school. The Oath demands that physicians 'abstain from anything deleterious or mischievous' to individuals and 'give no deadly medicine to anyone.'"*

The surgeon read through the articles, then picked up his pen and wrote across the paper absentmindedly, *Those who do not learn from the past are doomed to repeat it.* He inhaled deeply and proudly, and spoke out loud to the empty office.

"Someone has to take responsibility for injustice and the righting of wrongs in our society. Nothing is accomplished by Nervous Nellies and principle-spouting idiots like Fonderdorf. Look what I have accomplished in eleven months, and what I will continue to accomplish in the coming months and years, Marilyn. You and I have started a revolution in medical practice that will free surgeons from the bondage of fear, anxiety and financial ruin. You and I together, dear, will advance the cause of justice to all physicians. Everyone speaks about it, people have written about it from before the time of Shakespeare and his famous phrase, 'Let's kill all the lawyers,' but no one has done anything about it for a thousand years until you and I took these first few steps. And we have accomplished a great deal, Marilyn, a great deal."

"Hello? That you, doc?" It was one of the office building security men making his rounds on Sunday morning. The man unlocked the door and poked his head into the office.

The surgeon snapped out of his trance and answered. "Yes. It's me. Just getting a little work done. Thanks for checking. I'll be leaving in a short while."

"Okay, doc. Sorry to disturb you. Just checking up, ya know. You work too hard. Ought to take a day off, ya know."

"Yeah, I know. Thanks for your concern."

The man turned and exited the office, locking the door behind him.

The surgeon finished his coffee and muffin, discarded part of the newspaper and took the rest with him as he left his office.

–36–

Dr. Sam Fishberg was glad to get a few paid days off from his busy schedule as a general and vascular surgeon in Southern California. Having been an English and American literature major in college, he had kept up his interest in literature and writing for many years and had written several manuscripts, which he kept in a closet. In the past year he had published a book on *Comprehensive Breast Care* and one on *Understanding Surgery*, both volumes written for the lay public. It was these books that the medical examiner and his wife had read. The doctor had experience with medical malpractice attorneys, both defending himself and defending other physicians, and was well-qualified to see the issues from the physicians' point of view.

He was a middle-aged, silver-haired man, six feet tall, with an easy sense of humor, who lived with his second wife, a nurse, in a small village by the Pacific Ocean. Mac met him at the airport and drove him to the Hilton for his three-day stay. After freshening up, they went to a small restaurant near the hotel for a working dinner, where Mac reviewed the cases and his impressions of the perpetrator. The visitor remained silent throughout Mac's dissertation, then sat back thinking for a moment. Finally, he leaned forward.

"Getting a letter of intent to initiate a lawsuit is one of the most emotionally upsetting things that can occur for a physician. Aside from the legal aspect of the case, the letters are usually laced with terms such as *below the standard of the community, incompetent, wrongful*, and other such terms in reference to the physician. Now, of course, most of these are form letters with a few details added, but the effect is the same as if someone were screaming in your face. You are basically being told that you are a bad doctor, a bad person, and that they're gonna *get you*. It upsets the doctor for days because it threatens his ability to practice in his field. Whether there is any validity to the charges made is often unrelated or unimportant to the doctor.

"He is usually quite devastated, and this feeling persists until he speaks with his malpractice company or his own attorney. The same behavior holds true for the lawsuit itself. While in settlement conferences or in a court trial, the surgeon is so powerless and distraught that he is often unable to function well at his day-in, day-out job. Then, to boot, during a trial his case is being evaluated by a jury of his so-called peers, usually a group of twelve average citizens who cannot or will not be able to understand the key elements of what is usually a complicated matter. A jury of your peers is definitely not a jury of your peers, in this instance. As a specialist, a surgeon should go before a jury of specialists."

"But there are consultants and specialists on call in jury trials," said McClymonds.

"Ah. But you well know that there are always people who will testify to anything. It's no different with medical malpractice trials. Each side pays an expert to testify, and it really depends on who sounds the best or has the best credentials. I have seen cases won and lost for the flimsiest of reasons. But that is neither here nor there. Most physicians who have been sued have a deep dislike, even a hatred, for attorneys. But then we all have our moments when we hate something or other, and it doesn't express itself in homicide."

Mac was nodding his head in agreement.

"I'm sure you know," said Fishberg, "that everyone at some time or other makes a lighthearted or even angry statement to the effect, *I could murder the guy*, or *I'd like to kill my ex-husband or ex-wife.* But the number of times anyone ever follows through with such a threat, as we know, is minuscule. This surgeon has gone over the edge, and it makes me think that he's been harmed deeply by a malpractice attorney."

"We can't look through every case of every physician in the country," Mac explained. "We've been through the cases in New York City for the last five years, and that's led us nowhere."

Fishberg held up his hand. "I agree you can't trace every malpractice case, but let's look at the kind of cases that could instigate this type of behavior.

"One. Personal loss of his ability to practice medicine. I've found that if the physician can keep his insurance and continue to practice his craft, he can get beyond a bad malpractice suit and get on with his life. Most hospitals require a doctor to have malpractice insurance to practice in their facility. For a surgeon, losing a big malpractice case and being canceled out by his malpractice insurance carrier means the end of his job. That would be devastating and leave a wound that wouldn't quickly heal. I know one fellow who lost his insurance and then claimed disability due to some orthopedic injury just to keep on making enough money from his insurance to survive. So, under number one, I would be looking for a surgeon who lost his malpractice insurance and had to quit medicine."

"Aren't there many malpractice insurance companies?" asked Mac.

"Yes, indeed, but they generally go by the same standards; if one turns you down, the others will generally follow suit. Now, there are special companies that insure high-risk doctors, but the premiums are so high that only the most affluent can afford it. I'm talking around $100,000 a year for insurance. With decreasing reimbursements for physicians and escalating costs, even if a doctor were making a gross income of, say, $300,000 a year, he could barely break even after paying all his costs, overhead, employees, etc. So, getting back to our killer, I would look for the doctor who feels he was driven out of medicine by the actions of the malpractice attorney. Now, I'm not necessarily defending the doctor; he may well have committed a terrible error and deserved to get sued and lose his ability to practice. I'm just saying that individual would see himself as a victim and might well seek out revenge."

Mac was keeping notes. "Good point, Doc."

The waiter brought their main dishes, and Mac put his yellow pad away.

"Say, let's finish dinner, and then we can continue."

They both relaxed a bit and gave each other a bit of their backgrounds. Mac found himself actually amused by the California surgeon; he had never had much personal interaction with a medical specialist, and this guy seemed okay to him. By the time they finished and were sipping coffee, Mac pulled out his pad again, and they got back to business.

"Let's look at another scenario," said Fishberg. "I'll call it number two. You have a surgeon who has a member of the family or some loved one who has in some way been harmed by the actions of a malpractice attorney. Maybe a brother or wife was a physician who was harmed or even a son or daughter who went into medicine and was sued. Suppose that individual lost the ability to practice, and this surgeon decided to get even. Although I tend to doubt that would cause him to flip out to this extent.

"And this brings me to my third proposal. Suppose, as a result of some malpractice action, this loved one was so shamed or so depressed or so unstable that this person took his or her own life."

"A surgeon whose son was a physician and lost a suit and was so depressed that he killed himself?" asked Mac. "Sounds pretty far-fetched."

"No. Actually, there are cases of suicide surrounding malpractice cases. Look at one of the attorneys that our guy killed. That case involved a young surgical resident named Beaujolais, who killed himself after losing a malpractice lawsuit. Your guy killed the attorney of record, a woman."

"Right. Ellen Freemont. I'd forgotten that aspect of the case."

Fishberg continued. "Suppose Beaujolais had a father or uncle who was a surgeon and looked at that young doctor as a love that was suddenly cut from him. The right guy, the right circumstances could trigger this kind of reaction. Anyway, I would look for deaths of doctors somehow related to malpractice lawsuits, then look for family members."

Mac was taking notes rapidly and nodding his head. He thought, *The doc here makes sense.*

Fishberg continued. "The fourth situation would be the most difficult to deal with. Imagine a surgeon who is getting on in years, perhaps no family or wife, suddenly starts to go crazy and seeks an outlet for his anger. Let's assume he's just a nice ordinary guy who's had his come-uppances with malpractice attorneys, but nothing bad enough to cause him to lose his insurance or his ability to practice. But this guy has a psychotic side and starts to feel tired of taking it from the legal profession. He's bright and smart and clever and has some free time. He justifies to himself that he has, in some way, a God-given inspiration to rid the earth of this profession, which he sees as totally evil. Now, I know a lot of doctors, and I'm not proud to say that some of them are quite nuts. Not necessarily psychotic, but definitely a bit nuts. Take away any stable aspect of their life or insert something such as the death of a spouse or son or daughter or loss of money in the stock market, and some guy just might flip out."

The two continued to talk for a while, then walked back to the hotel. Fishberg was exhausted and went off to bed. Mac went to the bar, where he took up his usual seat and pondered the things the surgeon had discussed with him.

–37–

Fishberg slept late the next morning. Mac picked him up at 11 A.M. and took him down to the morgue to meet with the medical examiner, Birdwell, to see if they could come up with more helpful information. They had the list of victims and the surgeries performed on them.

Fishberg said, "This guy has taken the most care with the colon surgery, the gall bladder, and the thyroid. The enucleating of the eyes was coarse and showed no skill. This looks like the work of a general surgeon, as opposed to any of the other specialists, so I think we can narrow it down quite a bit. He used stapling devices, so he's been practicing the last twenty years; he's not retired, because he has access to a hospital or surgical center operating room where he can steal some staplers and other instruments.

"His use of English is clever at times, which might be difficult for an Indian or Asian or even European. I doubt he's African-American from the few descriptions we have. He closed the abdomen with large PDS sutures. Now, many surgeons use that, but it probably eliminates all those who don't. By the way, did you test the eyeballs for fingerprints?"

"What?"

"You know, the smooth shiny surface may have picked up something if he had taken off his gloves. Were there any prints on the grapefruit spoon?"

"No. It was wiped clean. Why?"

"Well, why bother to wipe the spoon clean if he had worn gloves when doing the enucleating?"

"Yeah," said Birdwell. "Good point. Unfortunately, the eyeballs were handled by our staff, and whatever was on them has probably been lost. But we'll give it a try, anyway."

Fishberg asked, "Did you find any gloves in any of the cases?"

Mac proffered. "You looking for prints inside the gloves? No. We thought of that, too, but there were no gloves found."

"What about the bullets? Any chance of identification?"

"Standard 22 caliber. Can pick 'em up in any munitions store and almost impossible to trace a 22 caliber pistol."

Fishberg paused a moment. "I was just thinking. Not many surgeons I know have weapons. At least, not firearms. Other physicians sometimes go hunting, but it's not common among general surgeons. I can't say exactly why, and maybe it's just among my acquaintances. Just another point you may want to look into."

Mac kept taking notes, and the three of them went over the profile as it was developing. Birdwell especially liked the initial characterizations of physicians who could be pushed into homicide.

Fishberg continued. "After reading some of the newspaper accounts of the murders, I've thought about what would cause me to take revenge. I know Mac and I discussed this yesterday, but I want to go over it again. I was thinking about the surgeon who has extreme resentments against malpractice attorneys, but is prevented from doing anything because he's afraid of being caught. I'm sure many people are deterred from crime of one sort or another purely by that fear."

Mac added, "We certainly hope so. And yet, crimes of passion occur without the perpetrator thinking sensibly about the possible punishment."

"But," said Fishberg, "these aren't like that. They're usually planned in advance, sometimes days or weeks, so they can't be spur-of-the-moment crimes of passion. The killer knows what and when and how in most circumstances. So either he feels he will not be caught or, in the long run, he doesn't care whether he is caught or not."

Mac listened carefully, then said, "I'm not sure I understand what you're driving at."

"Look at it like this," said Fishberg. "If the surgeon is so confident that he doubts anyone can catch him, he's obviously very naive. Serial killers always leave some clues and are eventually caught by their own mistakes. This guy must know this, so I doubt whether he really expects to continue indefinitely. So either he's going to stop completely after a series of these killings have satisfied him, or he's using these killings as a ruse to cover up a murder that he really wants to do. For example, he may have one particular attorney he wants to kill, but to do that would be too obvious. So he knocks off a half-dozen guys beforehand in order to set up a pattern before he goes after his real victim. Then he does one or two more and feels satisfied or vindicated. In that case, we need to look at every case of every murdered attorney and try to compare the surgeons involved with our vague descriptions."

"I've seen that scenario on two accounts with husbands killing their wives. One guy killed two women, then killed his wife, then killed another woman to cover his tracks."

"How'd you finally get him?"

"Last victim lived long enough to finger him."

"Oh. Well, there's another scenario we haven't discussed. That's the surgeon who has a hatred for malpractice attorneys and doesn't care if he gets caught."

"Why is that? Totally crazy?" asked Birdwell.

"We hope he's not totally crazy, because then he could do anything at any time. I'm thinking about the possibility that the surgeon may have a terminal disease."

"Terminal disease?" asked Mac."

"Yes. Suppose he has incurable cancer and knows he's going to die and wants to take a few attorneys with him."

"Wouldn't he be too weak or sick to perform these murders?" asked Mac.

"Not necessarily. Many individuals have very minor symptoms or have an incurable malignancy diagnosed by accident. They're strong and feel healthy, but there's nothing that medicine can do to heal them. Oh, they may be treatable with radiation or chemotherapy, their lives prolonged for months or even years, but there's no cure, and they know that, within a given period of time, they'll deteriorate and die. He may have had a routine chest x-ray or some other test and discovered there's this cancer that has already advanced beyond the possibility of cure.

"Our surgeon might not have any family or loved ones, and his only desire is to take vengeance upon malpractice attorneys before he goes to the big operating room in the sky."

"So we should also look for a surgeon who may have a terminal disease?" asked Mac, incredulously.

Fishberg saw his look. "I'm not saying this is the situation here. But these are just some possible scenarios you need to take under consideration. And maybe if you're lucky and the guy does have a terminal disease, he'll die before he kills anymore."

Birdwell looked at them and smiled. "And the guy would cheat the hangman? Damn, there'd be no satisfaction in that."

Mac and Fishberg glanced at him and tried to ignore the comment.

"You've given us a lot to think about, Dr. Fishberg. I'll get together with the team and see if we can start looking down some of these avenues. I know you have some plans for the rest of the day. Why don't we get together tomorrow morning for an hour or two before your plane leaves, and maybe we can iron out a few more points."

Mac and Birdwell shook the doctor's hand, and one of the officers drove Fishberg back to his hotel.

—38—

The diary was becoming a friend and he wrote as if he were speaking to it.

I love to walk through the city late in the afternoon. Philadelphia is one of the major historical, cultural and intellectual centers in the United States. Between the confluence of the Delaware and Schuylkill Rivers, the city is a walker's paradise. I often have time to explore the old and the new sections of the city, and it affords me the opportunity to think about the great men that walked, spoke and wrote here. From the Ameriport harbor to the central gridiron of streets designed by William Penn, I can walk through the four tree-lined, fountained squares, through Fairmount Park and even to Independence National Historical Park. Do you think it odd that one such as I should enjoy walking through these historical areas where the Declaration of Independence and the Constitution were written and signed? I am sorry that I must admit I was born in Australia and not in this cradle of democracy. You are perhaps too parochial in your thinking. I consider myself a free thinker, and I would have done well in those hallowed halls with the likes of William Penn and Benjamin Franklin.

*In a country so steeped in politics and legal
wrangling that a presidential election creates havoc,
there has been a deterioration of the free American spirit.
I used to walk here with Marilyn in her free moments, and
we talked about the history of this great nation. As a
physician, I felt I was close to those founding fathers
because I often extended myself to the common man
without regard to religion, creed or financial background.
Most personal injury attorneys or malpractice attorneys
seek out only financial rewards under the guise of helping
humanity. Their hypocrisy makes me angry, and I have
that strange feeling rise up in me. There is that need to
get back to the principles that the founding fathers
represented. They were standing up for their rights
against the tyranny of the British throne and were seen as
treasonable men who should be hanged. Perhaps that is
the way many in society will look upon me and yet, in the
right time and the right place, I should be looked upon
much as a James Madison, William Penn or Benjamin
Franklin would be. If they were here today, I think they
would have raised their flintlock pistols to wipe out this
abomination of attorneys.*

The surgeon walked through the park and into a side street,
where the three-story, red-brick buildings looked much as they
had over two hundred years ago. He was lonely as his mind
wandered to thoughts of Marilyn—those calmer, more pleasant,
happier times. He felt as if he were part of a large machine that
was slowly winding down to a close, soon to be shut off. He
wanted to make his mark before the plug was pulled and wanted
to be part of the great American dream. His vision, however, was
a great melting pot with all the malpractice attorneys melting at
the bottom!

He bought a newspaper and entered a restaurant with the
name of a signer of the Declaration of Independence and signaled
for a table. It was 7 P.M., and the place was just beginning to fill

up. He was seated near a multi-paned window looking out onto the street and ordered a drink, bourbon on ice. He felt the smoothness of the liquid as it went down and within a few minutes could sense himself relaxing. He fingered through the pages until he found another article about the malpractice attorney slayings. Very little detail was given, but there was a separate article about the downturn in malpractice cases.

If I were smart, I would probably stop the killings now, he thought. *But I can't be comfortable just about the decrease in the cases, can I, Marilyn? I shouldn't stop until every attorney has left the field or every case has been stopped. Perhaps I am foolish. Maybe I can even talk with the bar association and agree to stop my activities under certain conditions. Nah. They'd never consider it after only a few deaths...or would they?*

He took out a small pad he always kept with him and started to write a draft of a letter. Later, he would type it out on his computer and print it out on his personal printer. He felt sure this couldn't be traced. He began the letter:

To whom it may concern:

You have put some time into looking for me and I have put a great deal of time into the matter of malpractice attorneys. I have the ability to go anywhere and to continue purging society of these individuals whenever and wherever I like. I am careful, as you have seen, and the probability of your apprehending me is very small. I would, however like to come to an agreement with the legal community, if that is found to be acceptable.

Before any medical malpractice case can be brought to bear, it would have to be heard by a neutral arbitration board consisting of three physicians. If that board deems there is no malpractice, then no suit can be started. If they feel there has been gross negligence or other deviation from the standard of care, then a trial can be undertaken, but it must be with a jury of peers and these, too, must be physicians. Yes, I agree that this will significantly change the legal system as we know it, but changes were made in the system in 1776 that were thought impossible at that time. Please give this letter to the appropriate individuals and let me have a response in The New York Times *within two weeks. If you decide not to arbitrate this issue, there may be more surgical intervention!"*

He smiled after the last two words and signed his letter, *A Concerned American.*

When he returned home, he quickly transcribed the letter on his computer. In several of the articles about the serial killings, a single name had been mentioned, Lieutenant Septimus McClymonds, so he addressed his letter to him in care of the NYPD. He read through the letter several times.

Are my demands too radical to be considered? Perhaps, but at least it will get them thinking along the right lines. In the meantime, he would have two or three weeks to investigate another possible victim.

—39—

D_r. Fishberg, Lieutenant McClymonds and Medical Examiner Birdwell met for breakfast at the hotel. Just before the meeting, the letter arrived from the surgeon, and Mac had it with him.

He decided to hold onto it for a while before revealing the contents to these other two men.

Briefly, they reviewed the previous day's material, then Fishberg offered some more insights.

"If I was this guy, and I wasn't totally nuts, I would realize that I couldn't continue this activity indefinitely without being caught. So he might just stop for a while. Don't be surprised if he goes into hiding for a few months, then returns to the activity. Also, I would take his behavior very seriously. What I mean is, don't think this is a man without a motive. Recognize that he wants something and is not just killing these men and women for the enjoyment. Don't challenge him in any way. Try to get the media to downplay the aspect of his being crazy or demented. He probably sees himself as a justifiable vigilante."

Mac countered. "But he *is* crazy, and he *is* a danger to society. What happens next time he's killing an attorney and some innocent bystander who's not an attorney happens upon the scene? Do you think he'll just let him go?"

"I agree. He's very dangerous and probably crazy, if you want to use that word. But if you give him even a slight impression that someone is taking the situation of medical malpractice

191

under scrutiny, he may back down. He's very much like the terrorist who makes extreme demands, but will actually settle for much less, like any good businessman does in making a sale or purchase. The only problem is that the cards he's dealing are human lives that he feels no compunction about snuffing out."

"But if we were to even suggest this line to the Bar Association, they would start screaming so loud we'd all be fired. And what do we do, let the guy get away with these murders?"

Mac took the envelope out of his pocket. "I received this today, postmarked in Manhattan yesterday." He read the letter aloud to both men, then just sat while they digested the contents. "It's standard computer copy paper, no special marks or identification and no prints."

"I guess he and I think along similar lines," said Fishberg. "I think he must have read my mind. Now you don't need to make the suggestion to the Bar Association. Just give them the letter and ask how they want you to respond in the newspaper. That way you can't be kicked downstairs no matter what happens. Oh, and let me see the stamp. Is it one that has self-adhesion or did it need to be licked?"

"Looks like he licked it."

"Can you do a DNA tracing on that?"

"We've been successful with it before. I can have the lab give it a try," said McClymonds. "Well, Dr. Fishberg, you've given us some good suggestions, and we'll start following up as best we can. Of course, we've got this letter to consider. On the surface, I can't conceive of any legitimate response except refusal. But even if it opens up some line of communication with the guy, that's better than nothing."

"Run it by the attorneys and see what they want to contribute," said Birdwell. "Keep them in the loop. Also keep the Mayor in on this just to protect your own butt."

They said goodbye to the surgeon from California, and he thanked them for the free trip. "If anything comes up that I can help you with, just give me a call." They shook hands all around and parted company.

—40—

It was one o'clock in the morning when the phone rang.

"Hey, Doc. Good morning. It's Doctor Fred Bailey at the Samaritan Hospital Emergency Room. We have a fifty-six-year-old man here with free air in the abdomen and what looks like a perforated duodenal ulcer. I gave him the name of the surgeon on call, but he says he's heard of you and insisted we call you. Also, his family physician is Doc Morrison, and he recommended you."

"What time is it?"

"About one fifteen."

"You *sure* he wants me?"

"Absolutely. He's here with his wife and in a great deal of pain."

"All right. I'll be there in about half an hour. Get a CBC, urinalysis, electrolytes, chest x-ray and EKG."

"All done already. White count is 22,000 with a left shift. EKG and chest are okay."

"Then notify the operating room that we have a case, and we'll probably be ready to go in about an hour. Oh, and give him a couple grams of antibiotics intravenously now, would you?"

"Got it. Thank you."

"Goodbye."

He rolled out of bed and pulled on a pair of pants, shirt, shoes and socks and went into the bathroom to freshen up. He still liked the emergency work, but it took him a few minutes to wake up. He was out of the house in seven minutes, and the drive to the hospital was easy with almost no traffic in the early morning hours.

He parked in the emergency room lot, went into the hospital and into the urgent care section. The door had a coded lock to prevent unwanted visitors. There had been several emergency room shootings throughout the country in the last few years, and most hospitals had full-time guards and locked doors between the waiting rooms and the treatment area. He punched in the four digits and the lock snapped back, allowing him to enter the corridor to the nurses' station and the patients' beds.

The facility was half empty. As he walked in, one of the staff nurses called out to him.

"Good morning. Your man's in bed sixteen." She walked towards him holding out the chart. "The x-rays are on the view box."

He looked through the chart noting the ER physician's workup and laboratory results, then went to the view box where two films were on the screen. The x-ray showed the abdomen, and there was a sliver of shadow under the diaphragm on the right side consistent with "free air" in the abdomen, a classic indication of a hole in some intra-abdominal, intestinal organ.

He went to bed sixteen and introduced himself. A woman, the wife, was standing next to the patient, a Mr. James Dufour, who looked much younger than his age, with dark black hair and a chiseled face. He was obviously in a lot of pain as he extended a hand towards him.

"Jim Dufour, doc. This is my wife, Evelyn. Dr. Morrison recommends you highly. Says you're the only man for the job."

"I'll have to thank him, since it's almost two in the morning." The surgeon smiled. He took a complete history from the man and completed his physical examination.

"It's pretty straightforward, Mr. Dufour. You've had ulcer disease before, and it looks like you've finally perforated one of the ulcers. That means you have a hole in your stomach, and we have to go in and sew it up."

"Too much scotch whiskey, eh?" He tried to smile, but any motion caused him more distress. "I'm in the middle of a case right now. How soon can I get back to work?"

The surgeon felt a chill go through him. "What kind of work do you do, Mr. Dufour?"

The wife responded. "He's an attorney."

"I see. Hope you don't sue doctors." The surgeon smiled a bit.

The patient looked towards his wife and then to the surgeon. "Well, I go both sides of the road. But I promise I won't take it out on you." He tried to snicker, but couldn't.

The surgeon seemed to ignore the comment. "Well, my friend, I treat people, not professions. Be happy that I see you as a friend of Phil Morrison's."

The attorney grabbed his hand and held it tight. "Thanks, doc. I really appreciate your coming in at this hour. I promise I'll be the best patient you ever had."

"We'll be going to surgery as soon as the OR crew and anesthesiologist get here." He got a pen and paper and drew a picture of the stomach and duodenum and showed how he would be over-sewing the ulcer and possibly using a patch of Dufour's own abdominal fat, the omentum, to help close the hole.

"Is this a dangerous operation, Doctor?" asked the wife.

"It's major surgery, and this is an emergency, but I feel certain he'll do quite well." He looked at the man "You'll probably be here for about a week, and I doubt you'll be getting back to work in less than three or four weeks. Also, I'm going to call in an infectious disease doctor to manage your antibiotics and may even need an internist, if any problems arise."

"Problems?"

"I'm sure you're aware of all the potential problems, but I'll run down a few of them before we get going. They include infection, pneumonia, intestinal leakage, bleeding, blood clots to the lungs and possibly even the need for another surgery. However, you're in excellent health otherwise. and I think you'll do well." He looked over at the wife. "Any questions?"

"No. Thank you, doctor."

The patient looked towards him again. "I really appreciate your coming in and taking care of this, doc."

"Thank you. It's what I do for a living."

The patient grabbed his hand again and shook it firmly, stopping only when it caused him more abdominal pain.

The OR crew had arrived and were wheeling a gurney towards the patient's bed.

The patient gave a weak grin and said, "I know I'll do fine, just as long as you're not the guy knocking off malpractice attorneys." He put up his index finger shaking it at the surgeon.

"If I am, you're in deep trouble, eh?" They both laughed. The surgeon had a strange feeling inside. He turned and went to the nurses' station to complete his paperwork while the orderlies placed the patient on a gurney and took him to the operating room.

He went over to the wife. "Wait in the main lobby, and I'll see you as soon as I'm finished. The surgery itself will take about an hour, but it'll be at least half an hour before we get started."

"Okay, doctor. And thank you, again. Jim doesn't want to show it, but he's quite frightened."

"Don't worry. I'll take care of him." He picked up his paperwork and headed towards the operating suite.

It was two thirty in the morning by the time the patient was asleep on the operating table. Had it been during the daytime, the surgeon might have called for an assistant to help him, but seeing as the hour was ungodly and the case was relatively straightforward, he wouldn't need an assistant. He had done this same procedure at least a hundred times before, and it was not technically difficult. The only thing was the man's profession. On the one hand, he knew he could treat and cure the man without difficulty. Only the sickest patients with other complicating problems didn't pull through. After all, the guy was relatively young and in good health. No diabetes or heart disease and, although he drank, there was no evidence of liver dysfunction. Could he really do away with the guy on the operating table?

The abdomen was shaved, and an iodine solution was used for preparing the skin. The cloth towels were placed by the surgeon, and the suction and electrocautery apparatus set up with the proper grounding lines attached to the patient's thigh.

"All set?" the surgeon asked the anesthesiologist.

"Whenever you're ready. He's stable."

"Did he get his antibiotics?"

"All in."

The surgeon held his right hand out. "Scalpel!" The nurse placed it firmly in his palm. He made an incision in the skin extending from the xiphoid at the lower ending of the breast bone to the bellybutton. There was some bleeding, which he controlled with the cautery. Then, using the cautery stylus, he continued cutting down to and through the fascia in the midline of the abdomen. The operating room scrub nurse acted both as a nurse and a first assistant, retracting tissue when directed to do so. The surgeon took a scissors and a forceps and, carefully lifting the peritoneum, made a small nick and then a larger incision to open into the peritoneal cavity. There was no odor, but there was a watery, brownish liquid of stomach contents that had flowed out through a five millimeter hole in the duodenum, the first part of the intestine after the stomach.

The surgeon took a cotton-tipped swab and collected a sample of the fluid for culture and sensitivity to be sure he would be using the correct antibiotics, and then put an abdominal retractor in place to make the exposure easier. He irrigated the abdominal cavity with a large volume of saline and then with an antibiotic solution. Then he placed his hand in the abdomen and did a careful exploration of all the intra-abdominal contents. He took several medium-sized cloth towels and isolated the area of the perforation, then, using silk thread, closed the opening. After it was sealed, he brought a small part of the abdominal fatty apron, the omentum, over the area he had just closed and sutured it in place as a secondary protection.

He thought for a moment while he was placing the last few sutures. *There are so many things I could do here that no one could identify after the fact. I could cause bleeding or infection or even injure the pancreas with my fingers. He would develop severe pancreatitis and might not survive after weeks of misery. I could place a very loose suture around one of the major vessels that would surely come loose in a day or so and cause catastrophic bleeding. We might not get him back to surgery in time. I could injure the large intestine and blame it on the perforated ulcer, and he could develop another leak, this time from his large bowel or colon. He'd go into septic shock pretty quickly from that.*

"Doctor. Doctor." He heard a voice calling in the distance, and realized he was just standing there, staring into the abdomen. The nurse was looking at him expectantly.

"Yes. Yes. Just thinking whether there's anything else we need to do." He looked around the abdomen and reached his hand inside again. Everything was in order. This would be his last opportunity. He felt himself getting warm, and his heart beat faster. Decisions. Decisions. He felt for the spleen. Just a small flick with a finger could rupture the capsule, and there would be a delayed hemorrhage. He withdrew his hand from the abdomen and took a deep breath. He thought, *It would be too obvious. I must restrain myself.* He looked over the drapery screen separating him from the anesthesiologist. "I'm done here. I'll be closing."

"Thank you. He's doing fine," said the anesthesiologist. He started turning some dials to change the level of anesthesia and start the process of undoing the effects of the anesthetic agents that had put the man to sleep and paralyzed him.

The surgeon closed the abdomen with the large, looped #1 PDS suture and irrigated the subcutaneous tissue with the antibiotic solution. He stapled the skin edges together and backed away from the table. "Just put a small dressing on him. Thank you, all."

He nodded to the anesthesiologist, picked up the chart and exited the operating room. After taking off his mask, he went to the waiting area and spoke to the wife.

"He did just fine, Mrs. Dufour. Everything went well, and he'll be in recovery for an hour. Then he'll go to the surgical floor, and you'll be able to see him there."

"How long in the hospital?" she asked

"If all goes well, probably about five days to a week."

She grasped his hands in both of hers and looked down at them. "Thank you so much." She had tears in her eyes.

The surgeon finally disentangled himself and walked back to the recovery room to write his orders and dictate the procedure. *Son of a bitch*, he muttered to himself.

–41–

"**Y**ou must be out of your mind. You can't deal with terrorists or maniac serial killers." The attorney from the Bar Association threw the letter back at the mayor, and Mac just stood to the side.

"We thought you should see the letter so you can understand what we're up against. We have three choices. We can give no reply, give some response that you think might be appropriate, or you can leave it entirely in the hands of McClymonds here," said the mayor. "But if you decide to back off and leave it to us, I don't want to hear any negative comments from your group about the job we're doing. We've got a number of leads that we're working on, and hopefully we can find this guy before he strikes again."

Mac interrupted. "We may want to do some delaying tactics in the meantime. We have nothing to lose and may gain some time and prevent another death. He's gone from silent and careful to open and more reckless. That gives us more to work on."

The two attorneys spoke to one another, then looked at the two policemen and the mayor. "We're ready to help in any way possible. If you think you can stall him a while, then catch him, then let's do it."

"Agreed," said Mac. "From what we have and his easy access to New York, I figure he must live within about one to two hundred miles from Manhattan. He's called us and written the note from here and was within easy access of Boston. Any farther, and it would be too difficult to make the trips. He doesn't travel by plane, or we'd have tagged him by now. He either drives or takes the train or a bus."

"What about the Chicago death?" asked one attorney. "Unusual. It was the only one outside that radius, and we think
he may have taken a train or driven. It would be a long drive and a difficult getaway if there were a major problem."

"There was a major problem with that one, remember?" said an attorney.

"And that's why I think he went by train." Mac went over to a map of the United States on the wall. He swung his arm in an arc around Manhattan. "That radius of about one hundred to two hundred miles keeps him in the area bounded by Boston, New York, Syracuse, Harrisburg, Washington and Baltimore."

The attorney stood up and looked at the map. "There's also Philadelphia, Trenton, Newark, New Haven and dozens more cities. How the hell are you going to pin down any one area?"

Mac looked at him. "Police work is mostly just tedious plugging away at clues, narrowing down possibilities in a slow methodical process. A case like this has a million possibilities, but we've been narrowing them down every day. We got some good suggestions from the consultant surgeon from California, and we have more information now than a week ago. If you're impatient, nothing will get accomplished. This is not like some TV drama where all the round pegs are quickly placed into round holes. We're gonna have a lot of square pegs attempting to fit into round holes before this case is solved.

"We need cooperation rather than dissension, and that's why I want you all to work as a team. We have twelve operatives working on this case, and that's not including the secretarial force calling every malpractice attorney in the country and putting out warnings and information throughout the nation in every police department and every law office. It's a slow, tedious process, but it's the best we can do right now."

"So how should we answer the guy's letter?" one of the attorneys asked in a more sympathetic tone. "We're with you all the way."

Mac pulled a sheet of paper from his briefcase and read aloud to the assemblage.

> *To whom it may concern.*
>
> *We have received your letter and are giving it serious consideration. It is not easy to concede to your requests, yet, in view of the alternative, we have decided to attempt any solution which might be possible and agreeable to both sides. While we understand your situation, we also must take into consideration the families of the individuals involved. If the events stop as of now, we think that some agreement may be reached. Please allow us a few weeks to reach a decision and show your good faith by not continuing your activities. Sincerely,*
>
> *Septimus McClymonds*

The group each took a copy from Mac and read it over carefully. The mayor underlined a few items, then said, "This guy is very clever, and he'll know we're just trying to buy time."

"Probably," said Mac. "But at least we can hope he'll put his activity on hold for a while. And we'll have the opportunity to follow up on some of the suggestions given to us by Dr. Fishberg, the surgeon from California."

After a while, everyone left except Mac, his boss, the Chief of Police, and the mayor.

"We're walking on thin ice, Mac. I hope it doesn't come back to haunt us," said the mayor.

"I don't see how it could. Let me outline what we've started. We have four people on computers with the malpractice companies and newspapers going back twenty-five years for all major cases lost by physicians with resultant loss of malpractice insurance. In addition, we're checking all cases where the physician killed himself as a result of a case and seeing whether there is any other physician, preferably a general surgeon, related to the individual. We started this morning, and it will probably take several days to accumulate the information. Then we have to sift through the data and see if we can come up with a name. If we do, then at least we'll have someone to observe. As of now, we don't have any evidence on which to even give anyone a parking ticket."

"All right. Go ahead with the newspaper article in the *Times*. Keep it inconspicuous—back pages—and keep me informed of your progress."

"We will, your honor," said the chief.

—42—

He brought out the diary and began writing.

We're going to the Metropolitan Museum in New York today. Marilyn loves to see the Impressionists and the Greco-Roman sculptures, and now she can see them through my eyes. I do like to get there at least once a month. The sculptures appeal to our sense of anatomy and design. The figures are much like the torsos of Vesalius in his book of anatomy, and I am sure that many surgeons have been inspired by the magnificence of the human body looking at those sculptures.

I know which ones Marilyn likes and can see her admiring them in the grand hallways. I can feel her sense of awe and delight through my own visual and emotional senses. The Impressionists painted a fabric of sensuality over the structural integrity of the human body and gave us the sense of passion that we had together...that we still have together. The voluptuousness, the sexuality, the salaciousness of the Renoir bodies and the Degas dancers bring back memories to us, and we revel in them as we walk as one through the galleries.

You think me crazy? If this is crazy, then I accept the appellation. But, then, Aristotle was crazy and so were Copernicus, Darwin, Picasso and Salvador Dali.

Craziness is an aberration from the norm of society, and yet I am a sane, rational, functional man who performs his daily chores and contributes to society.

You think, because I am eliminating malpractice attorneys from that society, that I am crazy? You have the right to think what you want, but great minds often think differently from others and are often grossly misunderstood.

The surgeon put away his diary, locking it in his desk. He had kept it for twenty-one years, adding only a few pages each month. It gave him solace to read his words from so many years ago, and he was proud of his philosophy and his actions. He was doing what was best for society by doing what was best for himself.

It was his own adaptation of Ayn Rand's ethical egoism, the philosophy formed by a teenage girl and held throughout her life. He had grown up with it as a college student but, as he matured, he had grown away from most of the dogma. It contrasted sharply with his code of medical ethics, which emphasized altruism and service above personal gain, but it pushed him towards accomplishment of his goals with an emphasis on the ends justifying the means. The problem was that, for him, ethical egoism allowed him to define his own understanding of what was ethical and what was unethical. It was the joy of a democracy; the freedom to choose one's own philosophy of life without regard as to how it would affect others. It allowed him to be selfish for his own principles, being justified by a spurious, childlike philosophy.

The surgeon was not introspective. He rarely, if ever, looked inward and that, along with his intellectual pursuits, made it possible for him to decide upon his actions with little doubt or compunction. He rationalized that what he did was right and good, and never considered that his motivation might be flawed. He was, at times, a complete atheist and at other times held a firm belief in a power greater than himself—partially in the voice of

Marilyn and partially in something he could neither explain nor understand. It was the great unknown. There was never any question in his mind that he was intelligent, yet this eclipsed his ability to have moral values other than those he constructed in his own mind. He never felt guilty and never looked into himself to find the real driving force behind his all-consuming hatred for those attorneys.

The childish purity of an eleven-year-old was never replaced in the deep, dark recesses of his mind. He had maintained this eternal battle between good and evil right up to the present. While most adults, in maturing, realize the world is not black or white, but mostly gray, he saw only the extremes, and this made it easy for him to formulate his decisions about eliminating the malpractice attorney from the face of the earth.

Like Ayn Rand and her novels, he saw himself as a hero, and like the philosopher, he was disillusioned with life in that he could not be his type of hero. That is what started his thoughts about the legal profession. In conjunction with the passion he had felt towards Marilyn, he adopted a philosophy which allowed him to accomplish a cleansing of society. He could be the independent, vindicating, daring, and courageous man who would right the wrongs of this society, the wrongs that had led to the loss of his one and only love, Marilyn. But he could not hold with the objectivist philosophy that selfishness was a virtue and altruism a vice, a vice that didn't really exist. The surgeon, as he grew older, became a man with confusing philosophies of life interwoven into his practice of medicine. His only recourse became a hatred of one of the evils in his self-designed society, and that was the malpractice attorney.

—43—

The list had over one hundred names on it, but that was a marked improvement from the twelve hundred with which they started. The list had been developed by twenty-six temporary operatives who slowly ruled out all but one hundred with a cursory review.

From these one hundred, Mac and two associates, Don Rogers and Chuck Sharpman, had gone over each doctor until they came up with twelve who had possible motives and backgrounds. When he checked into these, he found that one was now a paraplegic, another was in a much weakened state from six months of chemotherapy and radiation for advanced lung cancer. A third was eighty-seven and couldn't manage the physical aspects of the murders. That left them with nine and, before going out to interview them and possibly letting the guilty one know how close they were, they decided to get as much information as possible to rule on these nine candidates.

Mac placed the list on the table. They had a separate sheet for each individual. Two of them, Dr. Mark Monson and Dr. Peter LaGrande, were general surgeons in their fifties who had lost their ability to practice medicine because of high frequency and severity of malpractice cases. Neither one had done surgery for at least ten years and were now in other lines of business. Monson was a teacher in a medical school, and LaGrande had become an attorney and was doing quite well. Monson was five feet six inches tall and weighed 138 pounds. La Grande had gained weight over the last ten years and was a voluminous 325 pounds, barely able to get from his car to his office without huffing and puffing. Neither of these seemed a likely candidate. He put their files in the *improbable* folder.

He looked at the other two detectives. "We're getting down to a number which is more reasonable. Each of you take two names, and I'll take three. Let's see what we can find. But I want to emphasize that we don't eliminate any names from the list unless all three of us agree."

The assistants nodded. They liked Mac because he was always open to suggestions and worked as a team when using his associates.

"You each have the days when the crimes were committed, and we can get most of what we need from computers without involving the individuals. If they seem highly unlikely as suspects, then come back, and we'll discuss it. Then you can go out, eyeball the guy and talk with him. Anyone who looks very suspicious should not be approached. We need proof before we can touch this guy and, if we confront him now, he might just disappear for a few months or even years. If you need help, talk with my secretary, and she'll arrange for someone to give you a hand. Agreed?"

They both nodded their heads. Although he was democratic in his attitude, his comments were generally accepted as orders, and his questions were statements for which he just wanted a nod of agreement. He had been around a long time and knew the ropes very well.

When they met in twenty-four hours, Rogers had already eliminated his two. One was in the military reserves, a full colonel in charge of a medical group. He had been on duty during two of the murders and could definitely be ruled out, in spite of the fact that he had a physician brother who had killed himself after losing his ability to practice medicine after a nasty malpractice case seven year before.

The other physician couldn't practice surgery after losing his malpractice insurance three years before. He had three lawsuits involving laparoscopic surgery: two the patients who died from injuries during the procedure, and a third who required two other surgeries to correct problems. The malpractice judgments had been well over three million dollars, and he could no longer find a company to insure him. He was sixty-six and had retired with his wife to a small apartment. He was not very athletic and had some back problems for which he claimed disability and was able to collect money on a monthly basis along with social security. They had accumulated some savings over the years and lived very comfortably, traveling every three months. Rogers had discussed the case with Mac, then went to visit the doctor on the pretense of finding out whether he might like to do some work for the police department.

"He couldn't strangle a small dog, much less a grown woman," said Rogers. "He's very small in stature with a balding head and small hands. His eyes are brown, and he seemed very amiable and talked to me about his lifestyle. He said he was retired and openly admitted his plight with his malpractice insurance. Said it was all his fault, and he'd learned to live with it. And, no, he wasn't interested in getting back into medicine. He had several grandchildren and likes to travel."

"You don't think he could be faking it?" asked Mac.

"Not a chance. Even though eye and hair color could be changed and a wig worn, this guy's hands were small, and his general demeanor was wrong. He was in the area for all but one of the murders, but for that one he was on a Princess Cruise through the Panama Canal. I've confirmed that he was actually on the ship all the time."

"Sounds good," said Mac.

Sharpman had returned with one definite negative, which he presented to the group.

"Dr. Charles Baker is a fifty-three-year-old surgeon in Washington, D.C., and lives alone with three dogs and a cat. He's into bodybuilding and fits the type for our guy. He has blue eyes and black hair with a bit of gray. He lost his malpractice insurance after operating for appendicitis and damaging a kidney during the procedure. He was shown to have been drunk when he was in surgery and not only lost his insurance, but also lost his license to practice for five years. Apparently, he sobered up and has been clean and sober in AA for seven years. Never did get his malpractice insurance back, but he works for the VA hospital system and seems happy with his work there. He was out of the country at the times of two of the murders, once in the Bahamas and the other time at a body-building convention in Tokyo."

"Did you confirm all this?"

"Absolutely. From a physical point of view, the guy looked good but, after speaking with him and confirming his absences, there's no way he could be involved."

Mac had gone over his three carefully. "I've got a guy named Dr. Melvin Garnsey, a six-foot-tall, sixty-year-old general and peripheral vascular surgeon who had a son who was a surgeon. His son had been in practice with him for two years when he operated on an elderly man with severe vascular problems in the left leg. The nurse had prepared the wrong leg prior to his entering the operating room, and he did an extensive reconstruction before realizing his mistake. He then went on to do the opposite leg and completed the surgery. The patient did surprisingly well and was walking in two weeks. However, the malpractice attorneys went after him and the hospital, and he lost a huge settlement, as well as his insurance. The young doctor was thrown off the staff of the hospital and eventually went into medical research. The father has been very vocal against malpractice attorneys since then, although he himself has never had a major case. Both the older surgeon and his son were out of the country with their families during the time of the Bevis murders, and they each had solid alibis for the times of at least two of the other cases. So I've ruled them out."

"We're left with three suspicious persons, and we need to go over each one carefully," said Mac.

Sharpman sat down with his second folder. He showed them the picture of a tall, heavyset, graying, brown-haired man. "This is Dr. Daniel Rudnick. He's fifty-eight, divorced and practices in Manhattan. He hasn't been on a vacation for six years and is a compulsive over-worker. He's been sued seven times and lost four big cases—the last one two years ago—and now can only get insurance with a very high-priced company. It costs him over $7500 a month in malpractice insurance just to stay in business. But he is very busy and manages to pay all his bills and still live pretty high on the hog. He has a seven-room apartment in mid-Manhattan and a second home on Long Island. He's got dyed brown hair and blue eyes, and works out daily in the gymnasium in his apartment complex. He runs a special practice doing only hernias and apparently is well-known for this throughout the country. I can't find anything to put him away from the scene of a crime without going into hospital records and operating room records. I didn't want to do any tracing until we spoke."

Mac looked over the information. The sheets of paper included education and training. He had no police record, not even a parking ticket. "All right. He's one we can put under surveillance, but I don't want anyone approaching him or talking with friends or hospitals yet. I've got two here I want to discuss with you, and one sounds very promising. The other is probably a rule-out. Let me tell you about the latter one first."

He opened a file and passed around a picture of Dr. Luigi Marcolendo. "This guy looks like he came off the set of *The Godfather*. Do you remember that guy, Luca Brazzi?"

"He's the big dumb hit-man that gets garroted in the bar."

"Right. Well, this guy looks like him. He's six foot three and has brown eyes and brown hair, huge hands and is strong as an ox. Used to be a wrestling champion at Purdue. He does general surgery and apparently has been sued twice, both with large outlays of cash from his malpractice company. The facts of the cases indicate that they were not major problems, but the guy comes across so arrogant and obnoxious that the juries went to town with him. The malpractice company wasn't very happy, either, and added a ten per cent surcharge and a big deductible to his policy. He hates malpractice attorneys and has been cited for his language against them in public. He has a small Italian practice in Brooklyn that keeps him afloat. In general, he's very temperamental and doesn't get along with anyone except his own family and friends. So he looked like a possible, but he goes to a gym almost every evening, and they have a sign in log there."

"Couldn't he have faked it or something?" asked Rogers.

"That's what I thought, so I followed up. On two of the murder occasions—once in Boston and the other, the woman attorney—he was giving wrestling lessons to teenage kids at the center. No doubt about it."

"Hey, Mac. Do you think there could be more than one guy doing this?"

"No. We haven't released the information about the notes or the surgical incisions. A copycat wouldn't know that. Has to be one guy."

"So we're left with two possible suspects. Let's hear about your possible," said Sharpman.

"Okay," said Mac. He opened the last file folder and took out the portrait of a distinguished man. "This is Dr. Oliver Johns, a sixty-two-year-old, British-born general and vascular surgeon. He lives alone in Washington, D.C., never married and openly gay. His partner died four years ago of AIDS-related problems, and Johns is very vocal about malpractice attorneys, since his partner was sued for supposedly causing a patient to become HIV positive six years ago. He had kept his HIV status a secret and that only came out during a trial when it was shown that the surgeon had cut his finger during a case and blood had gotten into the abdominal wound. The man lost his malpractice insurance after losing the case with a judgment for six million dollars. Shortly after that, the hospital revoked his privileges. His condition deteriorated rapidly, and he died about six months later. Dr. Johns has been tested and is HIV negative. He has a practice of surgery predominately limited to the gay community. There is no apparent time when he was away, and he seems like a good candidate."

"You think that's all of them?" asked Rogers.

Mac held up both his hands in frustration. "God, I hope so. We went back ten years and pulled up these twelve hundred and whittled them down to these two. We don't have enough computer data to go back any further without a completely manual search. That could take months or years."

"Do you really think one of these guys is the perp, Mac?"

Mac looked at the two folders left in front of him. "Could be. But I agree with you. It just doesn't sound like our guy, and that's very depressing. Anyway, let's keep a watch on both these characters. I don't want them out of our sight for even a minute except when they're at home, and I want a report of all activities. Get a judge to sign a permit for a phone tap on the two homes and offices, and we'll make sure it stays confidential."

"I already looked into it for my guy," said Sharpman. "Judge Daviling said there's not enough for him to give me permission to do a phone tap. Says the guy's an upstanding member of the community and has a lot of personal calls. He says to call him back if there's more evidence, but says what we have is not enough."

"Shit." said Mac. "I suppose he's right. It's probably the same with my guy—all supposition and no hard facts." He looked at the other two. "Let's see what we can do with the hospital records. Maybe they were in surgery at the times of the killings. But let's keep them both under surveillance."

—44—

January is the cruelest month of all. I always disagreed with T.S. Eliot, who felt it was April. The days are short, and the sky is often overcast in the Northeast, with snowfall and freezing cold. I am a man of variable temperament, and the weather affects me strongly.

I read the reply in the Times *today. About what I could expect, I guess. It was a foolish thought at best, and perhaps a dangerous one, to expose myself in any way to the authorities. If I look upon this activity seriously, then I can carry it out successfully; if I expect too much, too soon I will be disappointed.*

I am a surgeon. If I were a patient man, I probably would have gone into internal medicine where I could hand out pills and watch people slowly get better. Surgeons like to see things accomplished immediately; we get results now. And so it is with this whole malpractice attorney bit. I want to see them exterminated immediately. I've made great strides, especially in the Northeast where the number of malpractice lawsuits has fallen off sharply. But look at Texas or California or Florida. Oh, there was an initial decrease, but now they're coming back.

It's cold and overcast today. Very depressing, and I need something to cheer me up. I have only found a sense of fulfillment when I complete a good surgery, and when I

217

complete my extracurricular activities. My surgery schedule has been slow. It always is right after the New Year. No one wants an operation at this time, and also patients have to start a new year with their health insurance deductible.

I have several days free, and I found another candidate. This one is in Houston, Texas. I wondered whether it would be safe to fly there, but they always ask for picture ID's and that would be too easily checked. I did have a fake driver's license under another name with my disguised face, but it would still mean exposing myself to examination and possible recognition. I always have held that for emergencies.

I checked the train schedules, and AMTRAK has no direct trains from Philadelphia or New York to Houston. It takes two days, and you have to go either through Jacksonville or Chicago. I think I'll go through Jacksonville and pay cash at the last moment. Marilyn goes free, yet she is with me at all times. She encourages me when I am down and depressed. I used to take anti-depressant pills, but they never worked well. I don't take anything now. Better to be off all medications unless absolutely needed.

Just the planning and the anticipation are raising my mood.

He went to his back closet and picked out two outfits. He had a comfortable one for traveling with no added weight. He'd add a little facial makeup and perhaps a beard, but overall a light and easy disguise. The other one would be more cumbersome with the increased fatty look and greater change to his appearance. He was a bit apprehensive traveling so far from home for an activity, but it was time to go to farther and more fertile fields.

He looked up the weather forecast in Houston: fifty-two degrees and cloudy. *Too bad,* he thought. He had hoped it would be nicer, but the victim had already been selected, and he wasn't about to make any changes He'd already made preparations and would buy his ticket at the station. He wouldn't get a through ticket. He'd just purchase one to Jacksonville and buy a ticket to Houston from there. *Can't be too cautious. This one should shake up the legal community.*

He was getting tired. He noticed it in his work and found that getting up in the early morning for his usual hospital activities was becoming increasingly more difficult. He was losing some more weight and just didn't have the same appetite. *Probably depression.* Things weren't going badly, but he had this pervading sense of loneliness and failure. He didn't know why, exactly, but it would come and go. Sometimes, it was a kind of powerlessness over circumstances beyond his control. Sometimes, it focused on Marilyn and the attorneys, or sometimes on nothing in particular. He'd gone to a psychologist several years before and was told he had bouts of clinical depression. It was recommended that he take medications. He tried for a while, and it seemed to help, but when he started hearing from Marilyn on a more regular basis, he decided it was best not to take the drugs. She would take away his depression. That actually did help for a while, but when the weather was overcast and dreary, his spirits lowered with the barometer needle, and he recognized the change. He often thought of going back on the medication, but always seemed to have another reason to avoid it.

Yes, he was getting tired. Perhaps he would do one more attorney and then quit for a while. That might be best and safest, if he could manage it. Sometimes, it was as if a second person were helping him when he committed the murders. *The Benjamin Franklin or Isaac Newton side of me,* he thought. *Great men are spurred on to do great and dangerous things for the betterment of society. I am one of those.* He knew it, and Marilyn knew it.

It was Tuesday, and he had scheduled himself to be off for five days. He would be back in time for noon surgery on the following Monday. Two easy hernia surgeries. Dr. Sandy Blankership, a young surgeon building his new practice, was always happy to take his calls when he was away, or on weekends when he just wanted to be alone, quiet and undisturbed.

"Sandy. It's Alex. I'm going up to Boston for a few days, and I'll be signing out to you. No sick patients in the hospital. Should be fairly quiet."

"No problem. Thanks for the support."

Dr. Blankenship was happy to have any business that came along and proud to be associated with one of the most prominent surgeons in the community. If he had been starting out without that support, it would have taken him years to develop a practice. The surgeon's endorsement had helped him immensely, and he was very grateful and indebted to him. He never turned him down and, on one occasion, actually canceled his own vacation to cover for him.

Apart from his fine house, the surgeon kept a small one-room apartment in the city, for which he paid in advance every six months. No one ever bothered him, and no one there knew who he was. He came and went at odd hours and only used the room for changing and storing equipment. He had two months left on the lease and was thinking of letting it lapse. Time to rest for a while.

He gathered his things, went to the apartment at 3 P.M. and picked up his supplies. He walked the twelve blocks to the train station at six in the afternoon and bought a one-way ticket to Jacksonville. The train was on time at 8:37 P.M., he was told, and wouldn't be very busy. There would be no problem getting a seat unless he wanted to reserve a sleeper.

"No. Thanks. I'll just take a regular ticket."

The station was half-full with travelers. He walked away from the ticket counter and sat on a bench with his carry-on bag next to him under a large sign that said TO THE TRAINS. An hour and a half later his train was announced, and he walked casually onto the pavement between the two waiting trains until he saw metal steps and an open door. He pulled himself up with ease and walked into the passenger car.

Down the compartment, seven rows in front of him, was another passenger who had decided to take a leisure trip by train to Washington, D.C., to check out a physician named Dr. Oliver

Johns. The other passenger was a Lieutenant Septimus
McClymonds.

—45—

Mac was a man always aware of everything around him. He didn't take the train very often, but he was in no particular hurry and wanted some time to think. The train afforded him that kind of uninterrupted time, and he found it enjoyable. New York, Philadelphia, Baltimore, and then Washington. It was a pleasant and relaxing trip, and the lieutenant had ensconced himself in a location with a table between the seats. His papers were spread out in front of him, and he had a soft drink and a ham sandwich. He saw the gentleman who boarded the train in Philadelphia and looked at him as he took a seat. They nodded politely to one another, and then the new passenger sat down facing away from him.

A horn sounded. The doors closed with a clanking sound. The train picked up speed, and they were soon outside the city limits racing south with a clickety-clack heard faintly coming through the floor of the compartment. Mac had several files in front of him and was reviewing the composites assembled from the meager information supplied to them. The only surviving witness, William Forseman, had finally been able to sit down with a police artist and agree on a vague likeness of the man who had shot him. The most salient features were the blue eyes, the mustache and the large hands. As for the face itself, the image was far from photographic, and the descriptions could apply to a large number of people seen on the streets of New York every day. He had the troublesome feeling that the case was going to linger on for months.

He looked up again at the man sitting down the way from him. *It could just as well be the guy sitting in the same train compartment.* The man had raised his arms while reading a newspaper, and Mac noted the huge hands. He'd also noticed the piercing blue eyes. Mac bent over his work. He was getting distracted and, for all he knew, there were ten thousand men with similar descriptions within a five-mile radius.

Dr. Johns in Washington didn't seem like a likely candidate from his further investigations. Mac had spoken with the D.C. police, and they were cooperating, letting him take over the investigation in their city along with one of their own men. They had done a careful background check on Johns and made preliminary inquiries at the only hospital where he worked. He had been on a surgery schedule on three of the days in question, and they were pulling records to be sure of the times. A fourth case was just a few hours before the Boston murder, and it seemed that, unless Dr. Johns was a magician or exceedingly clever, he too would have to be taken off the list.

Mac had a cousin, Emily, who lived in Washington and decided to make it a long weekend. This was very unusual for him, but he felt he needed the R & R to give him some fresh insights on the case. He had only spoken to his cousin twice or three times a year for the last few years, although, when he was younger, he had considered her one of his only confidantes in the family. She was a literary editor at the Smithsonian, and it was always interesting to spend time with her. He had an appointment with Dr. Johns the next morning and, from his telephone conversations, he was extremely doubtful that this was his man. He would then stop by the hospital and confirm that he had been in surgery at the important times. He had the sneaking suspicion he had either missed his man in filtering through the twelve hundred originals, or else he was somehow looking in the wrong places.

Several seats apart from him, the surgeon sat huddled over *The New York Times*. He hadn't noticed McClymonds when he first entered the car, and only became aware of him when their eyes met as he was about to sit down. He felt comfortable that, in his present disguise, no one from Philadelphia would possibly recognize him, but one could never be too sure. And that man looked very familiar. He had been on the train, probably from New York, so he wasn't someone he might have known in Philly, or even an old patient. He remembered patients' faces, but almost never their names or their surgeries. Of course, the patients who stopped him on the street or in restaurants always assumed he knew their names and their anatomies. It was often embarrassing to have such a poor memory for names and surgeries.

But that face. He knew that face. He sat down and pulled out *The New York Times* and tried to concentrate on reading. On page two there was another note about the serial murders with reference to the Harvard professor being officially linked to the killings by Lieutenant McClymonds—and then it struck him like a sledge hammer. Of all the quirks of fate, he was riding in the same compartment as the lieutenant who was looking for him. He felt himself getting very warm and noticed a faint tremor in his hands. He tried to glance at McClymonds, but couldn't do it from his sitting position unless he made a marked effort and that, he thought, would be too obvious.

He hasn't approached. He hasn't walked back to look at me again. He probably hasn't the slightest idea what I look like except for that goddamned attorney in Chicago. But that guy barely had time to see me, and I was wearing a slightly different outfit. No. Wait. Damn. I was wearing the same thing I'm wearing now. Stupid. Stupid. I figured I'd never run into anyone outside of Chicago or New York who would know what I looked like.

Then he sat back. *They probably don't have much of a drawing, otherwise it would have been circulated or that policeman would have reacted differently. I'm still completely in the clear. If I can just stay calm and act normally. Damn. I hope he's getting off in Baltimore or Washington.* He shifted slightly in his seat so that he was more comfortable. *What the hell is a cop doing on a train? Probably the one goddamned time he's taken a train in his life, and it has to be this one. Why isn't he on a plane?*

The train stopped briefly at Wilmington, and then started towards Baltimore. Twelve people got in the car at that station, and the surgeon was thinking of moving to another car or getting off the train completely. After some consideration, he decided to stay put. Obviously, the policemen hadn't recognized him, or he would be in handcuffs by now. For the first time since he had started his activities, he felt like a criminal, and he was somewhat taken aback by the thought. It bothered him that he would be considered a common murderer or criminal when he thought of himself as a hero. He saw himself as a freedom fighter liberating Paris from the Third Reich or a soldier of justice; but for him to sit cowering in a seat on a train with a policeman just down the aisle seemed wrong.

No. I'll be okay. It's a natural feeling, and I'm sure those same thoughts went through the minds of many American patriots. He thought of the pilot, *what was his name, oh yes, I think it was Captain Paul Tibbett in that B-29, Enola Gay, that dropped the first Atom Bomb on Hiroshima and killed thousands of people in a few seconds. Was he a common killer or a hero? Someone always has to suffer when we are seeking justice for the many. The malpractice attorneys are destroying our country by destroying the lives of uncounted physicians.* He felt better. It was clear, and it was rational. He was not a common criminal, but simply a dutiful hero doing his part to make the United States a better place to live.

The conductor came through and punched his ticket. He sat back and closed his eyes until a food cart rolled down the aisle. He bought a cold drink and a ham and cheese sandwich.

McClymonds got up only once to go to the bathroom, but it was at the other end of the car. The surgeon didn't get up at all.

Mac held out his ticket to the conductor and had it punched. He held his police badge in his hand so only the conductor could see it and motioned for the man to lean down. The surgeon was facing the opposite direction as Mac described him to the train-man. "Just curious, and there is no definite problem, but where is that man going?" The conductor stood up trying to look as inconspicuous as possible and, recognizing the individual about whom Mac was talking, leaned back down to him. "He's got a ticket to Jacksonville, sir."

"Thanks," said Mac. "Don't say anything."

"Of course not, sir."

The surgeon was unaware of the goings-on.

The surgeon could not completely relax knowing that McClymonds was so close to him. When the train pulled into Washington station, he changed his position slightly so that, turning to his left, he could catch a glimpse of the man. McClymonds had put his papers into a briefcase, gotten up and was making his way to the exit. As he passed the surgeon, he again took a brief look, and their eyes met. Mac paused for ever so slight a fraction of a second, and then moved on.

He thought, *If there's a murder in Jacksonville, I'll know where the guy came from.* He smiled to himself and made his way to the exit door, down the steps and into the chilly Washington air.

Mac shook his head as he glanced back at the train. *Pretty soon I'm gonna be stalking everyone with blue eyes and large hands.*

—46—

Anectine is a depolarizing neuromuscular blocker, the surgeon read from his notes. *Five cc's injected intramuscularly should result in complete paralysis in about one minute. The individual will be alert, but paralyzed, and death should occur within about three to five minutes.*

He was satisfied with his accomplishments to date. Aside from the one extra attorney in Chicago, everything had gone well. His only regret was that the attorneys did not have a prolonged period of suffering before they passed on. The week before, he had been sitting in the doctor's lounge when several of the anesthesiologists and surgeons were talking about cases. Someone had brought up paralyzing agents, which are needed for complete relaxation of a sleeping patient during intubation and during surgeries where all the muscles must be completely paralyzed or relaxed to complete the procedure. He listened as they joked and described how the drug, given intravenously or intra-muscularly, would be great for the perfect crime, since the drug is metabolized out of the blood stream and disappears rapidly. The patient would be awake, but unable to move or breathe, and would die within a few minutes from lack of oxygen. The physicians had been laughing as they postulated perfect crimes.

The surgeon had listened intently and actually liked this method because, if he were going by plane under a false name, he would have difficulty sending a bag through with a pistol. There would always be the problem of possible metal detection and inspection. A vial of Anectine and a syringe and needle could easily be hidden and carried anywhere. It had been easy for him to steal the drug from the operating room, and he had needles and syringes in his own office. He smiled to himself. *I won't need to swab the area with alcohol before making the injection.*

He was angry and upset because the policeman had opened the door to reality a little bit, making him question the ethics of what he was doing. No. The policeman didn't have to say anything. His mere presence opened up an area of his mind to the actuality of his deeds, and it took a while for him to suppress it. He was happy when McClymonds got off in Washington, D.C., and he could have a peaceful journey for the rest of his trip. He liked being judge, jury and executioner. It seemed the natural progressive step from his surgery. Surgery was a parochial, professional adherence to rules and regulations. It was a conservative approach to life following strict guidelines and only allowing occasional deviation from the norm. Now he felt he was taking the giant steps beyond the rules of the society. He was making his own rules, because the society had failed to regulate itself and its attorneys. He was an extension of the arm of society correcting the errors. He felt that he was a present-day Darwinian and had redefined survival of the fittest to fit in with his philosophy of life. *I am a genius. It may not be the humble thing to say, but we are few and far between.* He defined genius as ability and capability, intellectual and master, the one who does not sit quietly while being led to the slaughter, but the active force that rises up against injustice and quashes it.

He had a blank subpoena with him in his traveling bag, and he was going to roll it up, tie it with a black ribbon and place it in the next victim's mouth. He had prepared the next note and printed it on the subpoena. It was very late. He closed his eyes and fell asleep to the cadence of the train on the rails. He didn't awaken until almost nine the following morning and had a small breakfast of coffee and croissants when the porter came through the compartment.

He arrived in Jacksonville at 12:08 P.M. and decided he didn't want to take another full day for traveling. He was getting anxious and decided to fly the rest of the distance. He knew he'd have to show some ID, but he had the fake driver's license with his new appearance, which he had obtained a year ago on the streets in New York City. You could find just about anything there: a driver's license, college diploma, even a passport. Cost was two hundred dollars, but he had it for emergency situations. Now he was tired and anxious, so he would use it. He took a cab from the train station to the airport and booked a flight from Jacksonville to Houston. He arrived late at night and checked into a small hotel. It had been a busy day for him emotionally, and he quickly fell asleep.

—47—

It had started four years before. A DNA strand had divided and two genes were incorrectly duplicated. A single cell developed, but it was not an identical clone of its parent cell. It looked different and acted differently. Mitochrondria were more plentiful, and a segment of the nucleus was bizarre, at least it would have appeared so if you were able to be present in that microscopic sphere. Several protector blood cells approached this new cell, but somehow it avoided their contact and sequestered itself beneath some fatty tissue, out of reach of the killer cells that would normally have eliminated it. It was very sick. It did not function normally and had difficulty metabolizing the raw materials it needed for healthy growth. It was much like a primordial cell millions of years ago. It had no consciousness and no awareness. It just functioned as a unique individual cell with an inherent ability for survival.

And so it grew very slowly, at times remaining essentially dormant for several months until, somehow, its nuclear material was stimulated, began to break up into a chromosomal arrangement again and prepared to cause the cell to divide and multiply. Initially, it took longer than the normal cell because it was so unusual in its structure, but after a difficult period it managed to replicate itself. The process was finally complete, and both cells were able to enter a resting phase for a short while. Then it happened again. The two cells multiplied to four, then into eight, sixteen, thirty-two and sixty-four. The process became easier. Several of the new cells died because they were so abnormal that they could not survive. Many of the remaining cells had progressive changes. Some joined with others to form incomplete ring-like structures, and others made attempts at forming glands.

The body sent in more of its defensive cells and even tried to produce a thick sheet of protective tissue around the new cells to wall them off from the rest of the tissue. It seemed to be successful for a few months, but then the aberrant cells became more active and broke through the capsule around them. The mass now forming was about one millimeter in size. As the weeks and months went by, this little accumulation of cells grew slowly. It had a need for nourishment, and chemicals inside it began producing a substance which caused tiny blood vessels to grow into the mass, supplying blood-borne oxygen, removing toxic agents and carbon dioxide from the mass. It was foreign to the body, yet the body did not react strongly to it, and this allowed it to grow larger, eventually reaching several millimeters in size. The body which hosted this mass felt no pain, no symptoms, and had no way of signaling the conscious brain that something was wrong, so the mass kept on growing, slowly and steadily.

Unlike other tissue in the body, this new growth, this neo-plasm, had no function. Skin or tissue surrounding and enclosing the body had a function to protect the body against intrusion of bacteria and to prevent fluid loss, among other things. Some tissue, like the bone marrow, produced blood cells; others, like the pancreas, produced insulin or enzymes. Some groups of tissue were muscular and helped move the organism, and still others in the liver took part in breaking down waste or producing substances, like bile, for digestion. And finally, a group of cells lined the intestine and produced mucous and absorbed fluids. These were called colonic cells.

The little mass of tissue belonged to the latter group, except it didn't function to help the body in any way. The little mass of cells tried to form a gland and almost accomplished this, producing a small amount of mucous. But its DNA was so abnormal that it couldn't coordinate its own development. One thing, however, set it apart from other cell groups in the body. It didn't have a regulator to tell it how much to grow or when to stop growing. It started to grow into an abnormal shape, and the body's regulatory systems couldn't control it. It had started in the part of the body called the ascending colon, a segment of the large intestine just beyond the cecum and the appendix. At first this little accumulation of wild cells grew in the inner lining tissue of this area called the mucosa.

That original parent cell had been part of a normal colon. But as months went by, with no way to prevent its growth and development, the entire body seemed just to forget and ignore this little group of cells. The mass grew from two millimeters to three, then five, then ten millimeters or one centimeter in diameter. It was growing more wildly now, and without conscious effect it had spread from the surface deeper into the wall of the colon called the submucosa and then into the muscularis. It started to grow so fast at the edges that the central portion didn't have enough new blood supply to keep it alive, and some of the cells finally died, creating an ulcer cavity. And, as cells died, they sometimes weakened the integrity of the entire mass; small cracks occurred in the mass which caused a little bit of bleeding, though initially not enough to be seen by human eyes without a special test for occult blood in the stool.

And what was this group of cells called? It was called *Cancer*. The body in which it was growing was unaware of its growth, and the little tumor grew and grew as the weeks and months went by. The body kept up its normal activities of eating, sleeping, working and excreting waste, without knowing that somewhere, deep inside, an accident had occurred, and something was growing that, if unarrested, would eventually destroy its host and itself.

—48—

Essau Kramer was sixty-one years old. He was on his fourth wife, a twenty-seven- year-old former Las Vegas showgirl, and his former wives and his six children never called him. He was the senior partner of Kramer and Dogwood, the largest personal injury and malpractice attorney corporation in the state. His personal net income each year was in excess of fifteen million dollars. He owned a large mansion and a one-hundred-and-twenty-foot yacht with a full-time staff of six that he kept in the Caribbean.

Essau Kramer was a powerful man and not one to cross, personally or professionally. He had handled many of the largest medical malpractice cases in history and had a smooth personality that seemed to endear him to judges and juries alike. The malpractice companies shuddered when he or his associates took on a case, because he invariably won excessive awards and left physicians groveling, defeated and humiliated. He had a coterie of physician experts in every area who would support and testify against anyone and any situation. He had personally destroyed the professional lives of other attorneys, as well as physicians, and was responsible for the closing of a hospital even though, after several appeals, the verdict was overthrown. The damage had been done and was too difficult to repair.

Essau Kramer had a finger in politics, business, and civic organizations, as well as the competitive legal world, and he was feared by many, liked by none, but respected and avoided by most. He paid his associates well, and his partners, mostly of the same ethical and personal ilk, stood by him to reap the financial rewards. A policeman who had inadvertently given him a speeding ticket in his Ferrari ended up losing not only his case but also his job at the hands of the vindictive Mr. Kramer.

Essau Kramer's name was mentioned with the most famous and infamous of trial attorneys, and he hobnobbed with the crest of society and sleaziest of the lower echelon in order to find out everything about everyone, especially for the good of his clients. Whereas many malpractice attorneys took clients on contingency, Kramer was so well-known that many of his clients paid high prices up front for his services. Frequently, Kramer wanted to take cases only on contingency, because he was assured of high payments, and he rarely lost any money on one of them.

When he received an envelope with $ 20,000 in one hundred dollar bills from a Douglas Monsarrat for a consultation and as a retainer on a very private matter, he took the situation as a serious offer for service. This was followed by a phone call setting up an appointment in a "private place" on a very personal matter with Mr. Monsarrat who would be arriving by private plane that day. The appointment was arranged for 7 P.M. in Mr. Kramer's office, and Mr. Monsarrat was assured it would be private except for Mr. Kramer's personal bodyguard, who was trustworthy and always accompanied him on private business for obvious reasons.

Mr. Monsarrat assured him that would be fine as long as the bodyguard could wait in an adjoining room once the serious discussions got underway. Kramer saw no problem with that arrangement since Franco, his three-hundred-pound "watchdog", would be a few steps away in the next room. The surgeon had expected something like this and had arranged for this slight inconvenience. It was easy to purchase a 22 caliber pistol in Texas, and he had done so just after arriving. An extra $1000 had made the deal easy and he felt prepared for his evening. He regretted having to add a non-attorney to his list, but it was unavoidable.

The office was in the Kramer Building, an eleven-story glass and steel construction completed six years before that stood as tribute to the mastery of litigation.

The surgeon approached at exactly 7 P.M., wearing his heavy outfit and a pair of white gloves. The temperature was falling rapidly, and he was glad, because his clothes were warm. He carried a traveling bag with him and kept the pistol in his right hand in the pocket of an overcoat. He felt confident, yet he knew there was more risk to the situation this evening.

When he entered the building, there was a doorman who nodded, so the surgeon kept his head low, just mentioning Mr. Kramer's name.

"Eleventh floor sir. He's expecting you."

The surgeon walked straight to the elevators without stopping to acknowledge the greeting, and the elevator door opened immediately. He entered and pushed the button for the top floor, feeling a bit queasy for the first time. Then he felt the slight waft of breath over his shoulder and felt more confident. "You're here, aren't you, Marilyn?"

The elevator door opened into a wide hallway with a shiny brass sign overhead—*KRAMER AND DOGWOOD*—and he was no sooner out of the elevator than a huge man in tie and jacket came forward to greet him with a smile.

"Mr. Monsarrat. Welcome. Mr. Kramer is in his office, and I'll let him know you've arrived."

The surgeon walked forward and made a gesture to remove his coat. The huge man took a step forward to help him and the surgeon turned ninety degrees, pulling the gun and silencer out of the pocket, extending his arm and firing point blank into the left ear of the huge man. The noise was minimal, and the bodyguard fell to the ground with a thud, never uttering a sound. The surgeon heaved a sigh of relief and removed his coat from the clutches of the man. There was no blood on it, and he placed it over his right arm, concealing the pistol. He moved quickly forward to the closed office door, where the name, *Mr. Essau Kramer, Attorney-at-Law*, was engraved into the glass. Just as the door opened, a large man moved towards him with a broad grin on his face. He must have heard the low sound of the pistol and come to see what had occurred. The surgeon was moving towards him with a broad smile. Then Kramer caught a glimpse of his bodyguard on the floor, and his face collapsed into an expression of combined confusion and fear.

"What's wrong with Franco?" he asked.

The surgeon held the gun directly at Kramer's head. "The same thing that will happen to you, if you don't cooperate completely."

He backed the man into his office and closed the door behind him. It was the largest office he had ever seen, with an original impressionist oil painting in one alcove and several bronze sculptures on pedestals. The huge desk was of fantastic, burled wood and, in spite of its size, was dwarfed by the size of the room.

Aware of the possibility of hidden alarm buttons, the surgeon motioned him to sit down in the center of the sprawling office. "No sound and no movement, and you'll do just fine."

The attorney had begun to sweat and at first adopted an attitude of strength. This was the first time in his life he had been spoken to in that manner. "How dare you come in here like this! What have you done to Franco?" He started to move forward, and the surgeon placed the gun directly between his eyes and stared him down.

"I have just silenced him temporarily. He will be fine, unless you get some smart idea. Now, just sit down." He pointed to the floor, and the attorney exhaled loudly and lowered himself, staring at the gun.

"What do you—?" He was cut off by the surgeon.

"We're here to discuss medical malpractice. Please be silent. You have been a very bad boy, Mr. Kramer. Turn over onto your belly and lie down."

"Are you going to kill me?"

"If I wanted to kill you, I could have done it already. If you cooperate, you'll be fine."

The man rolled onto his belly, but had a very concerned expression.

"Are you the doc who's been knocking off malpractice attorneys?"

"Of course not. That man sounds like he's crazy. I just have a few questions for you."

"You can take your money back." Kramer rose up a bit and pointed to the envelope on his desk.

The surgeon came over and put a foot on his back, pushing the man down onto the floor.

"Thank you. That's very kind. I may just do that." He reached into his bag and pulled out the syringe with 5cc's of anectine and, removing the cap from the needle plunged it through the trousers into the man's buttock, injecting the full amount.

Kramer flinched. The surgeon took his foot off the man's back, then said, "Now, turn over." Kramer did so, partially sitting, and was looking directly at the surgeon who had his watch in front of him as he looked down at the attorney.

"In exactly thirty seconds, you will not be able to move. You won't be able to talk or breathe or speak. You will be totally paralyzed, and I expect it will take about two or three minutes for you to become unconscious."

The attorney was starting to fall backwards onto the floor and was obviously having difficulty breathing. His eyes showed fear, and his last few movements were with his fingers and his eyes. He finally stopped blinking, and the surgeon stood over him.

"This is your last case, counselor, and you've lost it. You've punished enough people and enough doctors. Now you are receiving your just rewards."

The man was barely twitching, and his color was draining rapidly. His lips were turning blue. He was still alert as the surgeon took the rolled up subpoena with the ribbon around it out of his bag and shoved it forcibly into the man's mouth and down his paralyzed throat. As consciousness began to fade from the attorney, the surgeon held up a small white tag and read,

The defense rests.
The prosecution has swallowed his own words.

He leaned over and felt for a pulse. It remained for almost three minutes, began to fade, and then disappeared.

Initially, he felt elated. His entire body was shaking for a few minutes, and he had to sit down next to his victim. Then he felt weak. He put the gun and the syringe back into the bag and sat down. He didn't feel any better. *I better not do the surgery. I better get out of here before I feel worse.*

He stood up, bag in hand, and went to the elevator. It opened immediately. He pushed the button for the garage, and the door closed. He rode down the elevator twelve floors to the basement parking area, found his way to the exit door and left the building, unseen by the doorman. He walked several blocks and, finding a dumpster, discarded most of his clothing and the syringes, then hailed a taxi and went directly to the airport. He took the next flight out of Houston, which happened to be going to Atlanta, Georgia, and boarded the plane. He fell back in the seat and slept all the way to Atlanta.

—49—

The doorman at the Kramer building was on duty until midnight, at which time he would lock up and leave the premises. He made his usual rounds of the building at 6 P.M. to check the doors, and that would be sufficient until the morning crew came on duty. It was not unusual for conferences to take place lasting several hours, and he was instructed that it was all right to leave after his shift, even if some employees were left in their offices. He had not seen the client leave and, when the midnight hour passed, he assumed it was a long-term conference and just locked up and left. For this reason, the bodies were not discovered until ten to eight the next morning, when Mrs. Fritzoff, the office manager, came in to start the day. On exiting the elevator she was confronted by Franco's body, and she started screaming until one of the security officers came to see what was wrong. She was terribly frightened, and he escorted her down the elevator to the lobby, where he immediately called the police.

All employees were kept out of the building until the police arrived. The second body was not even discovered until thirty minutes later when the first squad car drove up and two officers, pistols drawn, entered the eleventh floor lobby. They found Marco sprawled on the floor with a small amount of congealed blood around his left ear. The officers immediately called for help and summoned the investigation squad. After this, they made rounds of the other rooms, soon finding the body of Essau

Kramer with the note attached to his right big toe and the subpoena shoved down his throat. They immediately sealed off the area until the investigation crew arrived. Within ten minutes, there were news reporters and video camera crews crowding the front of the building. The investigations crew immediately set about notifying the families of Franco and Kramer, but it wasn't until almost an hour later that chief investigator Parsons came to the front door and announced that a homicide had occurred. The question was immediately asked whether this was another in the series of malpractice attorney murders, and the chief politely declined to comment until further investigation was undertaken. The news channels, however, had a field day with the meager information they could glean from the sketchy reports. Investigator Parsons immediately called New York to speak with McClymonds, but took almost forty minutes to reach him on duty in Washington, D.C., where he was having an interview with Dr. Oliver Johns.

"It sounds like our man," said Mac, after Parsons had repeated the note and described the crime scene. "The only thing suspicious is the murder of the bodyguard and the lack of an operation. It might just be a copycat. The attorney wasn't shot?"

"No. The cause of death is unknown. Our medical examiner says there is a small puncture wound in the left buttock; he may have been injected with something. He says we'll have to wait for toxicology, although his purple color indicated he suffocated."

"Please, send me a full report when you get it done."

"We'll rush this one through. Should have everything in about a week."

"Thanks. By the way—you said the bodyguard was shot. What kind of gun? Can you tell?"

"Shot through the left ear, and it looks to me like a small caliber, maybe a .22."

'That's what we had before with our guy. Anything else?"

"Not yet. The place has been dusted, and it's clean as a whistle. No prints even in the elevator. The doorman had a brief look at the guy…says he was heavyset and hunched over…didn't get a good look at his face. He did say he was wearing white gloves. Never saw him leave, so either he left after the place closed up at twelve or he went through the garage on the ground floor."

"Okay," said Mac, giving him the fax and mailing numbers. "Keep in touch. Thanks."

"Absolutely. Good luck to you, McClymonds."

Mac had just about finished with Dr. Johns. The conversation with Houston, as well as his background checks, pretty much ruled out the Washington surgeon. Later that morning, he had a call from detective Sharpman, who had followed up on Dr. Daniel Rudnick.

"The guy's a complete asshole, but aside from that he has pretty solid alibis for the times in question. Real arrogant SOB, though; barely gave me the time of day."

"Well. I just got a call from Houston, and it appears our man may have killed two men there, a big shot malpractice attorney and his bodyguard. I'm not a hundred percent sure it's the same guy. He shot the bodyguard, but suffocated the attorney…gave him some type of injection. And there was no operation. But the note was there with the same type of wording, and no one but our guy would use the same language and paper."

"Houston?"

"Yeah. He's decided to go far afield."

"Shit," said Sharpman.

"My sentiments exactly," said Mac. "I'll be back in New York tomorrow, and we can start from ground zero again."

"Okay, Mac." The phone was hung up with a clunk.

Mac decided to cut his long weekend short and called his cousin. They would have dinner that evening, and he would take a late train home. He was fed up with flights and wanted to relax and think for a while.

He met her at an Italian restaurant at 6 P.M. and gave her a hug. They sat down, and she stared at him. "It's been a while, Mac. You don't look like you've been getting much sleep."

"I manage. This serial attorney killer just struck again in Houston, and it's getting on my nerves. The guy is too slick, and we still don't have any solid leads." He looked at her and changed the subject. "You're looking good. How's the family?"

Emily had been married for twenty-six years, but lived apart from her husband, a reporter for the Washington Post. They had two grown children and kept a cordial relationship.

"About the same."

"When you gonna get divorced and start looking for Mr. Right?"

"I had Mr. Right. I don't want another one."

The conversation ambled on until late, then Mac took his leave, and she drove him to the train station for the three-hour trip to New York. He felt tired, and she commented again how worn out he looked.

"Just the usual stuff. I'm not getting any younger." He leaned over in the car, gave her a peck and a hug, and got out, carrying his small bag with him. The train was on time, and he found a comfortable seat with a table so he could sit back and relax, possibly doze off for a couple of hours.

—50—

The surgeon made a telephone call to Dr. Blankership as soon as he returned.

"I've decided to stick around for the weekend. Were there any calls?"

"Nothing, Alex. Very quiet. If you need me to cover just call."

"Thanks again, Sandy." He hung up the phone. He had discarded the entire outfit in a dumpster downtown including the remaining anectine, and had shredded his backup driver's license. He would change to a different disguise in the future.

The entire trip had exhausted him, physically and emotionally. He was very happy to rid the world of that man, but had slight disturbing twinges of conscience about the bodyguard.

"This is a war, and there are always unpleasant casualties in war; it can't be avoided." He repeated it over and over until he felt almost comfortable. He must make a point of not facing that situation again.

He picked up a copy of *The New York Times* and saw the article at the top of page two. *Houston Deaths Linked to Malpractice Killer*. It followed with a description of the victims and a long article about Essau Kramer. The surgeon read every line very carefully and cut out the article. He had a scrap book that he kept in his safe at home, and in it was a compendium of malpractice attorney murder articles with editorials. There were a few that commented on the activity of malpractice attorneys, but none were supportive of the killings. He understood it would be journalistic and political suicide to write articles commending the serial killer, but he felt strongly that, in their hearts, most sensible people applauded his activities.

Several hundred miles away, on the train from Washington D.C., Mac was awakened from his brief nap by a generalized abdominal cramping pain. He had eaten pasta for dinner several hours before and figured it had given him a bad upset stomach. He was mildly nauseated and slightly lightheaded. They had passed through Wilmington, Delaware, about fifteen minutes before with the next stop being Philadelphia. Mac decided to go to the bathroom to get rid of some of the cramping. He set his paperwork to one side and got up slowly, standing next to his seat. He definitely felt a bit dizzy, but it seemed to get better after he stood for a minute. He walked to the bathroom, which was just around the corner at the end of the compartment. He went inside, closed the door and undressed, sitting on the toilet. He had a sudden explosive evacuation of mostly liquid with a foul smell and, in wiping, himself he noticed that it was all liquid blood and clots. He felt more dizziness and had to go again. More blood. He sat for a few minutes, and then felt more comfortable. He cleansed himself and dressed. He again felt dizzy as he stood up, but got to his feet, opened the toilet door and started back to his seat.

The cramping became more severe, and the walls of the car started to waver. The last thing he remembered was grabbing onto a seat to prevent himself from falling.

Two teenage boys were sleeping in the row as he fell partially onto the floor, draping one arm over one of the sleeping boys and awakening him with a start. The first boy nudged his friend, and one of them helped Mac lie down on the floor of the compartment while the other went to find the conductor. Another passenger had noticed the situation and came over to help.

"What happened here?"

"This guy just fell down."

Mac was breathing, but appeared very pale and was not conscious. The conductor arrived and immediately felt for a pulse. It was there. Very thready and weak, but it was there.

"Hey, mister. Can you hear me?"

No response. The conductor instructed the other adult passenger to stay with the man while he called out for a physician. A young man came by from the next compartment and immediately recognized the smell of rectal bleeding. He bent over him and after a quick evaluation, he propped Mac's legs on a couple of bags to increase blood flow to the brain.

"We have to get this man to a hospital as soon as possible. He's bleeding and needs fluid replacement."

The conductor looked at his watch. "We'll be in Philadelphia in six minutes. I'll call and have an ambulance waiting there." He left the prostrate McClymonds in the care of the physician and went to his portable phone to make arrangements. Another passenger got Mac's bag and his notes together, and within a few minutes the train slowed as it pulled into the Philadelphia station.

Mac was semiconscious, mumbling, but incoherent. When the conductor returned, he removed his wallet and noticed his police shield and his weapon.

He bent over and called out, "Officer McClymonds."

No response. "Officer McClymonds, can you hear me?"

Mac made a slight motion with his head and hands but there was no conscious awareness. The conductor looked at the physician.

"He's bleeding pretty badly," said the doctor.

"We're almost there, and the paramedics will be at the station."

"Fine."

The train slowed to a stop, and three paramedics entered the compartment. One started an intravenous and began administering fluids, then the other two placed him on a stretcher. They were very efficient, and Mac was out of the train, bags and all, within six minutes. The hospital was eight minutes by ambulance, and the paramedics had already called ahead.

"Fifty-eight-year-old Caucasian police officer collapsed in a train. He's unconscious with some movement of arms and legs. Blood pressure 70 systolic, pulse thready and 156. Grossly bloody stools. We've started Ringers Lactate. Pupils are small and react well. He appears very pale. No evidence of trauma. Arriving in four minutes."

"Good. Open the IV wide and pour in the fluids. We have a team waiting."

The ambulance pulled into the receiving dock of the Emergency Room at 11:57 P.M., and Mac was taken immediately into the treatment room, where blood was drawn for type and cross-match. Another large intravenous line was started with more fluid replacement. A surgeon and a gastroenterologist were called, and Mac became more alert as the fluids caused his blood pressure to rise.

The gastroenterologist initially wanted to examine his lower intestine with a scope, but found too much blood and couldn't see anything. He opted for an emergency bleeding scan to locate the source of the bleeding, and Mac was sent to nuclear medicine for the study at 12:30 A.M. The bleeding continued and, by the time the scan was completed, they were transfusing two units of blood rapidly with the blood pressure hovering around 68 to 70 and the pulse at 148. Mac remained semiconscious when they returned him from the nuclear medicine scanning to the emergency room. The surgeon, Dr. Alex Blanton, had arrived. He was the surgeon of choice of the gastroenterologist and had practiced at the hospital for many years. The radiologist came over with the scan.

"He has an active bleeding site in the right side of the colon, either diverticulitis or a cancer."

The surgeon looked at the chart and saw the name. Lieutenant Septimus McClymonds, New York City Police Department. He shuddered at this second, seemingly impossible, coincidence.

The emergency room physician called over to the surgeon. "I can't keep up with the blood loss, and his pressure is dangerously low."

"Call the operating room crew and tell them we're taking this man to surgery as an emergency. How soon for the blood?"
"Two units ready now and another four being cross-matched." The surgeon wrote some brief pre-operative notes and had an EKG and chest x-ray done while waiting for the surgical crew to call for the patient. The blood pressure hovered between 70 and 80, but Mac was only semiconscious. He would be unable to sign a legal consent and would be going to surgery as a life-saving emergency.

The surgeon looked at the comatose McClymonds.

"So, we finally meet, lieutenant. But it's on my turf and not yours."

—51—

It was one thirty in the morning by the time McClymonds was on the operating table and asleep under the care of an anesthesiologist. The abdomen was prepared and draped, first with towels, then with sheets, and the large overhead lights were adjusted.

"Scalpel," asked the surgeon.

It was placed firmly, but carefully, into his outheld right hand. Very rapidly, an incision was made through the skin down the center of McClymond's abdomen. Then, working rapidly using an electro-cauterizing device, the incision was carried down through the fatty tissue and the strong midline fascia. A sharp scissors was used to open the peritoneum, the enveloping tissue of the abdomen, and the surgeon then placed a special abdominal wall retractor to hold the skin edges apart so he could work more easily in the abdomen.

"Pressure's pretty low, doc. Can you get to the bleeding area quickly?" asked the anesthesiologist.

"Another two minutes," said the surgeon, as he reached one hand into the abdomen and began to mobilize the right side of the colon. Carefully dissecting out the major artery to the area, he placed a large clamp to occlude the blood flow.

"That should stop most of the blood loss."

"Good. I'm giving the second and third units of blood."

The surgeon felt the colon and could feel the tumor in the lower part of the right side. He then examined the rest of the belly and noted there were no enlarged lymph nodes and that the liver was free of tumor. It appeared to be a self-contained, small tumor and, potentially, completely curable.

It was two in the morning, and he had two nurses in the operating room with him. One, called the "circulating nurse," was not in a sterile gown and was free to get equipment and materials during the case. The other, the "scrub nurse," was in sterile gown and gloves, handing instruments to the surgeon and assisting as needed. Because of the urgency and the hour, there was no assistant surgeon. Dr. Alex Blanton was essentially alone to do what he could or would with Septimus McClymonds. He began mobilizing the end of the small intestine and the ascending colon, along with its supporting structures, the mesentery.

This was the man who might possibly find him and eventually arrest him. This was the man who could end his career and his life. That is, if he allowed him to live.

"Pressure's coming up nicely, doc. We're up to 90 over 70, and the pulse has come down to 96."

"Excellent," said the surgeon. He considered. All he had to do was slip the clamp off the artery and just let him bleed to death. It was all in the realm of possibility. No one would question his ability or intentions. He stared into the wound and reached for the clamp.

Was that a fine breath of air over my shoulder? he thought. *Is that you?* he said softly.

"What, doctor?" asked the scrub nurse.

He stepped back for a minute and looked first at the scrub nurse, and then over the drapes at the anesthesiologist. The words formed in his mind, *This man is not an attorney, and he has only done his job. I must do mine.*

"Are you okay, doc?" asked the nurse again.

The surgeon stepped back to the table and resumed his mobilization of the intestine. "Yes, I'm just fine. I was only thinking how fortunate this man is to have survived long enough to get to surgery. And he's lucky to have a small cancer that gave him symptoms before it was too large to remove and cure."

He prepared the ends of the intestine before and after the area with the cancer, leaving a wide margin, then called for the stapling device. The GIA was a large scissor-shaped apparatus that could be used to clamp and divide the bowel in one easy movement. It was a big difference from the days when the surgeon tediously had to place many sutures to accomplish the same function. A procedure that used to take twenty minutes now took only thirty seconds. He secured the large blood vessels with sutures and completed the entire internal operation in forty-five minutes.

"Blood pressure's back up to 120 over 76, and pulse is 84. He's doing well, putting out good amount of urine in the catheter, also. Looks like you've got a winner here, doc," said the anesthesiologist.

"Thanks," said the pensive surgeon. He knew he had done the right thing, but it caused him anguish to know that he had probably saved the life of the man with the greatest potential to harm him. He placed the large sutures in the abdominal fascia, then closed the subcutaneous tissue and skin in separate layers. He turned from the table, took off his mask, surgical gown, and gloves and picked up the chart. Because of the hour, the operating room was practically empty. He went into the recovery room, where he sat down and wrote out his operative note and the post-operative orders. He picked up the telephone, dialed the appropriate numbers and spent five minutes dictating the operative report. It was done.

He sat back for a moment, thinking about the acuity of the situation and of what he had done and what he had not done. McClymonds would live.

Fifteen minutes later, with all the dressings and tubes in place, the patient was wheeled into the recovery area. He was just beginning to regain consciousness, and there were three messages for the surgeon from the New York City Police Department for him to call as soon as the surgery was completed.

There was an automatic coffee machine in the doctor's lounge, and the surgeon went and had a cup while sitting back in a lounging chair. *Just play it cool and everything will be okay.*

Don't let your imagination get carried away. He's not going to implicate you. A concatenation of thoughts went through his head, each with a different outcome, and he finally rose from his chair and went back into the recovery room.

"He's awake and talking, doctor," said the recovery room nurse.

The surgeon came beside the bed and looked down at the awakening policeman.

"You're going to be fine, lieutenant. You've had bleeding from your large intestine, but everything's going to be okay."

McClymonds looked at him and nodded his head up and down.

"I'm Dr. Blanton, your surgeon." He held McClymonds hand and squeezed it in response to McClymond's squeezing hand. "We'll talk more tomorrow when you're wide awake."

"Thanks, doc," said McClymonds. He closed his eyes and dozed off.

The surgeon went over to the lounge and picked up the phone, dialing the number that had been left for him. It was answered by detective Sharpman, and the surgeon filled him in on some of the events in surgery. He did not think it appropriate to discuss the cancer with him until he had first discussed it with McClymonds and gotten his permission.

"How long will he be in Philadelphia?" asked Sharpman. "When can he be transferred to New York?"

"If everything goes well, he should be able to leave the hospital in four or five days. I don't really see any reason to transfer him to another facility."

"That sounds good. He'll probably stay with my wife and myself when he comes home," said Sharpman. "Is he gonna be all right?"

"Well," said the surgeon, "since you're not family, I really can't discuss his condition without his permission, but I would guess he'll be fine after three or four weeks convalescing."

He heard a sigh of relief on the end of the line.

"That's great doc, just great. I'll let everyone around here know that I spoke to you. Mac, I mean McClymonds, is pretty highly regarded by everyone in this department, and that goes for the Mayor on down."

"I'm glad everything worked out well. Of course, we have to be a little cautious, because he could still develop complications after the surgery. But everything seems to be doing well right now."

"So you think he'll be back to work in a month?"

"He can probably do some desk work in a couple of weeks, if everything goes well."

"He's the main detective on that malpractice attorney case, you know."

"Oh, yes. I've read about that. So he's the one investigating that case?"

"Yes. We'll carry on without him for a while, but when you get to know him, you'll find that he won't be able to sit still for a month. He won't rest until he gets his man."

"I see," said the surgeon. It was not exactly what he wanted to hear.

"Thanks again for calling, Dr. Blanton. When I called earlier you were in surgery, but the nurse told me you were the best man around. I really appreciate everything you're doing for Mac. I'll call again tomorrow. Goodbye."

The surgeon heard the phone disconnect, and he hung up the receiver. He repeated Sharpman's words with disdain: "He won't rest until he gets his man." He shook his head as he walked back to the doctor's lounge to change into his street clothes.

—52—

B y the following morning, Mac was already alert and aware of his surroundings. When Dr. Blanton came in to see him at 8 A.M., Mac was sitting up in bed and had already pulled out the tube that went through his nose down to his stomach.

"Good morning, doc. I'm sorry, but I had to get that thing out of my nose. Have you ever had one?"

"Good morning, lieutenant. No, I have never had a nasogastric tube, and I'm sure it is very uncomfortable. It's to prevent you from vomiting, so if you get very nauseated or vomit, we may have to reinsert it."

"Over my dead body, doc." Mac looked at the doctor and noticed the deep blue eyes and the huge hands. He thought to himself, *I am getting crazy. Now everyone looks like the perp.*

He smiled at the doctor between twinges of pain in his abdomen. "When can I have some food?"

"Couple of days. When things start moving through."

"How will I know when things are moving through?"

"You'll have flatus…you'll start passing gas."

"You mean farting?"

"Yes."

"Why don't you just say farting."

"Flatus is more delicate and professional." The surgeon laughed.

Mac was smiling. *The doctor has a good sense of humor,* he thought. "When can I get out of here, doc?"

"Aren't you jumping the gun a bit, lieutenant? You had emergency surgery last night and almost died, yet you haven't even asked me about it."

"I figure from the way the nurses were avoiding the questions I asked earlier that I probably have something bad. Correct?"

The surgeon was amazed by Mac's self-control. Under the same circumstances, he would be asking a hundred questions.

"You had a cancer of the first part of the large intestine, and it was actively bleeding. Another few minutes, and you probably would have bled to death. I stopped the bleeding and removed that portion of your colon."

"Well, how bad was it? Had it spread yet?"

"From what I could see, I think we caught it early enough to effect a cure."

"Who's the 'we' doc?"

"That's just an expression surgeons sometimes use. Like the royal 'we'."

"I see. I understand you already spoke to my associate in New York, Sharpman."

"Yes. But I didn't tell him about the cancer without your permission."

"Hell. You can tell him anything. I have an important case to get back to. It's just office work, but I can do it even from here."

"So I was told. Give yourself a chance to heal, lieutenant. Take a couple of weeks off."

"Tell you what doc, you just do your part and let me decide when I'm well enough to continue my part."

The surgeon was surprised at the man's condition. Eight hours ago, he was at death's door and now, after a major surgery, he was sitting up in bed as though he'd had a toenail removed.

The surgeon examined Mac's abdomen and listened to his heart and lungs. He was doing surprisingly well. *This guy is tough as nails,* the surgeon reflected, as he picked up the vital signs record and reviewed the intake and output.

"Well. You're doing better than expected. I'll see you tomorrow morning. Try to get some rest. Don't get out of bed unless someone is helping you."

"Okay, doc. And thanks."

The surgeon left the room and went to the nurses' station to write a progress report. He had thought seeing McClymonds would have made him nervous and upset. On entering the room, he had been very agitated, but the longer he spent with the man, the more he relaxed and began to like him. He wondered if that would turn out to be the fatal flaw.

He had decided to stay away from his extracurricular activities for a while and felt that this interaction with McClymonds was a good stimulus for deterrence.

That evening, he sat in his library with thoughts of Marilyn and spoke to her about McClymonds.

"He's a dangerous man for me, yet I like and respect him."

He felt curiously at ease. Somehow, a load had been lifted from him for a while, and the compulsion to act out had been dissipated.

He looked around the room. The shelves were filled with rows of finely bound books, his massive collection of first editions. He was happy in this world of old volumes with his Vesalius' Anatomy and a single page from a Gutenberg Bible. He loved to finger through the pages of the old books and play host to a thousand thoughts of the great physicians and scientists of the ages.

Once, physicians were able to practice without the threat of malpractice attorneys; they were respected and revered and loved by their patients and society. And what had happened? They were now a classless group of peddlers hustling their medical wares at the lowest bargain rates, waiting to be sued by these intolerable sludges of society.

"You're a good man, Alex. You're a good man. You have made me happy and have helped me. You are an avenging angel. My avenging angel, and I love you. I love you, and I will always love you." He drifted off to sleep with Marilyn whispering sweet nothings in his mind's ear.

—53—

It was the second visit by Dr. Blanton that caused Mac to think twice about the man. He had the feeling he had seen him before, but couldn't place where. Then it came to him. There was something about the eyes and the face of that man on the train that reminded him of this doctor. Then there were the huge hands and the blue eyes. It made him shudder to think of the possibilities, yet this man had just saved his life.

Had this guy been disguised and on his way to Houston? Was that just an incredibly fortuitous meeting? It seemed impossible, but it had awakened his curiosity. He called Sharpman at 9 A.M.

After a few words of greeting, he got right to the point. "I know this sounds crazy, but I've got a six-foot surgeon here with blue eyes and huge hands, and I think I saw him in a disguise on the train coming down to Washington. He's the guy who operated on me. I want you to do a background check on him without his knowing."

Sharpman took in a deep breath. "But I already joked with the guy about you and how you were on this big case and all. He knows you're the chief investigator on the malpractice attorney case. If he were the guy, I don't think he would have saved your life."

"Maybe he didn't know who I was."

"Come off it, Mac. Everyone knows who you are. Your picture has been in all the newspapers and the tabloids. The killer has to have been reading about it and must have paid close attention to the guy who's been looking for him."

"Well, maybe."

"Not maybe, Mac. Definitely."

"Well, regardless of what you think, I want you to check his background."

"Mac. You may be losing it. You yourself said that everyone you saw lately had been looking suspicious and, what with the surgery and all, maybe you should just take a rest."

"What the hell are you talking about? I'm still your goddamned boss!"

"Yes, sir," snapped back Sharpman.

"Oh, and Sharpman..."

"Yes?"

"Thanks for calling and being so concerned."

"Careful, Mac. You're coming across as a pussycat."

"Aah, shaddup. Goodbye."

Mac got a pain shot shortly after his phone call and fell asleep for four hours before he was awakened by the phone ringing. "Hello."

"Yeah...hi, Mac." It was Sharpman, speaking in a very conciliatory tone. "I just got a complete rundown on that doctor of yours. Can you talk now?"

"Yes."

"Well, he's very well-known in Philadelphia, listed among the very best by the medical society. He comes from a very wealthy family and apparently has plenty of money. He doesn't need to work. But listen to this. He's single now, but has been married twice. His last wife died in an accident in Europe several years ago. From what I gather, it wasn't a great marriage. But before that, he was married for a few years to a woman called Marilyn Fedderstall—Dr. Marilyn Fedderstall. I found only two people who remembered her, but apparently it was a very close, passionate marriage. Well, she was a bit unstable and after losing a malpractice case, she killed herself."

"You gotta be kidding."

"No. I looked up the newspaper reports, and it was quite a bloody mess, all over the papers, headlines, the whole nine yards. And your doctor apparently went into a deep depression for a couple of years. Then he apparently improved and eventually remarried after about five years."

"How long ago was the suicide?"

"Twenty-five years."

"And now, all of a sudden, he starts killing off malpractice attorneys? That doesn't make sense."

"I know. I know. I'm just giving you the facts as I found them. Maybe something happened in his life. Who knows? Or maybe it's not him."

"Thanks, Sharpman. Talk to Philadelphia PD; talk to Captain Marvin Wangh, he's an old friend. Tell him the situation and have him come see me in the hospital. Tell him I want to put a couple of men on this doctor. If he can't supply the bodies, speak to our chief and tell him to place two of ours on the case."

"Okay, Mac. I'll see what I can do."

"Just do it."

"Okay. Okay." He hung up the phone.

Mac lay awake in bed. His incision was hurting, and he rang for the nurse to come and give him another pain shot.

Son of a bitch. Son of a bitch, he thought. *My own damn doctor, and he might be a serial killer. But he must have known who I was. Why not just let me kick the bucket? The whole thing doesn't make sense.*

The surgeon didn't come in again until the following morning, and Mac was already feeling much better. When the surgeon walked into the room in his surgical greens, Mac tried to look at him in the most natural manner possible. The surgeon was certainly pleasant enough, but Mac couldn't keep his eyes off the huge hands and the blue eyes. The man was well-built with muscular shoulders and forearms.

"Lieutenant, good morning. How are we doing this morning?"

"Ah, there you go with that royal 'we' again, doc."

"Excuse me. How are you doing this morning?"

"Terrific. It's been two days, and I'm hungry and ready to go golfing. You golf, doc?"

"Nope. Used to, but no more."

"Well, it looks like you stay in shape."

The surgeon looked at him and smiled. "Well, I do work out a bit at home, and I like to hike. How about you?"

"Nah. I just work, drink beer and sleep."

"Not the healthiest regimen." He went over and examined the abdominal wound and listened to his heart and lungs. "You're coming along nicely. Probably start some liquids tomorrow."

"Great, doc. Aren't you going to ask me if I passed any," and he emphasized the syllables, "flatus?"

The doctor smiled. He stood very straight and asked, "Lieutenant McClymonds, have you passed any flatus today?"

"Heck no, doc. But thanks for asking."

The surgeon stared at him, laughed and turned to leave. "Say, doc," asked McClymonds. "You haven't been out killing malpractice attorneys, have you?" Mac still had a smile on his face and was eager to see the doctor's response.

The surgeon just turned casually and looked at him. "It's hard to fit in killing attorneys when you have to spend your nights saving policemen." He turned and started towards the door.

Mac countered with, "Touché, doc." He stared after him and thought, *the guy is cool as a cucumber, but I'll bet he's my man.*

—54—

*W*as he just being funny? Does he know anything? He wouldn't joke so casually about something as serious as that. Or would he? This Lieutenant McClymonds is a strange bird. Is he playing with me? He knows I just saved his life. He knows that I know who he is.

The surgeon was sitting in his office trying to make heads or tails out of the matter. *Damn. Why does he have to turn up at my doorstep?*

He had a pen in his hand and was making a list of possible actions. *Maybe I should just take off and go abroad for a year. I could turn the practice over to Blankership. Then they'd know for sure it was me, if there were no more killings. Either way, it would be best for me just to stay here and continue in my normal activities. They may think it's me, but do they have any real proof? No. Just supposition.*

He got up, put on his overcoat and buttoned it up to the top. It was cold outside. He locked up the office and went to his car. He got in and started to drive aimlessly as he thought about his situation.

Did the great activists in history stop because of fear and self-interest? No. They had a cause, and they pursued it to the end of their life. Think of Nathan Hale standing on the gallows. I must believe in my cause with more depth and strength. It's my destiny. And, if something were to happen to me and I should die,

I could be with you eternally, Marilyn. This is a win/win situation.
He drove around for almost an hour before returning home. He was no longer afraid, and he had resolved to continue his work. He parked the car in the garage and went into the house. He sat down in the library, read through three newspapers and felt much more relaxed. Marilyn was with him and life was complete. There were several articles about the serial killings, and he read every one several times trying to see whether there were any hints as to his identity. There were none. One was a psychological profile of the serial killer. He didn't think he fit the pattern at all. Another was a comment on medical malpractice: *A Boon or a Blot for Attorneys.* There was a biographical history of malpractice. He read about medical negligence and how malpractice suits were common in the United States, but very uncommon elsewhere. Malpractice was described as failure of a doctor to provide the skill, expertise and care that is a standard of the community in which he lives. The article emphasized that *outcomes in medicine can never be guaranteed, but that due care and skill must be provided.* He read on.

A valid medical malpractice claim must have breach of duty with either physical or monetary losses. The lay jury is educated by the presentation of facts and information by expert witnesses and data from the medical records.

He threw the paper down. "Crap. Just crap. They find some so-called expert physician who will testify to anything and confuse a panel of twelve people who don't know much about medicine. It's the damn attorneys who have coaxed the public into litigation for anything and everything." He walked around a few minutes, then sat down again and picked up the newspaper.

Statistics from Great Britain show that, in one year, there were 700 writs for medical malpractice, whereas in the United States, during the same year, there were over 42,000 claims. Even with adjustments for population, the

*per capita incidence of malpractice cases in the United
States is ten times as frequent as in England.*

He fumed as he read this aloud, then skimmed over the
sections he didn't want to hear about, namely where malpractice
cases had supposedly promoted more patients' rights and led to
better medicine practiced by physicians. He was angry again,
wanted redress for his anger and didn't know where to go to get
it. He pulled out his personal telephone book and wanted to call
one of the women he knew. He was about to dial a number, but
decided against it.

*Ten times the number of lawsuits in the United States. Ten
times. Ten times. Goddamned attorneys. We don't need attorneys
policing the medical profession. They need someone policing
their profession. I don't need them, and they don't need me. Since
they have inflicted themselves on my profession in their way, I
will inflict myself upon their profession in my way.*

He picked up his coat and keys again and went to the front
door, slamming it behind him as he left. It was only 7 P.M., and
the library would be open until eleven that evening. He wanted to
read more. He would find another suitable victim. He would
drive that percentage down to zero if he had to. It took ten
minutes driving at sixty miles an hour through the city streets. He
was focused only on getting there.

He parked carelessly and turned off the motor. Then,
suddenly, he regained his composure and sat for almost five
minutes, muttering to himself "Festina lente, festina lente; make
haste slowly. What am I doing? Just sit for a moment and take
some deep breaths. Don't act foolishly. You could have been
stopped for speeding. You could have had an accident. You could
have hit someone. Stay focused. Deep breath." He soothed
himself and spoke to Marilyn as he sat in the darkened car. Then
he got out, more controlled, and walked to the library.

Once inside, the automatic doors opened quickly, and he
went to the reading room. After gathering several newspapers, he
sat alone in a booth and started going through them page by

page. Not one advertisement for attorneys, not one report of a case—the field had suddenly dried up. He was caught between joy and sorrow, elation and disappointment. He felt like a war-hungry general who has signed a cease-fire. He was looking for his case and couldn't find it. After two hours, he found himself reading an editorial page about homeless children. He finally put down the papers, left the library and went home to bed. He would try again tomorrow.

—55—

By the fourth day Mac was able to take liquids and was doing so well that he was allowed to go home in the afternoon on pain medication and antibiotics. Before leaving, he met with his friend Captain Marvin Wangh of the Philadelphia police department and had worked out a plan to have the surgeon followed and observed. It would take several men on different shifts but, given the circumstances, it was important enough to warrant the expense. He saw his surgeon that morning and was discharged to the care of a surgeon in New York City, who could take out his skin staples. He said goodbye to Dr. Blanton, shaking his huge right hand, yet felt sure he would see him again, albeit under different circumstances. He was such a pleasant surgeon. Mac, realizing that Blanton had saved his life, had very mixed emotions about the whole scenario.

Mac was picked up by Sharpman and taken to New York by police helicopter, where Sharpman deposited him in a separate room in his own home.

The final pathology report had come back very positive, with his cancer involving the innermost layer of the colon and no positive lymph nodes. It was staged as I-A cancer with an excellent prognosis and no further treatment necessary. Mac was still very slow moving around and had a moderate amount of incisional pain.

The observers were in place, but the surgeon's schedule had been relatively uneventful: home, office, surgery, occasional dinner with friends or some social event. Then there were his several-hour periods in the library reading through newspapers. That latter activity interested Mac.

"What's he doing?"

Sharpman shrugged. "Looking for victims?"

"That's what I was thinking."

"Do you think he's on to us?"

"I doubt it. Our guys are being changed every day, and they're very good."

"Did you get a phone tap?"

"Yes. Judge Burgess agreed with us on that one." "No calls of significance?" asked Mac.

"The guy's a virtual hermit outside his office and practice," said Sharpman

"If this is our guy, and I think he is, we'll just have to keep tailing him until he tries again. Of course, if he's onto us then we're in for a long wait."

"That's fine," added Sharpman. "Fewer attorneys hitting the dust."

"Probably not," said Mac. "If he's as compulsive as I think he is, he'll just stay low for a while. Guys like him don't quit. They are answering to a higher power…a higher judge. He'll just have a hiatus in his activity for a while. We just have to stay on top and catch him in the act."

Sharpman smiled. "Well, right now he can't go to the bathroom without us knowing about it."

"Have you checked out his whereabouts during the times of the murders?"

"Very difficult. He wasn't in surgery, but there's no way to know where this guy is seventy per cent of the time. He's usually not working on weekends, sometimes takes three or four days off. I can't find one day when he has an airtight alibi. Should I pick him up for questioning?"

"No. He's too smart, and we have nothing but an interesting history and some circumstantial evidence. He could probably sue us for harassment and abuse. And, if he is innocent, I look like a completely ungrateful schmuck, seeing as how the guy saved my life."

"Well, the whole thing doesn't make sense," said Sharpman.

"I know, but that's the reality of the situation."

"Do I discuss this with the mayor?"

Mac thought for a moment. "Yes, we have to. But let the mayor know that if we pick him up now, we might just lose him entirely. We should know within a month if this is the guy."

Sharpman left Mac in the bedroom and told his wife, loudly, "Don't let him out of the house."

"Don't worry," called out Mac. "I feel like I've been hit by a truck. I'm not going anywhere." He stretched himself on the bed, picked up his files and began reading and writing. He'd lost four days, and that was enough.

–56–

If I were a detective, what and whom would I be looking for? They know I must be a surgeon, and they will be trying to tie it into some malpractice disaster, but they probably don't how what to look for.

The surgeon thought about McClymonds. *Let's suppose he is onto me. Maybe the disguise wasn't good enough; maybe the guy that survived gave him a good picture. But they haven't got enough to come after me yet. Right. I'm too well-known and prominent to accuse without facts. If they had facts, I'd be in jail now, and I'm not. So what do they do next?*

He was again in his library making notes and trying to put himself in McClymond's mind. *I'm sure he's looked into my background. Yes. And he must have found out about you, Marilyn. So he's more suspicious than ever. What would I do? What would I...* He put down his pen and stood up. *Of course. I would put a tail on the guy. I would watch everything he does and everywhere he goes... But I've been clean.* He began pacing up and back in front of the lighted fireplace, the heat making him warm and more excited with each thought. *Ah, but they've seen me go to the library and read the newspapers. Why is he reading the newspapers? That's not too difficult to figure out.* Then he stopped.

Suppose this is all a pipe dream. Is this the ranting of a lunatic serial killer? Am I just imagining all this? Maybe they've tapped my phone. Maybe someone's watching me right now.

He was about to go to the window, then stopped.

No. I don't want them to know that I know. There's one way to find out for sure.

He went and got his mobile phone. It had a block, so it couldn't be traced. He called the central Philadelphia Police Department.

"This is Lieutenant McClymonds calling from New York. I'm the one with the Dr. Blanton case, and I forgot the name of the man in charge."

"Captain Wangh, Lieutenant. He's not in right now. Shall I connect you with his secretary?"

"No. Thank you. I'll reach him later." He flipped off the mobile phone and then thought, *They'll probably give him the message, and he'll call him back. Oh, well. At least I know that they're onto me. That means I can't leave the country, so I might as well just continue to do my work as usual and let them wait.*

He was all bunched up inside. He felt walls caving in on him, and then she spoke to him.

"It's okay, my darling. It's going to be okay. I'm always with you, and we can continue after a few days or weeks. We'll find a way. God will help us find a way, because we are right. You are right."

The surgeon sat back in his chair and closed his eyes. He could picture her just as she was so many years ago. *My love. My only love. We will do great things together, and no one will stop us. I promise you.*

He took a sleeping pill and went to bed. She would be with him all night. He was glad of that, and he slept soundly. In the morning when he awoke, it was 7 A.M., and she was gone. He showered and dressed, leaving the house at 7:30, just as the housekeeper was arriving. She spent half a day, three days a week, cleaning and sometimes preparing and freezing some meals he could defrost and use for dinners. She knew what he liked and kept the pantry well-stocked.

He knew he was being observed, but he couldn't see the tail. He glanced furtively at cars and people who were standing still. He couldn't see the tracer. He went to the garage and got in his car. He pulled out and watched in his mirror. Then he saw the car. It was quite a ways back, but it followed him wherever he went. He parked in the lot next to his office and went into the building. His secretary was already at work, and he reviewed his schedule for the day. Six patients between 8:30 and 9:30, then two surgeries starting at 10:00: a laparoscopic gallbladder removal and an inguinal hernia repair. That left him most of the afternoon off.

He looked over some paper and lab work that had been sent to the office and signed off on them with his initials. Then he went across the street to the hospital to make daily rounds on his patients, stopping to get a cup of coffee at the snack bar. He passed many doctors and nurses, nodding or saying good morning, then went to the surgical units. The ward secretary had pulled his charts, and one of the nurses accompanied him as he went from patient to patient, reviewing the chart, examining an abdomen or other area, changing dressings as needed. He felt relaxed…in his element.

He returned to the office and saw several patients: two new ones and several post-operative rechecks. He made several phone calls to doctors and patients, and even called McClymonds to find out how he was doing.

"Just fine, doc. A little pain but, aside from that, just fine."

"Very good. Just don't overdo it. You need some rest before getting back to work."

"Right, doc. I already spoke with my own doctor, and he'll be seeing me next week to take out staples. Everything okay with you, doc?"

Mac was trying to rattle the man, but was totally unsuccessful. The surgeon was as calm and relaxed as could be.

"Fine, thank you. Well, lieutenant, if there's anything I can do for you, feel free to call."

"Okay. Thanks for calling, Doc."

After hanging up the phone, the surgeon sat looking at it for a moment before going in to see one of his patients. The time moved very slowly, but finally he was done for the day and drove home. He caught glimpses of the car following him and noted that there must be two different ones: a brown Ford and a gray Chevy. He spent the afternoon in his library looking through the yellow pages and jotting down names of attorneys. He was going to eliminate one right under their noses. He peeked through the window and noted that one of the cars had stopped almost a block away. The other was gone.

The housekeeper left at three in the afternoon. He went to his room and opened the sliding closet door. He opened the safe, took out the last of his supplies—some anectine as well as the .22 revolver—and placed them in a small bag. Then he waited until the sun had set and rechecked the car down the block. He went out through the back door. It was almost pitch black, but he knew his way in the dark and crossed the broad expanse of his back-yard into the trees behind the house. He walked another hundred yards to a side street, where he had a second car parked. He glanced around to see if he had been followed, but there was nothing suspicious. He got in the dark green Volkswagen and drove away from the neighborhood into the poorer section of the city.

He parked a block from his secret apartment. He exited the car and, taking his equipment with him, ambled up the front steps and inserted his key into the front door. It was a fairly deserted neighborhood, and he felt safe and alone. Once in the small apartment, he pulled down the shade before opening his bag and laying out the equipment he would need for his next job. He even had the white ticket made up to tie to the foot. He spent about two hours preparing a new disguise and then, locking the door after him, retraced his steps back to his home. The Ford was still there.

—57—

Three more weeks passed with no activity other than the normal events in the surgeon's life. Mac was back in his own apartment and, although he tired easily, he was able to put in about four to six hours a day of office work. He occasionally went out in the car to follow up on cases, but hadn't done any work himself on the serial murders. He had been getting regular activity reports from the combined New York and Pennsylvania groups that were watching the surgeon. There had been no more deaths since the Houston affair and no more leads except the one which Mac felt was the strongest. Namely, Dr. Blanton, whose name he had not released to anyone except the mayor, his own associates and several policemen in Philadelphia. Most of them, however, did not know why they were watching this doctor, and there was no connection made between him and the serial killings.

He sat in conference with the mayor. "It's been almost a month since the last murder," said the mayor. "Do you think it's over, or is he just taking some time off?"

"I think he's just biding his time for now," Mac replied. "He may know we have him under surveillance for the murders. But I don't think this guy will stop. I think we've got him temporarily stopped, although there's no definite evidence of that."

"So how long do we keep him under surveillance?"

"I can't say; but we better continue for now."

"And what do I tell the attorney groups and the newspapers and the public?" asked the mayor.

Mac thought a moment. "The best thing is to say next-to-nothing. We don't want to say he's stopped or that we have someone under observation. We could give a press release that the investigation is in high gear and several leads are being followed. The public will be happy with that for now."

The mayor threw up his hands. "You know, Mac, I don't need this."

"That's why I never ran for elected office, mayor."

"Well. Maybe you're smarter than I am. All you do is try your best, and you don't have to lose your job if you don't succeed."

—58—

Matthew Carstairs was an avid sailor. He used to go out every Wednesday with his son Arnold up until the time his son died after surgery. He had mourned for several years after the death and actually felt cheated when the surgeon of record, Dr. Marilyn Fedderstall, took her own life. Since the death of his son, he would go out sailing once a month to be by himself and think of the son he had lost. It was a regular event for him, like visiting a cemetery stone, and he was always on the sea on Wednesday afternoon unless he was out of town on business or vacation.

He kept a pristine old fifty-foot Swan sloop in a yacht club on the Delaware River and, although he had a man who cleaned and kept up the boat, he always went out by himself. The boat, *The Jolly Counselor*, was rigged for single-handed sailing, and had a powerful gas engine and generator for cruising. Its presence on the river on Wednesdays was a local tradition. He would leave from the club at ten in the morning and return at five in the afternoon to meet his wife for drinks and dinner. At seventy-five years old, he was a tough, wiry man with a mop of white hair, piercing brown eyes and an acerbic tongue that had led to hundreds of victories in the courtroom.

It had been many years since the death of his son, but he remembered it as yesterday, and it always brought anger and terrible sorrow to him.

"A father should never outlive his son," he would frequently say. He wanted to keep the memory alive, though his wife had long since stopped her mourning and gotten on with her life. "Is there no one who remembers my son Arnold?" he would sometimes call out when on the boat. It would always ring out against the wind or rain to a terrible silence, and it often brought tears to his eyes.

He was, however, wrong. There was someone who thought about his son and those terrible last few days. He was about to meet him again.

—59—

One weekend the surgeon made a trip to New York and was followed everywhere he went. That evening he disappeared out the back of his hotel and was not seen again until one in the morning, when he returned without any apparent reason. No one had any knowledge of where he had gone or what he had done. The police were frantic, but it turned out to be a relatively quiet night in Manhattan with no attorney deaths. Mac and his team breathed a sigh of relief and decided to place a tighter control on the surveillance.

A week later, in Philadelphia, the doctor was assembling all kinds of things at home, and it was apparent he was very busy doing something, according to the two policemen watching him. The surgeon was good at making arrangements. He went out the back door in the evening and went directly to the apartment. He had intentionally not taken the same care as he had in the past, and his activity was seen by one of the undercover policemen. This was a change from his routine, and it was called into headquarters immediately.

"He's left the house by the back and picked up a car five blocks away, a green Volkswagen, License XPLRR67. He's carrying a sizable bag with him. We've traced him to a small apartment house in the Inner City, and he's been inside for almost an hour. Do you want us to pick him up?"

Mac replied. "Absolutely not. Just keep an eye on him. I'm taking the next police flight out of here, and I'll meet you at the stakeout area in two hours. Keep me posted if he moves and, for God's sake, don't lose him."

The stakeout continued all night. Through the window, they could see him moving inside the room until midnight, when he appeared to be getting undressed and going to sleep.

Inside the apartment, the surgeon laid out the plans of the yacht club and the river and finalized his arrangements. The following morning, Wednesday at 4 A.M., he made his way to the roof and carefully went from building to building until he was almost at the end of the block. He entered a building through the roof door and walked down to the first floor. He exited wearing his new outfit. He was dressed as an elderly man and kept his beret low on his forehead. He had a thin mustache and a patch over one eye. He hailed a taxi two blocks from the apartment and went directly to the marina where he mixed with the early morning dockworkers. He had some breakfast at a small restaurant, then meandered down along the riverside. When he got to the yacht club, he walked casually in and then down to the docks, where he found *The Jolly Counselor* at dockside. He watched from a distance as the caretaker prepared the boat for the attorney. He had everything ready to go by eight thirty, then left the area.

The surgeon waited about fifteen minutes before moving casually onto the docks as if he belonged there. He walked directly to the boat and boarded it without anyone taking special notice. The hatch was already open in anticipation of the arrival of Carstairs, and he went below and placed his carry-on bag in an equipment locker out of sight. He found he would be able to hide in one of the smaller sleeping areas, then went into the main cabin, where he could watch for the approach of Carstairs through a small side porthole.

Carstairs arrived at 9:45 A.M. and hopped aboard with an energy that belied his seventy-odd years. The surgeon had concealed himself before the attorney came down the steps. Carstairs tossed a small bag onto the table in the main salon, then went directly to the instrument table and turned on the electrical power. Without waiting a moment, he pulled himself up the steps through the hatch, and went to the binnacle, where he inserted his key and started up the engine. A younger man, the caretaker, had followed him to the slip and was undoing the lines and tossing them onto the boat. He held the bow of the boat away from the dock to prevent the ship from moving forward and touching the dock.

"So long, counselor. Have a good sail," he said as he tossed the last line aboard.

Carstairs slipped the clutch into reverse and backed the boat out of the slip with the ease of a master. Turning outwards, he again shifted the clutch and headed from the dock area into the main channel at a steady four knots. When he was about a half mile out, he turned the throttle down all the way and put the clutch in neutral. He went around, pulled the bumpers up and threw them into the hold. He hadn't had a chance to do this while at the helm. There was only a bit of haze, and he could see several hundred yards in all directions. He was practically alone on the river.

The caretaker had taken the sail covers off and attached the mainsheet. All the sailor had to do was turn the boat into the wind and hoist the main. He had electric winches, a necessity in single -handedly sailing the large boat. He went back to the binnacle, switched the boat's engine into forward and turned into the wind. He was about to undo the straps holding the mainsail in place when he felt a tap on his shoulder. He turned in amazement to see an old man standing behind him holding a small caliber pistol at the back of his head.

−60−

Mac had arrived late in the evening and went directly to the stakeout at the apartment. It was fortunate that the surgeon's room was in the front, and they could see his activities through the dim light of the room. They saw him carrying things back and forth, yet they couldn't make out exactly what it was he was doing. By midnight the two groups of officers had placed themselves at the front and back exits of the building, and by 3 A.M. Mac went around and told them to keep a close watch. He was getting very tired and went to one of the cars and sat back after notifying the officers to wake him if there was any activity. He fell asleep after a few minutes.

The surveillance was in full effect all night, but there was no activity seen. By 8 A.M. Mac had awakened and made the rounds of his assistants. Nothing. No movement from the surgeon. Several others had already left the hotel, and the police were careful not to be fooled by any disguises. They had stopped one large man who turned out to be a baker on his way to work at four in the morning. Aside from a few others, there was nothing abnormal. By 9 A.M. they could see with scopes into the apartment and there was no activity. By 10, with no activity, Mac sent a man up to the apartment as a plumber from the landlord.

He knocked on the door, first gently, then loudly, with no response. He called McClymonds, and the entire stakeout crew went to the room. In standard fashion, they first knocked and then got the landlord to open the door. The room was empty except for discarded clothing, medical supplies and several sheets of paper on the one small table in the room.

"Goddamn. How did he get out of here?"

He sent two men up to the roof, and they returned in a few minutes.

"He could have gotten away by the roof, but it would mean jumping across some pretty wide gaps. Do you think he could have done it at his age?" asked one of the officers.

Mac was examining the papers on the table when the man returned. "No. He probably flew," he answered sharply. "How the hell else could he get away? He must have known we'd be watching, or else he's the most cautious guy I've known. Damn."

Two of the team were going over the room while Mac sifted through the papers on the desk. They were maps of the water-front in Philadelphia and a small map of the Yacht basin and the yacht club.

"What's he up to, Mac?" asked one of the men.

"I don't know, but I'm sure it's no good. The only clue is the waterfront. Maybe he's on a boat. Do any of you know this yacht club?" He pointed to the map.

One of the men stepped forward. "Yeah. I used to take lessons there. There are a lot of private boats down there. I know my way around pretty well."

"Then let's get over there and see if we can figure out what's going down," said Mac. "Better call in and have some men down there looking for him. And remember, he'll probably be in a disguise of some kind. Look for size and the hands."

The all went back to their cars and headed for the marina.

288

–61–

Carstairs started to raise his hand toward the pistol, seeing that it was only an old man. The old man suddenly turned much younger as he grabbed the attorney's hand and bent it backward until the older man screamed in pain and fell to the deck. "Now, now, counselor. Let's have none of that."

"Who are you?" asked the older man, grabbing his own hand. "You could have broken my hand." He looked up at the figure looming above him. The patch was off, and the blue eyes stared back at him. "How did you get on my boat? Do you know who I am?"

"Oh, yes, counselor, I know exactly who you are. Now, get below." He pointed to the hatch. "We have to talk."

The attorney sat up. "We'll talk right here!"

The surgeon grabbed him by the collar and practically lifted him off the deck, throwing him towards the hatch. "I think not."

The attorney, hair tousled and with a bruise on his arm, was shoved down the hatch. He fell into the cabin and onto the wood-paneled floor. The surgeon was down on him in a moment, placing the gun barrel into the surprised man's mouth.

"Let's have no more discussion for now, or you'll be missing a few teeth. I want you to turn over, lie on your belly and not make a sound." He stared into Carstairs' face. "Do you understand?"

The older man nodded his head up and down, his eyes wide with fear. He was shaking slightly, taking rapid breaths as he turned over.

"Look at him, Marilyn. Look at the sniveling piece of garbage we call a malpractice attorney. This is the man you took your life for. This is the man who didn't thank you for trying to save his son. This is the lowest creature on earth, who was willing to sacrifice one life for another. Look at him, Marilyn." The surgeon spat out the last syllables.

Carstairs turned his head to one side looking for the woman. Then a look of understanding came into his eyes. "You're the husband of that surgeon who killed my son." He started to rise up again, and the surgeon stepped firmly on his head, slamming it to the deck.

"Stay on your belly and don't turn your head, or I'll squash you like an ant, counselor. I've been waiting a long time for this."

It was at this point that the ship to shore radio came to life.

"Jolly Counselor, Jolly Counselor. Come in, please. This is the coast guard calling. Repeat. Jolly Counselor, Jolly Counselor, come in please. This is the harbor patrol."

—62—

The team arrived at the waterfront in less than twenty minutes, and several different teams fanned out. McClymonds went directly to the Harbor Patrol Office. He took out his portable phone and called for helicopter backup. Then he spoke to the harbormaster who was standing on the embankment near the office.

"Has any boat left the harbor this morning?"

The harbormaster, with his pipe looked like the quintessential old man of the sea. "We had about thirty boats out so far this morning."

Mac felt his heart skip a beat. "Thirty?"

"We have a small fishing fleet that leaves about 5:30 or 6 A.M."

"What about private boats?"

"Oh, it's kinda cold for the average boater right now. The only one that goes out regular on Wednesdays is that lawyer, Carstairs. He's been pretty regular for years."

Mac paused a moment, then recalled the relationship between Matthew Carstairs and Dr. Alex Blanton.

"That's it. He's after Carstairs. It was Carstairs who sued his dead wife and led to her killing herself. How do we reach that boat?"

The harbormaster looked at him in amazement. "You want me to call ship to shore? It all depends whether his radio is on. A

291

good sailor always leaves the emergency channel on, so we can reach him on that line."

"Yes. Yes," said Mac. "See if you can contact Carstairs. It's an emergency."

The men walked into the Harbor Patrol Office, and the old harbormaster took up the radio handset and punched in some numbers. He depressed the switch and spoke into the microphone, *"Jolly Counselor, Jolly Counselor. Come in, please. This is the Harbor Patrol."*

At first, there was no response, then there was a familiar voice, which Mac recognized immediately.

"This is *The Jolly Counselor*, over."

Mac took the microphone from the harbormaster. "Dr. Blanton. This is Lieutenant McClymonds. We know you're aboard. Is Carstairs there?"

The surgeon took the hand microphone from its holder and depressed the speaker switch. "Lieutenant. You seem to have found me. That's a pity. It will be too late for Mr. Carstairs."

In the background Mac could hear a voice screaming, "Help me. Help me. This man is mad." This was followed by a loud thud as the surgeon pushed the attorney to the floor. Then there was silence.

"Blanton, what have you done to Carstairs?"

"Not too much yet. The best is yet to come."

"Dr. Blanton. Why not give yourself up now? You can't get away, and there's no point to harming Mr. Carstairs."

"'Lieutenant. How are you feeling?"

"Blanton, this is no time for small talk, and you know it."

"There's always time for talk, lieutenant. Where's your bedside manner? Oh, pardon me. I'm the one with the bedside manner."

"Blanton. Mr. Carstairs was upset when his son died, but he didn't kill your wife. She was emotionally unstable. She killed herself."

"Lieutenant, lieutenant, lieutenant. Let's not confuse the issue. Mr. Carstairs is a malpractice attorney, and his actions led directly to the death of my wife. I am sure his behavior and lack of ethics have led to a great deal of misery and suffering over the last forty years, and he is going to be punished for it."

Mac was calmed down by another officer, who told him to keep the man talking. Maybe they could get to the boat before he did anything to the old attorney. Mac turned to the harbormaster.

"Can we find the boat out there?"

"We can look, and we'll eventually find her with visual sighting or radar, but it could take half an hour or more. We'd arrange for a helicopter, but that might be a couple of hours."

"Let's get started as soon as possible. We'll stay in contact with him all the while."

"Whatever your pleasure, officer," said the harbormaster. He arranged for a large Harbor Patrol ship to pull up.

Mac went back to the microphone.

"Dr. Blanton. Why don't we meet and talk for a few minutes? I owe you my life, and I want to help."

"Now, really, lieutenant, how do you suppose you can help me?"

"Please, doctor. We could discuss the psychological possibilities. If you don't give up, you'll be shot and killed, and I don't want that."

"I see. Maybe I could plead insanity?" He laughed.

"Doctor. You are a sensible and brilliant man, a gifted surgeon. You know that to commit serial murders is the act of an unbalanced mind. You need help, and I can be instrumental in getting that for you. But you have to let the attorney go and give up."

"Thank you, lieutenant. I do think you are speaking from the heart. But let me tell you that I am doing what I am doing because I firmly and intellectually believe that it is right and good for society. Sometimes, we must be judged by a future generation. That's what will happen in my case. Only a few will stand and be counted, and I am one of those."

Mac looked at the other policemen who were listening and rolled his eyes.

"You accomplish this higher end by killing attorneys?"

"Malpractice attorneys, lieutenant. Only malpractice attorneys."

"What about that bodyguard you shot and killed?" asked Mac, trying to buy more time. The Harbor Patrol craft had just arrived, and all the men got on board. It was slightly foggy out and visibility was down to about fifty yards. A bad day for boating and certainly for sailing!

"We must sometimes make sacrifices in love and war, as the expression goes," said the doctor. "Think of all the innocents killed during the bombings of German cities during World War II."

"That was a war, doctor."

The surgeon cut in immediately. "This too is a war, lieutenant. Our definitions are just a bit different. I am killing off unethical, money-hungry attorneys catering to the lowest standard of society, ruining the practice of medicine by driving up malpractice rates, causing doctors to lose their ability to practice their art and directly or indirectly leading to the death of some physicians. And yes, I hold Mr. Carstairs directly responsible for the death of my wife."

Mac thought for a moment. "Can you and I talk face to face in private, alone on the ship except for Mr. Carstairs?"

"How can I possibly trust you not to pull something, lieutenant?"

"I can only give you my word. I owe you my life, and you must believe that I will keep my word to you. Anyway, you have Mr. Carstairs as a hostage, so I wouldn't try anything that might get him injured or killed. And, more importantly, I give you my solemn word."

"I see. And right now I can hear a boat motor through the microphone. I assume you are in the Coast Guard patrol boat. To show good faith, I want you to stop the boat immediately."

Mac was taken aback by the man's keen perception. He glanced around him, and then at the Harbor Master. Then he signaled with his hand to shut down the motor.

"Okay, doctor. You are correct, and I have shut down the motor. I will give you five minutes to think about what I've offered you; then I must restart the motor and come after you."

"Okay. And no helicopters, either. Give me twenty minutes, and I'll give you an answer. If you come sooner or I see any helicopters, Mr. Carstairs will die. Twenty minutes, lieutenant."

Mac looked around at his colleagues. He turned the microphone off. "Tell the helicopter to stay away for a while. We have nothing to lose and possibly may be able to save Carstairs. Any objections to giving him twenty minutes? It will take us at least that to find him, anyway." He looked around the cabin. No one seemed to object. He turned the mike back on.

"Dr. Blanton. I will give you twenty minutes, and then you have to give me an answer. Agreed?"

"Thank you, lieutenant. I will give you an answer in twenty minutes. I need to think about this carefully. Remember. If I see your boat before then, Carstairs will die." He shut off his radio.

—63—

The surgeon had expected this response. He turned to the attorney who was moaning on the floor and raised him up to face him.

"I hold you responsible for the death of my wife. She had tried to save your son, but you only saw evil, and your actions led to her taking her own life. For that you must be punished."

The attorney had a look of fear on his face. "Please, doctor. I'm sorry. I'm truly sorry. He was my only son, and he died after that surgery."

"We're wasting time." He held the pistol with a silencer up to Carstair's forehead and pulled the trigger. The man slumped onto the floor.

The surgeon took out his instruments and quickly made several cuts and placed tissue into a small plastic bag which he tied to the man's foot. Then he took the note and placed it in another plastic bag and tied that to the other foot.

He went to the deck and looked into the mist. He glanced at the binnacle and the compass and cried out, "I love you, Marilyn, and I have done all this for you." He took the rest of the equipment out of his bag and went below. It was nineteen minutes and thirty seconds since he spoke to the lieutenant. He switched on the microphone. "This is *The Jolly Counselor* calling the Harbor Patrol boat. Come in, please."

"This is Lieutenant McClymonds, doctor. What have you decided?"

"I have decided that I will talk with you. I will turn on a signaler so you can locate us. You can come within fifty yards and then turn off the engine. Get in a rowboat and row over to the sailboat. You may come aboard, but you must not be armed. Understand?"

"I understand," said Mac. "Is Carstairs okay?"

"He's fine. Remember. I have a gun and, if you are armed, Carstairs and you will both be shot. Understood?"

"Yes, doctor. I understand."

The surgeon turned on the signaler.

"We are getting your signal now, doctor. Is it all right to come ahead?"

"Yes. I must leave the cabin and go on deck, so I will turn off the microphone now."

He reached into the bag and took out several surgical instruments and a timed detonator.

Mac heard the microphone switch off and told the harbormaster and crew to start the engine.

"Can you tell how far he is from here?" asked Mac.

"He's about half a mile east and about hundred yards from shore. We can be near him in about fifteen minutes."

"Okay," said Mac. "Remember to stop fifty yards from him."

"Yessir," responded the man at the helm. The big boat powered through the water.

Slowly, as the motor launch moved along, they began to see the outline of a sailboat in the distance. They slowed their speed until they were about fifty yards from the bow and then shut off the engine. The crew very quickly launched a rubber life raft with oars and gave McClymonds a life vest. He took off his service revolver and stepped towards the ladder at the side of the large craft.

"You're not taking a weapon, Mac?" asked Sharpman.

Mac turned back and looked at his associate. "No. He just saved my life. He's not going to shoot me. I may just be able to talk him into giving up. It's Carstair's only chance."

He climbed down the ladder into the rubber raft and took up the oars. The sailboat was fifty yards away, but the water was smooth and there was almost no wind.

It was a peaceful moment. Because of the slight fog there were small craft warnings against sailing and motoring, and there were no other boats to be seen. The only sound was the raft moving through the water, the water dripping from the oars, and the sloshing as they pulled the boat forward.

The silence was suddenly broken by a tremendous explosion. Mac turned toward the sailboat. It seemed to lift out of the water with a flash of red, throwing the mast upwards. The sky was filled with debris raining down, almost reaching the rubber raft and causing a large wave, which reached him in a few seconds and caused the raft to rock violently back and forth. Mac held tightly to the seat, but was almost knocked into the water. When the shaking stopped, he looked ahead of him at the remains of the sailboat surrounded by debris. It was sinking and disappeared below the surface in a few seconds.

Mac turned the raft quickly back to the Harbor Patrol launch and was back on board in a couple of minutes. "Do you have divers available?"

Everyone was in shock, looking at the debris.

Mac said, "Call for another boat to get out here as soon as possible with some divers. We'll stay here and look around to see if anyone survived."

The others looked at him. The harbormaster said, "Nothing and no one could survive that explosion, lieutenant."

The big boat powered up and slowly made its way through the debris.

—64—

The second Harbor Patrol boat was next to them in thirty minutes with two divers aboard in wetsuits with Scuba gear. "The water is relatively shallow at this distance from the shore, only about thirty feet. We should be able to find the wreckage quite quickly and any bodies, if anything remains," said the first diver. He and the other man dropped over the side into the cold water.

Mac looked at the others. "The guy was crazy. Who could anticipate such a thing?" He shook his head.

"The attorney was doomed no matter what you did, Mac. I don't think any of us held out any hope for him," said Sharpman. "You did the best you could."

Mac called ashore, first to the police chief, then to the Mayor's office, informing them of the situation.

"Any bodies yet?" asked the chief.

"We've got two divers down there now, but I can't see how anyone could survive."

"Could he have dived off and swum away?" asked the chief.

"It's always possible, but we're situated close enough to the boat where we would have seen something, and I did speak to him just a few moments before the explosion."

He hung up, and they all waited thirty-five minutes. The divers reappeared.

"We located the debris and we're getting a body and some body parts. We should be done in about half an hour."

They disappeared beneath the surface again. About forty minutes later, they reappeared carrying a large net and two smaller bags. They were pulled up onto the boat with them.

When they were aboard, it was apparent that they had a body and some body parts. The men took off their gear.

"There's quite a bit of wreckage, but it's only in a small area. We found one guy close to the wreckage and some body parts nearby."

The body was badly macerated and burned. The harbormaster looked at him.

"Oh, my God. It's Mr. Carstairs." The body was partially dismembered, and the face seemed partially destroyed, the eyes gone and the ears blown off, but the old sailor said it was definitely Carstairs. The neck and upper chest were blown open and the lower body was intact. Then they noticed the two plastic bags tied to the feet.

"Don't tell me," said Mac. He reached for the bags and placed them on the deck drying them with a towel. "We've got too many fingers here. There were two extra digits found near this body, but the body has all ten fingers and toes. These must be from the other guy."

Mac went over to the containers and looked down at the fingers, partially burned. The diver held up one of the fingers and placed it into a specimen bottle. "The other guy must have disintegrated with the explosion; this is all we found."

He reached into his bag and pulled out another 3 inch specimen. "Oh, and there's some clumps of burnt skin and hair also. Must be from the second guy cause the first guy's scalp is intact."

Mac looked down at the scalp hair and fingers and then at the others.

"I think we're done here. Just get this stuff to the lab and be sure it's Dr. Blanton. Anything else you can retrieve down there now?" he asked the divers.

"No, the bottom's pretty clean. There may be some more body parts strewn farther away, but we've combed the area."

"We'll go back down tomorrow with a full crew. There's not much more we can do today."

He opened the first sealed plastic bag and almost vomited when he saw two eyeballs, two ears and a large segment of the throat. The second contained just a small white tag with the inscription,

The defense rests.
The prosecution can
see no evil, hear no evil, speak no evil.

"Okay," said Mac.

He called the chief and the mayor again and told them about the findings.

–65–

Twenty-four hours later the lab called Lieutenant McClymonds and confirmed that the isolated fingerprints from the two fingers were from Dr. Blanton. DNA studies completed a week later from the fingers and scalp confirmed that they were both the same. The scalp came from Blanton also.

Mac notified his boss and the newspapers of the conclusion to the case, but he felt sad that it had to end this way. The doctor had saved his life and was obviously very disturbed. He had sincerely hoped he could have talked to him and saved him. But then he thought, *Would this guy have wanted to spend the rest of his life in a sanitarium? Perhaps it was the best conclusion possible.*

Epilog

It was getting colder and everyone was bundled up tightly. The overhead speaker announced, *"Swiss Air 645 for Zurich is now boarding at gate 62."*

A tall man in a gray overcoat holding a cane in his right hand, wearing a green alpine hat with a feather, walked slowly up to the counter.

"Can I help you, sir?" asked the attendant.

"Yes," he said. "My name is Martin Welch. My wife and I have two seats in first class on the Zurich flight, but she won't be able to make it. Can I cancel her ticket?"

"Certainly, sir. The flight is full, and we can use the ticket for a standby. May I see your passport?"

The old man set his cane on the counter, reached into his pocket with his right hand, withdrew his passport and handed it to the woman. He held his left hand in his bulky overcoat pocket.

The woman looked him over. He was tall but slightly bent over and looked somewhat infirm. "Do you need some help, sir?"

"No," he said. "Just recovering from a boating accident."

"I see. Well, I'll just cancel your wife's ticket if you'll give me her name."

"Yes," he said, looking directly at the woman with his large blue eyes.

"Her name is Marilyn."

CPSIA information can be obtained
at www.ICGtesting.com
Printed in the USA
LVHW011421180121
676803LV00037B/787